"What?"

Jules shot Callum a glare.

"I didn't say anything," Cal said.

She pushed her uneaten burger and fries away.

"I thought you were starving."

"Lost my appetite."

"Want to tell me what that was all about? I'm an expert at determining when I'm being lied to, so don't even try."

"How about 'none of your business'?"

"Maybe so, but considering I could feel the waves of tension rolling off of you while that guy was here, it certainly begs the question."

She stayed silent.

"I'd like to help if I can. You know, I have resources at my disposal..."

"Forgive me if I'm skeptical of your offer. I've asked law enforcement for help in the past, and they've failed me, spectacularly."

"I'm sorry to hear that. How did they fail you?"

"By failing my sister."

"Is this related to the reason you moved here? You said the other night that you came here for your sister. To protect her."

"Yes. To protect her. Because law enforcement and the court system refused to do their job."

Cal's expression was full of compassion. "Is there anything I can do to help?"

Dear Reader,

I recently celebrated the twenty-year anniversary of my first published book with Harlequin. Back then, Harlequin Romantic Suspense was called Silhouette Intimate Moments, and my editor was Allison Lyons. In a full-circle moment, after editorial shifts and department reorganizations at the publisher, Allison recently became my editor again. I was thrilled! Not that the other editors I've worked with through the years weren't terrific—they were!—but working with Allison again made me realize how far I've come, how many books I have under my belt and how lucky I am to write for Harlequin!

This month, my latest offering kicks off an exciting new Colton continuity set in North Dakota. In the quiet community of Red Grove, North Dakota, illegal drugs and murder have shaken the citizenry and threaten the tourism industry. The popular sculptures along the Enchanted Highway draw thousands of visitors every year, but one summer morning, a tourist discovers a dead body at the foot of one of the sculptures. Sheriff Callum Colton is one of the first on the scene. While interviewing witnesses, he discovers another mystery in the form of a sarcastic enigma named Jules Bailey. Jules has her own crime to solve, and when these opposites team up, sparks fly like Fourth of July fireworks!

Happy reading,

Beth

COLTON'S DEADLY EVIDENCE

BETH CORNELISON

Special thanks and acknowledgment are given to Beth Cornelison for her contribution to The Coltons of North Dakota miniseries.

Recycling programs for this product may not exist in your area.

ISBN-13: 978-1-335-18501-3

Colton's Deadly Evidence

For questions and comments about the quality of this book, please contact us at CustomerService@Harlequin.com.

Harlequin Enterprises ULC
22 Adelaide St. West, 41st Floor
Toronto, Ontario M5H 4E3, Canada
www.Harlequin.com

HarperCollins Publishers
Macken House, 39/40 Mayor Street Upper,
Dublin 1, D01 C9W8, Ireland
www.HarperCollins.com

Printed in Lithuania

1 2 3 4 5 6 7 8 9 10 LIT 28 27 26 25

Beth Cornelison began working in public relations before pursuing her love of writing romance. She has won numerous honors for her work, including a nomination for the RWA RITA® Award for *The Christmas Stranger*. She enjoys featuring her cats (or friends' pets) in her stories and always has another book in the pipeline! She currently lives in Louisiana with her husband, one son and three spoiled cats. Contact her via her website, bethcornelison.com.

Books by Beth Cornelison

Harlequin Romantic Suspense

The Coltons of North Dakota

Colton's Deadly Evidence

Cameron Glen

Mountain Retreat Murder
Kidnapping in Cameron Glen
Cameron Mountain Rescue
Protecting His Cameron Baby
Cameron Mountain Refuge
Her Cameron Defender
Her Cameron Bodyguard

The Coltons of New York

Colton's Undercover Seduction

The Coltons of Owl Creek

Targeted with a Colton

The Coltons of Alaska

Colton's Second Chance

Visit the Author Profile page
at Harlequin.com for more titles.

For Allison Lyons, who helped launch this incredible ride all those years ago. Thank you for all you do!

Prologue

He needed a yank. Bad.

John Harper ambled through the little store full of tourist crap and tried to look interested in the postcards and key chains. When his hands twitched, he shoved them deep in the pockets of his loose blue jeans and tried to suppress the shudder that raced through him. When he imagined the relief that would come when he finally had his Scooby snacks, the need that had been building all day roared in his head.

The little bell over the shop door jingled, and he cut a glance over his shoulder. A man in a red UNLV hoodie walked in and swept a look from the front counter to the back of the store, where John stood. With his hood worn up, the man's face was hidden. Not that John knew what his contact looked like. The message he'd gotten just said where to meet and when.

While there could be a nip in the North Dakota summer night air, John scoffed at the man's choice of clothing this early in the evening. He had to be sweltering. John sure was. He wiped the beaded moisture from his upper lip and waited impatiently for Hoodie to meet him at the back wall. As the man approached, John jerked a nod and in a quiet voice asked, "Hey, is Tina with you?"

Barely raising his head to make eye contact, Hoodie gave him a dark glare then shot a subtle glance toward the front counter, where the store clerk sat staring at her phone. "Tonight. You got cash?"

John glowered. "I know the drill."

One eyebrow twitched up on the man's grim face. "Five minutes. Behind the shop. Blue sedan."

Four minutes later, John strode up to the passenger door of the blue sedan parked in the far corner of the dirt lot behind the gift shop. He slid into the sun-baked car and handed a wad of bills to Hoodie, who still had his face hidden behind the voluminous hood. John chuckled. "What's up with the Little Red Riding Hood bit?"

Hoodie only pinned him with a narrow-eyed glare as he started thumbing through the cash.

"It's all there. When do I get the ice?"

"Midnight. You'll like it. It's a special local batch."

John's hands fluttered against his legs in anticipation. "Here?"

Red Riding Hood seemed to be considering, then nodded toward the prominent sculpture a short distance down the highway. "At the geese."

John scowled. "I don't like it. Why not here? Fewer eyes. I don't wanna go back to prison."

Red Riding Hood tucked the wad of cash in the hoodie pocket and repeated, "At the geese."

At midnight, John was waiting at the base of the geese sculpture when Red Riding Hood pulled up in his blue sedan. He marched over to the car and was jonesing so hard for the Tina that he thought he'd die before he could shoot up. "About time. Where's the goods?"

Red Riding Hood didn't reply. Instead, he slid out of his

car, strolled over to the base of the sculpture and gazed up at the flying geese. "This one was always her favorite."

"*Her* who?" John asked, then snapped angrily, "Stop stalling. Where's the ice?"

Red Riding Hood angled a churlish look at him. "Chill out. You'll get what's coming to you."

John could feel his heart dancing in his chest as Red Riding Hood reached in his hoodie pocket and pulled out a small vial of powder. "Try this first. Free sample."

Without questioning the largess, John snatched the vial and pulled a pipe from his pocket. Soon, he'd lit up, and the first zip rippled through his system. Bliss. Finally. After another few drags on the pipe, he faced Red Riding Hood and offered him the pipe. "You?"

Red Riding Hood shook his head. "I don't use that poison. It'll kill you."

Then, with a lightning-fast move, Red Riding Hood grabbed John's wrist and jabbed him with a syringe.

"What the hell?" John barked, then clutched his chest as he felt his heart throb so hard he thought it would explode. He convulsed once, then as he collapsed at the foot of the sculpture, a veil of darkness descended.

Chapter 1

The first dim rays of morning sun peeked over the horizon as Jules Bailey parked at the far end of the lot in front of the Enchanted Highway Mile 0 gift shop. She sighed heavily before dragging herself out of her car. She might as well give up the tiny room at the Catch-a-Wink Motor Inn and throw a sleeping bag on the floor of the gift shop. Even though she had a teenager from town to help out during the busiest hours, Jules practically lived at the little store. In the midst of tourist season, the store stayed busy from opening until she could kick the last stragglers out at closing. Outside regular hours, she stayed late to close out the register and balance the books. Prior to opening, she restocked the shelves, tidied the store and paid vendors.

This routine was not the way she'd intended to use her almost-PhD in chemistry, but she knew her current circumstances were temporary. Once the jerk stalking her sister was behind bars where he belonged…

Something moved at the edge of her vision, a fleeting shadow, and she heard a rustling noise behind the store's trash bin. Jules stumbled to a stop, her heartbeat tripping. A wild animal? A prowler? The wind?

"Hello?" She crept forward cautiously, dreading the necessity to pass the trash can to reach the back door of the store. She was not eager to find out what form of goblin—or rat—was lurking in the shadows. "Who's there?"

She heard another rustle, like a plastic bag, then swallowed hard as she moved forward, staying several steps back so she could angle a look around the garbage can… and spotted a black cat. A kitten, really. She both exhaled in relief and felt her heart twist in sympathy, because the skinny cat, clearly a stray, had a plastic grocery sack stuck around its neck.

"You poor thing!" she cooed, edging closer. "Have a little problem there, doncha?" She hung her purse and lunch bag straps on the knob of the back door and turned to the kitten that cowered near a corner created by the building walls. As she inched closer, still cooing softly, the cat hissed and scuttled back until it was trapped by the brick walls. "Easy, fella. I won't hurt you."

She crouched low and reached for the bag, but with another loud growl and hiss, the cat bolted past her with the bag flapping behind. After crossing the dirt lot behind the gift shop, the kitten disappeared into a field of low scrub bushes. Jules pursued the tiny cat, searching for a hole where it had hidden or a sign of where it had gone. After several minutes, she'd found nothing. As if the cat had vaporized.

Grumbling her frustration, she turned and went inside. She had work to do before the store opened. She couldn't spend all day searching for a stray cat that clearly didn't want to be found.

Once inside, she placed her lunch in the dorm-size refrigerator in the break room and started stocking the display of chips and candy. She was always surprised how many tourists waited to buy their picnic and snack food at the overpriced gift shop rather than packing their own at home. Every day, she sold dozens of picnic-size packs of cookies, tiny pop-top cans of tuna, chicken or ham salad and enough bottled soda to float a boat.

As she refolded all the T-shirts on the shelf and sorted them by size, she couldn't stop thinking about the cat. Would the bag choke the poor thing to death if she didn't help? And the kitten was so thin, you could see the starving animal's ribs.

Sympathy plucked at her as she moved to the office and retrieved the cash for the register. While she vacuumed the thin carpet and mopped the bathroom, her gaze drifted to the back door again and again. Finally, exasperated with herself, she took a can of tuna from the shelf, marched outside and popped the top. "Here, kitty kitty!"

Nothing. No sign of the critter. With a grunt, she set the can on the ground and went back inside.

She could already hear automobiles on the highway and the crunch of tires on the parking lot as she turned on the neon Open sign in the front window.

The bell over the door jingled before she'd made it behind the counter.

She opened her mouth to call a greeting, but instead, the tall man who led his family inside the shop grumbled, "About time! The sign says you open at seven. It's seven oh six. Where were you? On coffee break? Some of us value other people's time!"

Her muscles instantly tensed. Wow. The grumps and whiners were out early this morning. A number of stinging retorts flashed through her mind, but she shoved them down, opting for a sour smile and a churlish tone. "My apologies, sir. Please forgive me."

The man's wife, decked out in a Grand Canyon T-shirt,

Bermuda shorts and a straw sun visor, sent Jules a glare as she moved into the shop, mumbling, "So rude."

The family's children played with every toy in the shop, pulled the spinner off a pinwheel they didn't buy and loudly demanded their parents buy them candy for breakfast. The wife unfolded at least a dozen shirts, looking for her size, even though the stacks were clearly marked, and Mr. Time Police griped about the price of every item he picked up. Finally, after what seemed an eon, the family paid and left with their booty of knickknacks, trinkets and sugary treats. Jules had no time to gather her wits and once again question why she was working with the public before a young couple, their hands clasped, entered the store.

"Good morning," she called to the new arrivals. They ignored her.

Jules rolled her eyes and set to work refolding the T-shirts. Sure, she could save the constant straightening in the wake of shoppers for Bonnie, her teenaged summer helper, but the busywork helped her pass the time. As she collected the broken pinwheel left discarded on the floor, she heard what sounded like a scream outside.

The terror in the sound sent a chill down her spine, but she shook it off. The gift shop, located a stone's throw from *Geese in Flight*, the first sculpture along North Dakota's famous Enchanted Highway, was privy to all manner of noises throughout the day, from screeching children and shouting parents, to honking horns and raucous laughter. Tourists were nothing if not noisy.

After moving back behind the checkout counter, Jules lifted her phone to check the time. Seven thirty-eight. She goggled. She felt like she'd already been in the shop for hours, but her day had barely begun.

The shop bell jangled loudly as the door was thrust open.

Mr. Time Police charged into the store, his whimpering family on his heels. "Call the police! Hurry!"

Jules straightened her spine and arched an eyebrow. Before she could catch the snark, she asked, "Why? Did somebody hurt your feelings?"

"No, smart-ass!" the woman screeched, her hands flapping toward the door. "There's a body under the sculpture! I think the man is dead!"

A frisson of alarm snaked through Jules, but she was determined not to panic until she'd confirmed the couple's theory that the person under the sculpture was dead. She'd heard from locals who drifted through the shop from time to time that *Geese in Flight* was a popular spot for teenagers to hang out and drink late at night. She hoped what this tourist family had discovered was simply someone sleeping off a night of excessive partying.

Jules headed out to the sculpture with the squawking woman trailing behind her.

"You don't need to look! You need to call the damn police!" the woman shouted. "We tried to call, but our phones don't get reception out here in this miserable, godforsaken tundra!"

Jules stopped and turned to face the loud woman. "If it's so miserable in this godforsaken tundra, why did you come here for your vacation?"

The woman blinked, puffed up with indignation, and sputtered, "Wh— I—"

Without waiting for a reply, Jules marched the final distance to the sculpture. Her steps slowed as she neared the iconic art installation. She could see that there was, indeed, someone sprawled at the base. With each step, as the rising sun brightened the landscape and shone on the prostrate figure, she became acutely aware of two things. The man's ghostly white skin and fixed, cloudy-eyed stare left no doubt that he *was* dead.

And Jules had seen the man before.

Chapter 2

Sheriff Callum Colton cruised to a stop amid the collection of other emergency vehicles responding to the report of a death at the first stop along the Enchanted Highway. He climbed out of his patrol car, calling to the cluster of civilians crowded around to gawk, "Stand back, please. This area is now a crime scene and closed to the public. Please clear the area."

As he approached the scene, he found the first deputy on the scene had pulled aside a few individuals who stood apart from the rest of the crowd. Two young children clung to a woman with a sour expression, while the deputy spoke to a man, whose voice was raised and who was gesturing wildly. A second, much younger and extremely attractive woman stood nearby watching the proceedings with a scowl. Callum suppressed a sympathetic and situationally inappropriate smile. He'd be scowling, too, if he'd had to start his day being questioned about the discovery of a dead man and listening to the portly man rant.

Oh, wait...that was *how he was about to start his day.* Cal sighed and thought despondently, *Yay.*

He touched the brim of his campaign hat as he joined the deputy and nodded a perfunctory greeting to the witnesses being questioned. His gaze lingered a second too long on the attractive twentysomething brunette. His pulse gave a kick when she lifted her eyebrows slightly, a telltale sign of interest, and gave him reciprocal up-and-down scrutiny. But her scowl returned quickly as she moved her gaze away and folded her arms over her chest.

"Is this going to take long? I have to get back to the gift shop. I'm the only one working the store, and this is our busiest time," the brunette asked, her green eyes flashing with impatience.

Cal cocked his head and rubbed his chin as he studied her. "Ma'am, you do understand the nature of our business with you? A dead man takes precedence over gift shop trinkets."

She arched one eyebrow sassily as she met his gaze and chirped, "You think? I would have never guessed. Thank you for educating me, Deputy."

Cal tapped the star in his chest. "Sheriff. Sheriff Callum Colton." Then, because he couldn't resist, he quipped, "And you're welcome. Glad to help, Ms...."

He drew out the courtesy title, inviting her to introduce herself.

She rolled her eyes. Sighed. "Jules Bailey. I'm the manager at the gift shop." She aimed her thumb over her shoulder to the drab, one-story building a few hundred feet down the highway.

Cal pulled a pen from his breast pocket and a notepad from the back pocket of his uniform pants. "Perfect," he said. "I was going to have to speak to you soon to get the security camera footage for the past twenty-four hours."

She shook her head, her mouth twisting in scorn. "No cameras. The owner said he didn't see a need, because he's never had a problem since the store opened in the—" she hesitated, flipping a hand in frustration "—Neolithic era or something." In a quieter voice, she added, "And doesn't *that* just make me feel *so* safe when I close alone at night?"

Cal grunted his own discontent over the lack of cameras. Not just because he didn't have that source of evidence, but because he didn't like the idea of Jules Bailey, or any woman, working alone at night without any security measures in place. He made a mental note to look up the owner of the gift shop and recommend changes.

Hearing another vehicle arrive, Cal turned to see not only the coroner's van, but also the Stark County Sheriff Department's lead forensics guy. He walked over to greet the arriving team and huddle with them around the corpse for the initial assessment of the scene.

"Any sign of foul play or are we looking at a junkie overdose?" Ronnie Goldman, the forensics officer, asked.

"Aren't I supposed to ask you that question?" Cal said with a grin, shaking the man's hand.

"I suppose. Just thought you might have made an initial assessment." Goldman squinted at the body, giving the corpse careful scrutiny.

"Just arrived a moment ago myself. This is my first up-close look," Cal replied. He moved so that the rising sun wasn't in his eyes and studied the position of the body, checking for signs of foul play. "Plenty of scar tissue and old needle marks on his arm. That supports the idea he was shooting up with something."

Goldman aimed his finger at a tiny pinprick of red on the pale arm. "This one is recent. He injected something last night. Although…the bruising around the injection site shows internal bleeding. It wasn't a clean or careful prick."

"So he was already high when he shot up the last time? An unsteady hand?" one of the responding deputies, rookie Ben Holder, asked.

A rumble of discontent rolled from the coroner's throat.

"Mike? You have thoughts?" Cal asked.

Mike Palmer, the coroner leaned in and waggled a finger near the dead man's arm. "Look there. That pattern of bruising. Like a real tight five-finger grip near his wrist."

Cal nodded. "I've seen that sort of bruising before on domestic violence calls." He took a step back to view the body from another angle. "Do you see other signs of violence or rough treatment?"

Goldman used a clean tongue depressor to part the dead man's hair near the ground. "We have some bleeding back here. He didn't lie down gently and drift to sleep. He hit the pavement hard enough to crack his noggin."

Cal straightened. "Okay, I've seen enough to work under the assumption this man had help getting to this condition." Looking to the coroner and forensics officer, he added, "I'll let you two get to work. Send me a full report on what you find, ASAP?"

"Naturally," Goldman said. "And I'll brief your brother, as well. If drugs are involved, as we all seem to suspect, Detective Colton's drug task force is going to want in on this."

Cal turned up a palm. "*If* drugs prove to be involved, I'm more than happy to let Wyatt take the lead on the investigation. But I still want to stay apprised of developments in the case. The body was found in my jurisdiction, after all."

He pulled aside his deputy, asking the new recruit for a quick rundown of what Ben had learned so far in his interviews. Not much, as it turned out. The couple Ben had been questioning had discovered the body but seemed to believe they had better things to do with their vacation time than talk to law enforcement. The gift shop manager had been the one to call the authorities on the store's landline.

"Okay, finish questioning the couple. Be sure to ask if

anything about the scene has been touched or changed, and get all the details on where to reach the family later if more questions arise."

"Yes, sir." Ben squared his shoulders as if bracing for battle as he returned to finish interviewing the querulous couple.

Giving his pen a few clicks, Cal returned to the spot where Jules Bailey waited, her arms folded over her chest. "If you'd rather, we can have our conversation inside the store," he offered.

"What if I'd rather not have a conversation at all?" she asked, one eyebrow hiked over those mesmerizing green eyes.

"I'm afraid that's not an option. You have information I need in order to figure out what happened here last night."

"You make it sound like you think I did something wrong," she said, dropping her hands to her sides and balling her hands into fists.

"Did you?" he asked, more to needle her and see her cheeks flame than because he believed she had.

She frowned in consternation. "No."

He grinned. "Good. Then you don't have anything to worry about. Shall we?" He waved a hand toward the gift shop and started in that direction.

She hesitated but finally fell in step behind him. As they neared the gift shop, she paused, and he shifted his gaze to see what had held her up.

Her attention was focused on something at the back of the shop.

"Problem?" he asked, moving closer to her to have a better angle to see what held her attention.

"I need a minute. Wait here." She held up a hand, directing him to stay put, the way he directed his search-and-rescue cadaver dog, Pilot.

He gave a low chuckle. "And let you escape or destroy evidence?"

She snapped a startled look over her shoulder. "What? I'm not—"

"Just the same, I'm coming with you. What's caught your attention back there?" He waved his pen toward the dirt lot and low scrub brush behind the store.

"Well, I guess you'll see, if you insist on coming. But stay back, *and be quiet*! No sudden moves."

He grinned to himself, rather liking the fact Jules had the temerity to order him around, seemingly unphased by his authority as sheriff. She had gumption.

He unsnapped the top strap over his service weapon and rested a hand on it, prepared for whatever—or whomever—might be behind the gift shop. What he found was not even in the top ten of what he'd expected.

Jules crept quietly up behind a black cat near the back door. The feline was eating something voraciously despite having the handle hole of a plastic bag stuck around its neck. As she neared the cat, it heard her and spooked. With a hiss, the cat tried to run, but Jules lunged for it and grabbed the animal's scruff. Irate at being held, the small cat growled, spit and thrashed.

"Easy, baby," Jules cooed as she dodged flailing paws and slashing claws. "I just have to— Ow!"

He moved forward, his hands spread. "Can I help?"

She didn't answer. Instead, she continued crooning gentle words in a kind voice, until she managed to remove the tangled grocery sack. She bent to release the cat, but the ungrateful feline chose to push off and leap away, leaving long scratches on her wrist.

Jules hissed in pain and clamped her opposite hand over the injured wrist. "Son of a biscuit!"

"More likely the son of a cougar or panther based on its temperament," he teased as he reached for her arm. "May I have a look?"

"I'm fine," she insisted, pulling away.

Settling his hands on his hips, he watched her peek at the wound. "You'll want to clean that. Disinfect it."

"So now you're a doctor *and* the sheriff? Lucky me." She pulled a face and strode to the back door of the building.

He followed, chuckling. "You're only lucky because I don't charge for my medical advice. That's free of charge. A little something I learned from my father, who *is* a doctor."

"Hmm," she grunted, clearly unimpressed. She marched into a small, sparse break room and searched the cabinets until she found a plastic box with a red cross on top. After opening the first-aid kit, she removed the items one at a time, checking labels.

Enough of her stubbornness. He closed the distance between them and gripped her forearm lightly. "You should wash it first. Come with me."

To his surprise, she complied without a fuss as he led her to the sink and helped her wash the scratches with soap and water, then blotted the area dry with paper towels. She sat in a rickety chair by the small Formica table and allowed him to administer the disinfectant, then tape a large bandage over the wound before stepping back to admire his handiwork. His father, a surgeon at the local hospital, couldn't have done any better, Cal decided.

Jules, too, studied the bandage, but instead of thanking him, she said, "At least he ate something. The poor thing was starving."

He tipped his head. "Pardon?"

She gave him a look that said her meaning should be obvious. "The kitten. He ran from me earlier this morning. I put the tuna out hoping he'd come back and eat. Didn't you see how thin he was?"

"Can't say I noticed that while you were dodging claws." After removing his hat, he set it on the table and sat in the chair across from her. Studying the way her chestnut hair framed her delicate heart-shaped face, he clicked open his pen again. As he pulled out his notepad, he asked, "So what time was it when you arrived this morning?"

The roll of her eyes told him she was unhappy with the transition to his investigative duties. She sighed, then said, "Early. About six thirty."

"Did you notice anything unusual when you arrived?"

"Besides a starving stray kitten at the back door, you mean?" she asked, her tone full of attitude.

"Yes. Besides the kitten. Although I'll want to interview Mr. Scratchy next. No telling what he saw before you arrived." He couldn't stop the grin that tugged his cheek. Despite her sarcasm toward him, he saw something softer below the surface. Her concern for the cat, for example. She had a soft heart, despite the hard shell she presented to him. And ducking her verbal darts reminded him of the give-and-take that was common between him and his five siblings. He could joust and tease with the best.

Did her cheek just dimple with the beginning of a smile? He was almost certain he'd seen a hint of amusement before she'd turned her face away and assumed her resistant arms-folded position again. "No. I didn't see anything suspicious. I came in the store and started setting up as usual."

"Okay." He made a note of her reply. "When did you become aware of the body outside?"

"When that tourist family came back into the store screaming for me to call the police."

"What time was that?"

She gave him an exasperated look. "Didn't check the clock. Sorry. Maybe you could consult the 911 recording for a time stamp. Huh?"

He jerked a serious nod. "A very good suggestion. Thank you."

She snorted and looked away again.

"Did you go out to see the body at that point?"

Jules sighed. "I did. I called 911 after I went out to see the body for myself. Mainly I wanted to verify the man was dead before I raised the alarm. I've had drunks sleep off a bender in the parking lot before."

"And how did you verify that the man was dead?" he asked, taking down her comment.

She shot him another expression that said his question was stupid. Despite the grim tenor of the glare, he was intrigued with the glint of intelligence and spark of mettle in the emerald depths of her eyes. His body stirred as if answering a battle cry, a challenge to match wits or win her over. A whisper in his ear exhorted him to seduce her.

"I knew by looking at him. Did you see his pale skin? His glazed eyes and fixed stare?" Her description of the dead body grounded him quickly. He was here to do a job, not find a date.

His grip tightened on his pen. "Did you touch him?"

Her face reflected revulsion. "Lord, no! Why would I want to do that? Gross!"

"Just clarifying for the record. We have to establish a history regarding the evidence. Do you know the man? Can you tell me who he is?"

"Nope."

Cal tapped his pen against the pad, disappointed by that dead end. And what did he think? He'd waltz out here, ask a few questions and have all the answers presented on a silver platter? That he'd have the case tied up with a ribbon by lunchtime?

He flipped the page on his notepad and changed angles. "How long have you worked at the gift shop, Ms. Bailey?"

"Only a couple of months. And I'd like to keep my job. Do you mind if we move this interrogation out to the sales floor?"

"Actually, I think it would be wise to close the shop for at least a while. The forensic team will need the whole area around the body cordoned off until they can gather all traces of evidence. For example, how did the dead body get there? Are there tire tracks or footprints?"

"You should ask the guy that was with him," she said.

Callum looked up at her and frowned, replaying what she'd said mentally. "Come again?"

"The guy that was with him in the shop last night. He'd be a good place to start," she said, her facial expression once again suggesting "well, duh…"

Cal straightened, his heart ticking faster. "Hang on. You saw the dead guy alive last night? With another man?"

She nodded. "They came in the shop, right before closing."

He grunted and shook his head. "Why didn't you say so earlier?"

"You didn't ask!"

"I asked if you recognized him. You said, 'No.'"

"No, you asked if I *knew* him. If I could tell you *who* he was. And I don't, and I can't. Not only am I new in town, I don't make it my business to get to know the local drug crowd."

Again Cal's pulse tripped. "Drug crowd?" Now she'd really piqued his interest. "What makes you think the guy is involved with drugs?"

She scoffed. "It was pretty obvious."

"Obvious how?"

Jules shrugged. "Because I don't live under a rock. I may not do drugs myself, but I can tell when somebody is stoned and when I witness a drug deal."

When his eyes widened, she waved a hand and clarified. "Maybe not the *actual exchange* of money and goods, but…" She shrugged. "Clearly a precursor. They barely spoke before they left, but it was obvious they were going to do business later."

He pulled out his cell phone and swiped through a few screens until he opened a voice recording app. "I want you to start from the very beginning, from the minute the first man arrived in the store and tell me everything you recall. Every detail no matter how minor it seems. I'm going to record your statement. All right?"

"Would it matter if I said it wasn't all right? Don't you law enforcement types do what you want regardless of whether it's all right with the public?"

He hesitated, giving her a hard look. "Is there a reason for your dim view of law enforcement? Have *I* done something to upset you?"

She groaned and shook her head. "Not you." She flicked a brief glance at him, then added, "Yet."

"Yet?" He gave a wry chuckle. "I'll consider myself on notice."

She stared down at her hands, and he noticed how ragged and raw her cuticles looked, as if she'd spent a lot of time chewing or picking at them, typically a habit that reflected stress or anxiety. But what had Jules Bailey stressed? What had given her such a bad impression of law enforcement? He made another mental note to do a background check on the shop manager. A niggling suspicion told him there was a story here he needed to know.

"Ready?" he asked, his finger hovering over the screen of his phone.

She exhaled heavily and frowned. With an uncaring flap of her hands, she said, "Fine. Record me."

He pressed Record, and said, "Sheriff Callum Colton in the break room of the Enchanted Highway Mile 0 gift shop. Voluntary interview with Jules Bailey, shop manager. June 30th at eight thirty-five a.m." He slid the phone closer to her and said, "Start at the beginning. Tell me what you saw and heard last night."

Chapter 3

Jules swallowed hard, her mouth suddenly dry. How many times had she or her sister given statements to the police that amounted to nothing? Unreliable witness accounts, circumstantial evidence, contradictory alibis. The cops always seemed to have a reason to dismiss what she and Abby told them, and her sister's stalker would go free...again.

Now this North Dakota sheriff wanted her statement, her help in solving a crime? The irony galled her.

But if he was forcing her to keep the gift shop closed while he conducted his investigation, she might as well tell him what he wanted to know. The sooner the shop reopened, the sooner she could start earning her meager salary again.

Yippee, she thought, heaving a desultory sigh. She made a mental note to call Bonnie and tell her not to come in today. The teen would probably be glad for the day off to... well, do whatever teenagers did these days. She'd never had the luxury of being a carefree teenager, thanks to her parents. She'd had to work and look after Abby and—

"Whenever you're ready," the sheriff said, drawing her out of her thoughts. "What happened last night?"

Jules huffed out a breath and mentally reconstructed the events of the previous evening. "So...the dead guy was the first one to come into the shop." She paused, giving an involuntary shudder as an image of the man's ashen skin and cloudy eyes flashed in her mind. She drummed her fingers on the table restlessly as she tried to erase the gruesome memory and concentrate on reconstructing the events from the night before. Focusing was hard enough given the sheriff's distracting appearance and confusing manner. Every time she met his blue eyes, her thoughts scattered, and his habit of brushing off her sarcasm with lopsided grins that made his chiseled good looks even more strikingly handsome rattled her. The fact that he could so easily shake her composure was reason enough to keep her guard up, but considering he was in law enforcement, she knew she needed to double down on her caution around him.

So give your statement and get rid of him.

She cleared her throat and continued, "He came in at about five fifty-five. I remember the time because the store closes at six on weekdays, and I was just about to lock the door for the evening."

Sheriff Colton bobbed his head once in acknowledgment. "Okay. What did he do while in the shop?"

"Wandered aimlessly for the most part. He didn't act interested in the merchandise, just stayed by the wall of T-shirts, which is the wall farthest from the register. He acted jittery, kept his back to me. I tried to keep an eye on him, thinking he might be considering shoplifting or, I don't know, pulling a gun and robbing the shop."

"You said there was another man. When did he arrive?"

She scowled at the sheriff. "I'm getting there. You said tell you everything, so..."

He raised a hand. "Apologies. Please continue."

"I called to him once, saying the shop was closing, but he

didn't react, didn't answer. Just kept hovering by the back wall and glancing at the front door every minute or so."

"As if he was waiting for someone? Expecting someone?"

Jules nodded. "Exactly. The second guy came in around ten after six. I can't close the store while customers are still inside, so I was kinda peeved about the late arrival." She traced the fake marble pattern in the Formica tabletop. "But once the second guy showed up, he only stayed thirty seconds. They talked for a few seconds and left the store about a minute apart." She snorted. "As if they were trying to play it like they weren't together, leaving separately." She shook her head. "I know a drug deal when I see one."

"What made you think it was a drug deal? Could you hear what they said?" the sheriff asked, his blue eyes bright as he narrowed his incisive gaze on her. "What did the second guy look like?"

She gave a short wry laugh. "Impatient much, Sheriff? I'm getting there…in an orderly manner."

His laugh bubbled up like spring water, clear and refreshing. His gaze mirrored the same mirth as he grinned at her. "More apologies. My family is always telling me I get overeager. Please continue…in an orderly manner."

His grin stirred something light and warm inside her, and she felt as if her chair were tipping. She splayed her hands on the tabletop to steady herself and pulled out her practiced defenses. Sharpening her tone, she asked, "Are you mocking me?"

He blinked as if startled that someone could think his charming demeanor and ready smile were fake. "No. Certainly not. I appreciate thoroughness and order. Please, finish." His expression sobered as he pinned her with a look that burrowed to her core. "Why did you think they were dealing drugs?"

She lowered her eyes to the table again, unable to focus while she looked into that sky-blue stare. She didn't want to tell him how many drug deals she'd seen her father conduct, so she just said, "I recognized the signs. I'm not naive, Sheriff."

"Didn't mean to imply you were. I meant what specifically told you it was a drug deal?"

She sighed. "The first guy acted jumpy. Not nervous so much as edgy, needing a hit." She knew the difference, having seen it in her father so often growing up, but the sheriff didn't need to know that private detail of her life. "The second dude was wearing a UNLV hoodie and kept his hood up, shielding his face. He clearly didn't want me or any cameras to identify him."

"But you said there are no cameras here," he said.

"Doesn't mean he knew that. Do you want me to tell my impressions or not?"

He waved a hand. "Please continue."

She knitted her brow as she dredged up memories of the night before. "The first guy was kinda scrawny, but the second guy was more average height and seemed to have a large build. But that could have been because of the big hoodie. Again, I couldn't see his face, and, honestly, I couldn't tell you for sure what race he was. His hands were in his hoodie pocket. Only reason I know it was a man is because I heard him talk. His voice was low and deep."

She sensed that the sheriff wanted to ask another question, and, flicking a glance at him, she held up a hand to stay him. "The first guy, the dead guy—" she jerked her head in the general direction of the *Geese in Flight* sculpture, where the body had been found "—he asked UNLV guy if someone named Gina or Tina or some such was with him."

Sheriff Colton perked up and began scribbling in his notepad. "What did UNLV answer?"

"Not sure, he was mumbling. But his tone said he didn't like the question. Dead guy said, 'I know'…then something I didn't catch. But UNLV's reply was clipped. Just a couple grunted words. I did catch *five* and *blue*, or maybe *two*—something with an *oo* sound—before he turned and hurried out, his back to me. Dead Guy acted all the more restless and jittery after UNLV left. Like he was impatient to leave. So I kindly reminded him I was trying to close, and that seemed to be all the encouragement he needed to hustle out of the store." She fell silent, exhaling the coil of tension inside her. If she never had to talk to cops again, it would suit her just fine.

When Sheriff Colton said nothing, she risked a glance at his penetrating blue gaze. He was studying her closely, and when their eyes met, he curled his cheek up with a grin. Oh, Lord. He had a dimple.

She scowled, internally stomping on the giddy trill that buzzed through her veins. "What?"

"Just making sure you're finished before I speak" His smile brightened, and she matched his mirth with a darker glower.

"You *are* mocking me! Didn't your mother teach you manners?" She folded her arms over her chest, determined not to be mollified by the rich timbre of his chuckle.

"She did. My many siblings, however, taught me to tease." He fingered the brim of his hat, his expression unrepentant. After another beat, he reached in the breast pocket of his uniform shirt and extracted a business card. When he handed it to her, the paper was warm from having been tucked against his body heat, and a shimmy of sensation rolled through her, wakening nerve endings and stirring up hormones she'd kept under lock and key for the last few years.

Displeased with her reaction to the sheriff, she gritted her back teeth, trying to rein in the feral attraction to him. But like wild horses, the feelings flaring in her bucked and fought constraint.

When he pushed back from the table and rose from his chair, she couldn't help but notice how tall and fit he was. His broad shoulders and muscled arms stretched the fabric of his uniform shirt in all the best ways. He rested his hand loosely on the service weapon at his hip and started for the door. "That's all for now, but please stay available in case we have more questions for you. Since the victim, by your account, was in the shop prior to his death, I'm sure the forensics team will want to have a poke around. We'll have to keep the shop closed until they finish." He jammed his campaign hat back on his head. "To be sure no evidence is disturbed."

She winced. He noticed.

"What?" he asked, his gaze narrowing.

"I've cleaned the store since last night when those men were in here."

"Cleaned?"

She squared her shoulders and lifted her chin. "Yes. Cleaned. The shop doesn't clean itself, you know. And after a day of tourists plowing through T-shirts and tracking in mud, and grubby children touching everything that sparkles or makes noise, it's plenty messy."

"Define 'cleaned.'" He took a step back into the break room.

"Dusting stock, cleaning fingerprints from the glass

door of the drink cooler, vacuuming, refolding T-shirts for the hundredth time…"

He held up a hand to stop her. "Okay. Well, don't clean anything else until my men have a chance to go through here. Save the contents of the vacuum bag."

She arched an eyebrow. "Really?"

"Really." He flashed another annoyingly handsome smile. "No one ever said forensic work was glamorous. Sometimes it means tediously picking through the contents of a vacuum for hairs or skin cells."

She grunted. "Sounds like weekends I've spent in the lab looking for evidence of one molecule."

He cocked his head. "Pardon?"

She waved off the comment. "Nothing. Forget it." Then, recentering her composure, she said, "I will save the vacuum contents, dust rag and not clean another thing until cleared to do so."

He ducked his chin once. "Thank you. If you think of anything else that could be helpful to the investigation, please *call me*."

He waved a finger toward the business card she still held.

Was it her imagination or was there something more in his voice when he asked her to call? A plea? A personal request? That damnable tremor raced through her again.

She squeezed her hands into fists, which crumpled the business card, then she firmed her mouth. "I will."

He disappeared into the short hall, and when she heard the squeak of the back-door hinges, she released the breath she'd been holding. Too soon.

He stepped back into the break room…grinning, of course. "You have any more of that tuna? Your little wild friend is back."

Chapter 4

Because cell service was spotty at best out on the Enchanted Highway, Cal drove straight to the Red Grove police station to drop in on his brother Wyatt. He found Wyatt at his desk, his chair kicked back and his feet up while he laughed with someone on the phone. When Wyatt spotted Cal at his door, he put his feet down and said, "Hey, let me call you back later. The sheriff is here, and I have to look busy now."

"Detective Colton." Cal laughed as he shook his head and took a seat across from Wyatt. "Working hard or hardly working?"

"Would you believe me if I said that was work?"

Cal lifted both palms toward Wyatt. "You don't have to justify yourself to me."

Wyatt scrubbed a hand over his unkempt mop of brown hair, his Colton-blue eyes twinkling when he teased, "I don't? I can remember you appointing yourself boss over all of us kids a long time ago."

Cal grinned smugly. "Eldest's prerogative." Then he sobered and said, "Have you heard about the body found out at the sculpture at the zero mile marker on the Enchanted Highway this morning?"

Wyatt nodded pointed to his desk phone. "That's what

the call was about. Because of the needle tracks on the victim's arms, the coroner believes drugs were involved. The case has been assigned to my task force. I'll be heading up the investigation." Wyatt paused and shot his brother a mock dubious frown. "That is, if you approve, Mr. Prerogative."

Cal took a pen from the cup on the edge of the desk and threw it at his brother. Wyatt deftly caught the pen and chuckled. "I'll take that as a go-ahead."

Leaning forward, his legs splayed, Cal braced his forearms on his knees. He turned his hat in his hands idly. "I hate this trend of increased drug traffic. This town was quiet and safe for so many years, and now people are dying at the foot of landmarks."

"So your gut says the victim this morning was an overdose?" Wyatt asked. "We don't have anything official yet from the coroner on cause of death."

"No, nothing official. Although…"

When he didn't finish the thought, Wyatt prompted, "Although…? Spill, Callum. If you have an instinct on this case, I want to hear it. You're usually pretty spot on."

"Well, I don't think foul play should be ruled out. The team working the call and I noticed evidence of a physical altercation on the victim—bruising and a wound on his head that indicates he fell or was hit pretty hard. Plus, I talked with somebody who can place a second man with the victim last night."

"Interesting. Go on," Wyatt said.

Cal waved a dismissive hand. "It will all be in my report." Pushing to his feet, he added, "Which I should get back to the office and write up now." He started for the door, then turned to face his brother. "I know you're officially in charge of the case, but—"

"I will keep you apprised, Sheriff."

Cal chuckled. "You read my mind."

Wyatt gave a shudder and winced. "Scary place to be, your mind. It's so dark and empty."

Barking a laugh, Cal slapped his hat onto his head and wagged a finger at his brother as he strolled out of the office. "Good one, Wy."

After calling the shop owner to tell him about the ordered closure, Jules put another can of tuna outside for the stray cat and received another hiss for her efforts.

"Well, aren't you just a joy?" she said, shaking her head. She backed up from the tuna, and the kitten rushed over to gobble her offering. She watched from the doorway, her heart breaking. The little thing was just scared, she knew. Alone. Hungry. Just trying to protect itself with its angry noises. When the kitten stood and cast a wary glance toward the parking lot, where teams of law enforcement personnel were working the crime scene, she got a better look at the cat's back end. A girl, if she was right. "So *Joy* might be a good name for you, eh? If only for the irony?"

Finishing her meal, Joy licked her whiskers and scampered back to the safety of her hiding place in the scrub brush. As Jules went back into the gift shop and added the cost of the tuna to a tab of what she owed the shop till, her gaze landed on a collapsed box from her last shipment of stock. She could fashion a cathouse from it. Put a blanket inside, maybe.

She grunted. Not like she had anything else to do with the police ordering the gift shop to remain closed until they did a sweep for evidence. She didn't want to go back to her sad, stuffy little motel room to kill time, so…

Jules carried the box into the break room and put it on

the tiny table. She inhaled deeply as she glanced around, deciding what she could use to resecure the flaps of the box. The air contained the faint scent of a woodsy smelling soap or aftershave. A reminder of the sheriff and his bright blue gaze. His engaging grin. His square jaw and handsome—

Jules caught herself and rubbed both hands over her face as if she could erase thoughts of the sexy sheriff from her brain. She had not come to North Dakota to find romance. Her one and only focus needed to be on doing everything she could for Abby. That meant helping her sister feel safe and loved. And finding a way to get Abby's stalker off the streets.

Jules dug in the drawer where she kept the box cutter and found a roll of tape. She arranged the box on the table and ripped off a strip of tape to hold it together before setting about finding some makeshift comfort items in the shop for the box. Well, that used all of one minute. Now, what was she supposed to do with her day?

Not for the first time since coming to North Dakota, she yearned to be back in the laboratory, finishing her chemistry research. She'd abandoned her PhD studies in order to follow her sister here to Red Grove when Abby was at her lowest point. Abby mattered more than a degree, and Jules was willing to work this retail job for a while to pay her expenses until…

Until the man responsible for Abby's hospitalization was caught and Abby was safe again. Which could take weeks… or months? She held out no hope that the law enforcement here in Red Grove would be any more helpful than the previous police or judges she'd dealt with on Abby's behalf.

Her thoughts flickered briefly to the Stark County sheriff again. Dang it, why couldn't she stop thinking about him? Idle hands?

Refocusing on her impromptu project, she stared at the plain brown cardboard box and shrugged. It might not be ground-breaking organic chemistry research, but it was better than going back to her dreary motel room.

After gathering a few more supplies, she set to work drawing, trimming, creating. A window here, colored-on flower box there. A roof? Definitely a sign over the door identifying the structure as Joy's House and a scrap of carpet for comfort. She'd hoped the silly craft project would keep her mind occupied, but her thoughts drifted back to the dead body outside, the drug dealers that had been in the shop…and especially to Hottie McSheriff.

Huffing her frustration, Jules carried the box-turned-cat-shelter outside and set it up near the weeds where the cat had disappeared. Satisfied with her efforts, she returned to the shop to find some other way to push images of Callum Colton from her brain. Perhaps time and distance were all she needed. After all, she would likely never see the man again.

He wanted to talk to Jules Bailey again, Cal decided later the same day. He drummed his fingers on his desk at the sheriff's department. Her odd comment about searching for a molecule had left him wondering about her past. She'd said she was new to town, having only arrived a few months earlier. The fact that she'd given a local address that was nothing more than a motel room at one of the area's lowest rent—in other words, seediest—establishments spiked his interest, as well.

So he'd gotten on his desktop and done some digging. First, he found news of her winning an award for her research in chemistry at the University of Manitoba. This news had given him pause.

Chemistry. In Canada. Near where the task force believed many of the drugs flooding the area were originating. The award had been presented just last autumn, which meant less than a year ago she'd been in Canada. In a graduate program. Working in chemistry. Those key facts kept jangling in his mind.

But now, she was managing a gift shop and living out of a cheap motel? That didn't add up.

I'm not naive, she'd said when asked about her determination that the murder victim had been part of a drug deal. Did that mean she had personal experience with illicit drugs? Could she have been a user herself? Or a producer and distributor?

That didn't make sense either. She wouldn't admit as much if she had something to hide, would she?

He also knew better than to be deceived by appearances. While she seemed sober and clean of drugs on first blush, she was quite thin and had signs of stress and fatigue on her face. Dark circles under her eyes. Tiny creases around her unsmiling mouth. Her pouty, tempting mouth…

Cal shook his head to stop that line of thought. She might be sexy and engaging with her sassy retorts, but he needed to maintain his professionalism. He needed to look closer at her history, her social connections, her family. He couldn't find a social media profile other than an out-of-date and apparently unused Instagram account. Further searching took him to an Idaho high school's website. She'd graduated early…with honors. The school's website also listed an Abby Bailey, who definitely had to be related, based on her picture. Same high cheekbones, pert nose and bright green eyes.

Going back to his original page of search results, he scrolled down, looking for more tidbits about Jules Bailey.

An hour later he'd found that she'd won the science fair in fifth grade at a school outside Seattle, had been listed as a surviving daughter of a Julian Bailey, age 56, who died in Pocatello in 2020 and…most interestingly, had been arrested for contempt of court two years ago in Portland.

Cal scratched his chin and tried to make sense of the incongruous bits of knowledge. Jules was clearly highly intelligent, yet she'd left her graduate program in Canada to move to North Dakota and work in a gift shop. She seemed to be a model student yet had been cited with contempt of court?

He chuckled remembering her snarky attitude. Maybe he could understand this, especially if she'd run up against a judge with no patience or sense of humor. But why had she been in court to begin with? The court record didn't say.

Yep. He definitely wanted to ask Jules a few more questions. But…because he suspected her of something related to the death of the man near the gift shop or because he was intrigued by the mysterious and sharp-tongued gift shop manager? The tingle that skittered over his flesh when he thought about the attractive woman would suggest his interest was personal. But he also couldn't deny the fact that her schooling in chemistry, in Canada, her seemingly random move to Red Grove and her proximity to the scene of a presumably drug-related death were all too coincidental for his comfort. He wouldn't bother Wyatt with his hunch unless his private investigation uncovered anything more incriminating. But he *would* talk to her again.

He shut down his computer and headed out of the office. As he climbed into his county-issued Jeep, he decided to swing by his house and pick up his dog, Pilot. Though Pilot, a golden Labrador retriever, had been retired from the SAR program after years of service, the old boy still had a keen nose and good instincts. In fact, Pilot had done so well when he'd originally trained in search and rescue, Cal had him trained in cadaver detection as well.

He'd let Pilot have a sniff around the *Geese in Flight* sculpture and surrounding area and see what, if anything, he turned up. Not that Cal thought the local forensics team had done shoddy work, but… just in case.

Cal scoffed at his flimsy justification. *Okay.* He wanted to see Jules again because he was attracted to her and was curious what made her tick. There. At least he could be honest with himself.

He called Wyatt, told him his plan to take Pilot to the crime scene and got the go-ahead. "The forensics team has gotten what they need, but, of course, the area is still cordoned off so—"

"Way ahead of you, little brother. I knew how to preserve a crime scene before you were a wet-behind-the-ears rookie. I'll be mindful and share anything of note with you." He scratched his chin and asked, "Speaking of the investigation, I know it's early hours, but…do you have anything yet? An ID on the victim? An estimated time of death? Anything?"

"As a matter of fact, the ID was a simple matter, because the guy was in the system."

Cal perked up. "Do tell."

"Dude's name is John Harper," Wyatt said. "He's a known drug mule who likes to sample the product. He's been a guest of the state twice and only got out a couple weeks ago from his last stay at the James River facility."

Cal mulled the news for a moment. "Sounds like he wasted no time returning to his old habits. Maybe got sideways with somebody higher up the chain?"

"Everything is on the table. We'll follow where the leads take us."

Cal rose from his desk chair and headed out of his office. "Well, anyway…if Pilot finds anything of note, I'll give you a ring."

"You better. I'd hate to have to lock you up for obstruction or hindering an investigation," Wyatt said.

Cal snorted a laugh. "Buffalo patties! You'd like nothing better than an excuse to put me in a cell for a few hours."

His brother's answering chuckle filtered through the phone connection. "You're right. That would be kinda fun. Got any unpaid parking tickets, man?"

"I'll never tell. Later, bro." Cal disconnected, grinning to himself.

A few minutes later, with Pilot wiggling excitedly and thrashing his tail against the Jeep's front seat, Cal headed back out to the zero mile post on the Enchanted Highway.

Yellow crime scene tape marked off the area around the base of the *Geese in Flight* sculpture and fluttered in the light breeze. Closed signs and sawhorses warned tourists away from stopping at the first sculpture on the scenic highway. Cal maneuvered around the barriers and parked at the edge of the small lot.

Pilot bounded out of the Jeep, and his canine nose instantly sniffed the air, the ground, the scrub brush. Callum gave the order to search, and Pilot's whole body seemed to tense as he visibly shifted into work mode. Within seconds, Pilot was at the foot of the sculpture where the body had been found and had a sniff around the crime scene. His dog promptly sat and gave a distinctive bark that said, "I found something."

"You've still got it, ol' boy. Good job." He praised Pilot and rewarded him with a good scratch behind the ears and a chunk of his favorite kibble. "Now let's expand the perimeter." He gave his dog the command to search again and followed as Pilot went to work beyond the spot where John Harper's body had been found. If Harper had been killed somewhere close by and the body moved, would there be decaying traces of blood the forensics team had missed this morning? Or, more significantly, had anyone else been killed last night, before or after Harper had been? The second guy that Jules Bailey had seen in her shop, for instance. Had he run afoul of the same person who killed John Harper, or had the guy in the UNLV hoodie been the one doling out the lethal violence?

He followed Pilot as his dog sniffed his way across the parking lot, then wandered into the short dry grass. His dog's heightened sense of smell took him on a meandering path, and he paused now and then for a longer sniff before moving on. While Pilot searched, Cal scanned the area for visible clues. Crushed grass that could indicate a body had been dragged, footprints in the dust, or—

He stopped, his gaze snagging on something odd at the back edge of the lot behind the gift shop. At first, it looked like a pile of trash, but as he got closer he realized what he was seeing.

Chapter 5

Was that a cardboard box…with decorations? Drawings and writing. Cal moved closer, confused by what he was seeing. A scrap of old carpet peeked out from the open end of the box, and *Joy's House* had been written on a flap over the open end of thc box. Was it a child's homemade dollhouse? He walked closer, as did Pilot, who had smelled something of interest. An empty tuna can inside the box.

He dragged a hand over his mouth as he realized what this was, who had made it and what it said about the snarky gift shop manager. She had a caring, creative and even whimsical side.

Even as he thought of her, the back door of the shop opened, and Jules Bailey stepped out into the early evening sun. She drew up short when she spotted him, frowned, then braced a hand on one hip.

"Sheriff? There a reason you're back here so soon, poking around?"

He whistled to call Pilot back, then strolled across the dry lot to meet her. "Same reason I had for poking around this morning. Looking for evidence to help us figure out what happened last night." He cocked his head to one side as he studied her, trying not to notice how her sexy, slim, bare legs looked. Since this morning, she'd changed into shorts that hugged her bottom and left what seemed like a mile of long, tanned thighs and calves exposed. "What are you doing here still? With the shop closed, I'd have thought you'd be enjoying the day off." He paused and narrowed his eyes. "You haven't disturbed the sales floor, have you? It's off-limits until forensics is finished with it."

She pulled her mouth into a slanted pout that matched the disdain in her eyes. "No. I know better than to mess with a crime scene. But the break room isn't off-limits."

He raised a hand in appeasement. "All right. Just wondering why you're not catching a movie in town or getting a mani-pedi. At a minimum, you should be relaxing at home with a book or your favorite binge-worthy reality TV show."

She gave a dismissive sniff. "A gift shop manager's salary is not sufficient to blow money on movies or professionally applied nail polish. I can do that for myself for free."

He fought the urge to check out the color of her toenails, although the effort to appear uninterested in her feet was a physical ache.

"As for reality TV," she said, looking down her nose at him, "never watched it, never will. I have better things to do with my time and plenty of drama in my own life without wallowing in the manufactured drama of others."

Her comment on drama reminded him that she'd been arrested for contempt of court. He was about to ask her about it when she said, "I'm perfectly capable of staying busy without frivolous expenses."

His cheek twitched, and he couldn't help grinning. "Like building cathouses for strays out of cardboard boxes?"

Color stained her cheeks, and she gave a quick telltale glance to the structure behind him. For the briefest moment, she appeared embarrassed, but then her shoulders squared and her mouth tightened. "Yeah? What of it? Joy needed a shady place to hang out, and I had time on my hands. What's wrong with making a shelter for her?"

"Joy? You've named the cat?"

One dark brown eyebrow sketched up. "So? What of it?"

"Joy?" he repeated. "The wild, three-pound, hissing ball of razor claws?"

Jules rolled her eyes. "It's called irony, Sheriff."

"Cal."

She shot him a now familiar scowl. "What?"

"When I'm here on unofficial business, I see no need for formality. Call me Callum. Or Cal for short, like my siblings and most of my friends do."

"So this isn't an official visit? You're snooping around the field behind the gift shop for fun?"

"Sorta. It's business-related but on my own time. Call it curiosity and a chance to keep my dog's skills on point."

Her gaze shifted to Pilot, and something warm lit her eyes. "That's your dog?"

"Huh? Oh, no. *That* dog just followed me here. I have no idea who that dog is," he said, keeping a confused look on his face. He glanced around as if looking for something. "You seen a miniature poodle around here? Pink bow, top-knot and painted toenails? Foofoo, where are you?"

She sneered. "Very funny."

He chuckled and turned to whistle for Pilot, who'd wandered toward the side parking lot, still sniffing the ground. On command, Pilot raised his head and loped over to sit at Cal's feet. "Good boy, Pilot."

Jules's eyes widened. "Wow. Impressive. That's an obedient dog."

"He's been trained to be obedient and has had years of practice." Cal fished in his pocket for another dog treat and tossed it to his Labrador retriever.

Without asking, Jules crouched by Pilot and ruffled the fur along his neck and behind his ears. "Aren't you a good puppy? Hey there, handsome. How are you?"

"Um..." Cal cleared his throat. "He's a working dog, and it's bad form for the general public to pat working dogs without permission. Especially when they are on the job."

Jules shot a guilty look up at Cal. Her mouth opened and closed before she stood, her cheeks pinking again, and muttered, "I know that. But aren't working dogs supposed to wear a vest identifying them as working dogs?"

Cal bobbed his head once in concession. "True. Usually. Pilot has a vest at home. But it's hot, and I wasn't expecting to see anyone out here, so I left it at home."

Pilot, tail wagging, walked over to Jules and nudged her hand with his nose.

She peered down at his Lab and crooned in a sweet voice, "I'm sorry. Your mean daddy says I can't love on you."

Cal blew a raspberry. "Go ahead. Our search hasn't turned up anything new, so he can go off duty."

"Duty?" She pulled a face as she squatted again and gave Pilot the sort of hearty scratches and face-to-face interaction he loved. "That sounds so serious. What kind of working dog is he?"

"Pilot's a retired search-and-rescue and cadaver dog."

Jules's head snapped back, her wide-eyed gaze flying to his. "Cadaver?"

"He helps find dead bodies." Her expression said she might be regretting her choice to allow Pilot to lick her face, as if he'd just been eating a corpse instead of sniffing out the scents of one.

She blinked. Sobered. Then sent him another baleful

look. “I know what cadaver dogs do, thank you. If he’s retired, why is he working tonight?”

“I still put him to work now and then, like tonight, when I think he can help with an investigation in an unofficial way. His joints aren’t what they used to be, but he gets bored, so…”

She continued ruffling Pilot’s neck and baby talking to his dog in dulcet tones. “You’re a good boy. Yes, you are. Does that feel good? So handsome.”

When Pilot licked her face and made happy snuffling noises, Jules smiled and chuckled softly, rewarding Pilot with nose kisses and more ear rubs. Pilot loved the attention from his new friend.

Cal, on the other hand, felt an unwelcome prick of… what? Jealousy? Surely not. And yet on some level, he didn’t like that his dog was getting all the affection and lighthearted attention from Jules while he got only frowns and sarcasm. At least this display of warmth toward his dog gave him more proof that a soft heart beat beneath her prickly exterior. He cut a glance toward the cathouse she’d made for the grouchy stray. Definitely a soft heart.

After a moment, Jules glanced up at him again, her expression wary. “So…why did you have Pilot out here now? You think there’s another dead body out here somewhere?”

That was exactly what he’d thought possible, but he didn’t want to alarm her. Cal shrugged. “I thought it was worth seeing what he turned up. Sometimes it’s not a body but clothing or something else with the scent of decay on it. While our local police and sheriff departments are among the best in the business, we’re small and spread kinda thin during tourist season. Just giving the task force a helping hand searching the grounds.”

"And?" she said, her voice anxious. "Did he find anything?"

"He was spot on identifying where Harper was found this morning but he found nothing else. Although he didn't get too far out in the field." Cal turned and scanned the surrounding area of gently sloping hills and higher elevations rising across grassy plains. "I may send him back out in a minute to finish searching the fields."

"Harper? Does that mean you've identified the body?" She gave Pilot another nuzzle and scratch before rising to full height again.

"They have. He was known to authorities—his prints are in the system."

"He'd been arrested before? For what?" As if cold, she shivered and wrapped her arms around herself, despite the warm July evening.

"Nothing you need to worry about. The shop—this town—is safe, all things weighed out. Until evidence says otherwise, I see no reason to believe John Harper's death at this location was anything other than random."

"Somehow, I don't fine that reassuring," she said darkly.

He considered her point. He really couldn't say for sure if the *Geese in Flight* sculpture had been selected for whatever went down last night or if it had been a random happening. "Tell you what, I can come by in the evenings at closing time to walk you to your car until the killer is caught, if you'd like."

She gave him a dubious look and pointed to the small sedan parked behind the building. "I have all of twenty feet to walk to reach my car. It's not like I have to venture into a vast parking garage or megalot."

"Just offering," he said, flipping up a hand.

"And what about the other twelve-plus hours a day I'm here at the shop, often working alone?"

"Twelve hours a day?" he repeated, aghast.

"Yeah. Don't forget, those men came into the shop last night. I was there alone with them!"

He sobered. "I'm aware."

The notion that she'd had a brush with these men disturbed him more than he cared to admit…as did the idea of her working long hours by herself in this remote location, where cell service was spotty.

"And what about the second man? The one in the UNLV hoodie? Do you have an ID on him yet?"

"Unfortunately, no. Forensics is still sorting through the dozens of fingerprints and hairs they collected from the sales floor. Without a facial description from you, or a camera, it will be quite a while before our limited staff sorts through everything." He lifted an eyebrow. "Which reminds me…if you and any other shop employees could swing by the police station to be fingerprinted, it would help with eliminating your prints from customers'."

"I'll let Bonnie know. She's my summer help." She twisted her mouth as if in thought. "How long are you going to keep the shop closed?"

"That's not up to me. I'm not the lead on the case. But once the forensics team is sure they've recovered any evidence there might be in the store, you'll be free to reopen."

"You're not in charge? You were sure acting like it this morning," she said.

He forced a grin, trying to shake the needling disquiet that had crept over him. "Are you calling me overbearing?"

"If the shoe fits…" she said under her breath.

"My brother is a detective with the Red Grove PD, and

he's leading a task force looking into the drug traffic in the area. He's taking lead on the case."

"So I was right about the guys that came in the gift shop? That was a drug deal?" Her expression reflected a combination of disgust and satisfaction, presumably for believing she'd been right about Harper and his cohort.

"Too soon to say for sure. Suffice to say, the task force will follow all leads." He reached down to rub Pilot's ears when his dog sat on his foot and leaned against his leg. "I'm surprised you're not thrilled to have the shop closed for a day or two. If you're working as many hours as you say, the closure is like a minivacation. You don't have to spend money to relax. Sleep in tomorrow. Do something fun."

She aimed a withering look at him. "Something fun? At the Catch-a-Wink Motor Inn?" She shook her head. "Sheriff, I'm here now because even the closed shop with the sales floor cordoned off is more fun than my motel room."

"Cal. Remember? I'm Cal when I'm off duty." When she didn't respond, he followed an internal nudge. "If you're avoiding your motel room out of boredom, what about joining me at Pie Works for a pizza?"

She blinked at him. "What?"

He chuckled at the note of horror in her tone, as if he'd asked her to join him at a satanic ritual instead of dinner. "Is that a problem? Have you already eaten?"

"No, but…" She appeared truly flummoxed, her mouth open, her brow puckered in bewilderment. "Why?"

Her question startled a laugh from him. "Why? Because I'm hungry, and I thought you might be, too."

And because I find you fascinating. And because you're fun to verbally spar with. And because it would give me an excuse to ask more questions about your confusing and slightly suspicious background information.

Hitching his mouth in a lopsided grin, he added, "Pilot's going. If eating dinner with me is uncomfortable for you, you can consider this a date with Pilot instead."

Now the color washed from her face as her eyebrows shot up. "A date? You're asking me on a date?"

He exhaled and swiped a hand over his face before shaking his head. "I didn't mean to imply—" He spread his hands. "It was just an offer of dinner. I know today was upsetting, and you said your motel was nothing to write home about, so…" He lifted one eyebrow, inviting a response.

She studied him for several seconds, the dent in her cheek telling him she was biting the fleshy part inside in mouth.

Finally, he said, "Never mind," at the exact moment she said, "Okay."

"Okay?" he asked, on top of her "What?"

He gave his head a small shake, then aimed a finger at the back door of the shop. "I'll wait here while you get your purse and lock up. All right?"

She tipped her head at a haughty angle. "My purse, huh? You invited me to join you. I think that means *you're* buying dinner."

The corner of her mouth twitched *just a little*, but enough to tell him she was enjoying the verbal jousting as well. A full smile spread across his face as he gave a nod of assent. "It's a deal."

Chapter 6

Why had she agreed to have dinner with Cal Colton? Forget that pizza was her favorite food, and she hadn't indulged in a good restaurant meal in months, since she was trying to pinch pennies. And forget that he looked as good as homemade sin on a Saturday night, as her college roommate used to say. He was a cop. Not just any cop. The county *sheriff.*

No part of this arrangement made sense, given her experiences, both with law enforcement and too-handsome men. The former were unreliable and left vulnerable people helpless and prey to the wolves of society and the latter were just…well, window dressing. Self-centered, self-serving and shallow. She'd not make *that* mistake again.

Yet here she was, devouring a deep-dish pepperoni and mushroom pie with a man who looked like he'd walked off the set of a Hollywood Western…and having a good time. The man really did have the most engaging smile and melodic laugh…

Stop! her brain shouted.

Must. Not. Let. Guard. Down. And especially don't be sidetracked or fooled by anything as superficial as a handsome face and easy grin. *Sheesh, Jules!*

"How old is Pilot?" she asked as Cal took a bite of pizza.

The dog in question was lying quietly at his master's feet while they dined at the pet-friendly local pizza joint.

"Ten."

While he chewed, she queried, "Did you train him or did someone at the sheriff's department do that?" The more questions she asked about his dog, the fewer he could ask about her. And since learning more about Cal was off the table—no sense getting personal with anyone in law enforcement—she had to find safe, neutral topics to pass the time.

"The department found him through a search-and-rescue training facility. I've had him since he graduated the program, almost nine years ago."

She raised her pizza for a bite, and he used the same ploy she had, hitting her with a question when her mouth was occupied. "Do I detect a hint of Canadian accent?"

She shrugged. "Maybe a little."

"Oh? You've spent a lot of time in Canada then?"

She ignored the question for a couple of seconds, hoping he'd move on to another topic if she chewed long enough. When he didn't, she finally nodded. "About four years."

"Hmm. What took you to Canada?"

She rolled her eyes. He was acting like this was a blind date, asking all the trivial personal questions and making irritating small talk.

But the pizza was really good, so she supposed she could play along until they finished eating. She sighed and wiped her mouth. "I was there for graduate school. The University of Manitoba."

His face brightened. "Oh, yeah? What specialty?"

She frowned, hesitating. "Chemistry."

He pulled a face that said he was pleasantly surprised. "Wow. Impressive. So then what brought you to Red Grove?

Why is someone with an advanced chemistry degree working at a tourist gift shop?"

He said it casually, but she detected more than an idle curiosity behind the question. She plucked a slice of pepperoni off her pizza and popped it in her mouth, trying to think of a way to steer the conversation away from her past, her life choices. "I have my reasons." Before he could press her further, she asked, "You mentioned a brother earlier. The one leading the investigation about the dead guy from this morning? Is he your only sibling?"

"No. I have two sisters and three brothers. All younger. What sort of reasons?" he asked, without taking a breath to give her a chance to deflect. "Why not work in the chemistry field if you did all that work to earn an advanced degree?"

"Who says I earned the degree? All I said is that I was at the University of Manitoba for school, that I was specializing in chemistry." She realized her mistake as soon as she spoke. Rather than put him off with a sassy retort, she'd intrigued him all the more with her implication she'd not finished the degree program. Dang it!

"Why did you leave early?" he asked. Of course…

Jules gritted her back teeth, frustrated with herself as she decided whether to change the subject, tell him to buzz off or give him a surface understanding of the truth. The pizza she'd been gobbling now sat like a rock in her belly. She hated looking at the situation that had brought her to Red Grove too closely. It broke her heart. And made her blood boil. And kept her awake at night trying to find a way to correct the situation. Which she couldn't. Not by herself. Not without the cooperation of the legal system, which had so far been anything but cooperative.

She dusted crumbs from her hands and lifted her chin as

she met eyes the color of copper sulfate. “Why?” Her tone was sharp and loud, and she didn’t care. “I’ll tell you *why*. Because I *had to*! Because my sister needed me. I have to protect her, because no one else will! That’s *why*.”

She knew she’d attracted the attention of the diners seated around them. Even Pilot had lifted his head and given a small whine and head tilt. But she only cared about the reaction of the man across the table from her. Technically, he was one of *them*—a member of the profession that had so failed her and Abby for years and contributed to her sister’s fragility.

Cal put down his slice of pizza and leaned back in his chair, a cocktail of sympathy and curiosity brewing in his gut. The scorn in her tone was plain enough, but there was an edge of something else. Grief? Fear? Pain? Clearly, he’d picked a scab, and Jules was bleeding. Compassion nudged him to staunch the flow of heartache, but knowing he’d uncovered something important about her, he couldn’t back off the line of questioning…yet.

“What are you protecting your sister from, Jules? What’s important enough to pause your degree work and move to the Middle of Nowhere, North Dakota?”

Her mouth tightened, and she didn’t answer immediately. When she finally did respond, she evaded his question. “Nowhere? That’s rather derogatory for the local sheriff, don’t you think? Would local voters be happy to know that’s what you think of Stark County?”

He wiped his greasy fingers on his napkin and shrugged casually. “There’s plenty to love about my hometown. And I *do* love it. But there’s no denying it’s isolated. Not the sort of place someone used to life in Winnipeg usually chooses.”

"Again, Sheriff," she said pointedly, her mouth tight, "I have my reasons. And they're none of your business."

"Maybe. Until your reasons become part of my murder investigation."

She stiffened, clearly shocked by his statement. "What?"

"Why were you arrested for contempt of court?"

Her eyes widened. "How do you know—" Rather than finish her question, she clamped her jaw tight and narrowed an angry glare on him. Cal marveled at how bright and deeply green her eyes became when she was mad. Finally, in a low tone she asked, "Is this an interrogation? Should I call a lawyer?"

He held her gaze for several long seconds, fascinated not only by the rich color of her eyes, but also by how fast his pulse ticked as they stared at each other. Did she sense the crackle and snap of attraction that he did?

Realizing that, like a wild animal, she might take his continued stare as hostility and a challenge, he dropped focus to his plate and rubbed a hand on his cheek. "No and no. Not an interrogation. I guess your evasive answers just triggered my interrogative instincts. When criminal suspects won't answer questions with a direct answer, they usually have something to hide."

"So we agree that you're treating me like a criminal?" She haughtily arched an eyebrow.

"I—"

"Clearly, you've snooped into my past. That's the only way you'd have known about the contempt of court charge."

He raised a hand, conceding the point. "I did look into your public records. For good reason. You were the last person we know of to see John Harper alive."

"Except his murderer," she corrected. Then, as if she realized what he'd said, her eyes flared wide, and she added, "I didn't kill him!"

"I'm not saying you did. But we have to dot all our i's and cross all our t's. The fact that I'm asking you these questions here—" he gave a subtle nod to the pizza place's dining room "—instead of at the sheriff's department is proof I don't consider you a suspect. But when, in the course of an investigation, I learn that a key witness has had a brush with the courts, it does give me pause."

She folded her arms over her chest and turned to stare at the pinball machine in the corner of the room, her mouth pinched. When Pilot stood and moved to put his head in her lap, as if sensing she was upset and needed comfort, he covered his grin with his napkin and wiped his mouth.

Jules stroked Pilot's head and rubbed his ears, moisture sparkling in her eyes. After taking a breath, she seemed calmer and muttered, "I lost my temper at a court proceeding that didn't go the way I wanted, and I called the judge a..."

Now his cheek did curl up in a grin. "Yes? You called the judge what?"

She sighed. "A useless tool."

He muffled a chuckle. "I'm guessing he deserved to be called much worse."

"For the record, I'm not proud of my behavior, but sometimes my mouth shoots off before I think."

He feigned shock. "No!"

For his teasing, she crooked an expressive eyebrow again and grunted. Fixing her attention on Pilot, she said, "That useless tool is only one reason I knew if I didn't protect my sister, no one else would."

Cal picked up his pizza again, and after taking a bite

and swallowing, he asked, "So is it a safe assumption that your sister lives here in Red Grove?"

Jules dusted dog fur from her hands before lifting her own pizza slice. "In a manner of speaking."

When he shot her a look for her equivocating answer, she held up a hand. "Look, Sheriff—"

"Cal."

"Humph. When you stop acting like the sheriff and more like a regular Joe—"

"Cal. A regular Cal. Or Callum if you want to be formal."

The expression she flashed was one of irritation… but he saw a glimpse of humor as well. Was he breaking through her icy facade at last? She looked down at Pilot, who thumped his tail on the floor when he saw her attention shift to him. "Tell me, Pilot. Is he always this annoying?"

Pilot woofed, and she rewarded him with a slice of pepperoni. "That's what I thought."

"Hey now!" He flashed a faux scowl. "No fair asking my loyal companion to break the implied dog-owner confidentiality agreement."

Jules shrugged and took a bite of pizza.

While her mouth was full, he leaned forward, bracing his forearms against the table. "For what it's worth, if there's anything I can do to help protect your sister, I'm at your service."

She blinked as if startled by his offer. A moment later, she lowered her brow as if skeptical, then continued eating. "I'll only believe that when I see it."

Chapter 7

Jules felt a little lighter as she followed Cal from the pizza parlor out to his Jeep Wrangler. But was that because they'd shared the best meal she'd had in weeks? Maybe. Her stomach was definitely happier. Or was her mood better because she was starting to find his ability to match her snarkiness...*amusing*? Possibly, although she'd never admit as much to him.

She considered his offer to help protect Abby, and her initial spike of hope was quickly squashed under the weight of experience and practicality. Reassurances from law enforcement, like Cal's "anything I can do," always proved empty words. For that reason alone, she doubted she'd see Cal Colton again after tonight. She was on a solo mission to keep Abby safe, and no blue-eyed, charming small-town sheriff was likely to change that.

A pity, a renegade voice in her head whispered. *He's easy on the eyes and easy to talk to as well.* As they crossed the parking lot, she cast a side glance toward him, admiring the cut of his jaw and shadow of stubble on his cheeks. *Oh, yeah. Very easy on the eyes.*

Gritting her back teeth, she shut up that voice fast. Until she knew Abby was safe and happy again, she had no room in her life for distractions. Not her schooling, not side hobbies and certainly not a romantic relationship.

When they reached his vehicle, he opened the passenger door for her, and Pilot hopped in and settled on the seat, panting and content.

She had to crack a grin.

"Sorry, pal," Cal told Pilot. "The lady gets to ride shotgun tonight." He pointed to the back seat, and with a chuff of disappointment, Pilot crawled into the back.

She settled in the passenger seat then twisted to pat Pilot's head. "Thank you, puppers. Who's a good boy?"

Pilot wagged his tail and moved to the open window to sniff the night air.

As Cal drove her back to the gift shop to pick up her car, he resumed quizzing her, this time about the kind of stuff that might be discussed on a first date. But since this wasn't a date, she saw no need to give him more than terse, evasive answers.

"Where do your parents live? Do you get back to see them often?"

"No. Mom's in Portland, last I heard. Dad died."

"What do you like to do in your free time?"

"What free time?"

"Read any good books lately?"

"If I don't have free time, when am I supposed to read?"

"Okay. Umm, do you follow any sports teams?"

"Yes."

He shot her a lopsided grin. "Just *yes*? Am I supposed to guess which team, which sport?"

"It's a free country. Guess if you want."

He seemed to relish the challenge. "Okay then. You lived in Canada for a while. Maybe the hockey bug caught you?"

When she said nothing, he said, "No? Okay, baseball? If Mom's in Portland maybe…the Mariners?"

More silence.

"Although I hear there's a movement afoot to bring an MLB team to Portland."

"Don't know. Don't care."

"Huh. Football then? I know a lot of women like football."

She yawned.

"Am I even close?" he asked, dividing his attention between her and the road.

"You seem to think only men play sports." She turned a smug look toward him. "What about the WNBA? Or the National Women's Soccer League?"

"Touché," he said with a nod. "So women's basketball and soccer?"

She shrugged. "Not really. Just calling out your sexism."

He laughed. "My bad. I do know better. Don't tell my sisters, or I'll get an earful from them as well."

She should have told him she doubted she'd ever meet his sisters, but he'd just pulled his Jeep into the gift shop parking lot, so she let it drop.

As she climbed out of the Wrangler, she modulated her attitude long enough to thank him for the meal. She could be snippy, but she wasn't an ingrate.

"My pleasure," he returned, and the twinkle in his eyes said he meant it. But had he enjoyed dinner because he had skillfully cracked her reserve with his charming grins and gotten her to admit things she didn't usually share? Or was his delight based in some ill-formed belief that they shared an attraction?

Before she closed the Jeep door, she reached in the back seat to scratch Pilot behind the ears and tell him goodnight.

Cal rolled down the passenger window and called out, "If I wanted to talk with you again tomorrow, where should I look? At the Catch-a-Wink or here at the shop?"

She squared her shoulders. "You tell me. Will the police still insist I keep the shop closed tomorrow?"

He raised his hand from the steering wheel, gesturing vaguely. "Initially, I'd think. The investigation is only a day old. We're lucky to have an ID on the victim this quickly."

"Because he was in the system."

He hesitated. "Right. So where should I look for you tomorrow?"

"You're still acting like I'm a suspect. I already answered all your questions this morning—plus some at dinner—and if I am a suspect, I should have been allowed a lawyer present." From the corner of her eye, she saw the black cat creep around the corner of the gift shop and huddle by the down spout.

"*Should* we consider you a suspect?" Cal asked, bringing her full attention back to him.

She scowled. "Do you really think I'd tell you if you should?"

"Likewise. Do you really think I'd tell you what evidence we might have where you're concerned?"

She stiffened. "That sounds like you *are* investigating me." The notion was appalling and fed her distrust and dislike of police.

"Do you have something to hide?" he asked, arching a dark eyebrow.

She gritted her back teeth. "Can you give me a straight answer?"

The corner of his mouth twitched. "Does it bother you to have your question answered with a question?"

"Are you always this annoying?" She folded her arms over her chest, scowling at him.

"Have I annoyed you?"

She started to mutter something dark under her breath, but caught it on her tongue. He was teasing her, goading her. Recognizing his game, she refused to let him win. She chewed the inside of her cheek, deciding on a worthy comeback.

"Your ability to state the obvious is impressive, Sheriff. Did they teach you that in 'Duh 101' or did you hone those *keen* detective skills all on your own?"

Sheriff Colton threw his head back and let a musical belly laugh fly. "Good one, Jules. Well played!"

He wiped the corner of his eyes with a finger, and a self-satisfied grin quivered on her lips. She faked a cough to cover it, lifting a hand to hide her mouth.

After bringing his amusement under control, Cal raised four fingers to his temple in a salute. "Good night, Ms. Bailey. Count on seeing me again tomorrow. I will find you, wherever you choose to spend the day."

With that, he pulled away, the bits of gravel in the parking lot crackling beneath the Jeep's tires.

She stood, frozen for a moment, letting his parting words replay in her head. *I will find you, wherever...*

Chase Hamilton, Abby's stalker, had said much the same thing to Abby time and again. Not always in such pointed terms, but always with a subtle promise that she would never be rid of his menace.

Jules shivered, but not because of the dropping temperature as the sun disappeared below the horizon. Before Cal had tossed out that final promise, she'd actually found herself equal parts amused and irritated by their repartee. The teasing back-and-forth allowed her to maintain her snarky persona while safely exploring the boundaries of Cal Colton, a man she found surprisingly engaging.

She shook her head, reminding herself she'd be foolish to fall for any vague promises or put her faith in *any* law enforcement officer again. She'd been down that road and disappointed too many times already. With a sigh, she tried to set aside the disquiet of his parting words, the reminder of Chase's stalking and the tension that had hovered all day since the body had been found near the gift shop. Good grief! A *murder* at her doorstep was the *last* thing she needed if she wanted to lie low around law enforcement.

After digging her car key out of her purse, she shivered a bit thinking about the creeps who had been in the store last night and the body found beneath the sculpture this morning. A new possibility occurred to her and she paused, her heart thrashing.

Could Chase be connected to the murder? Was he the man in the red hoodie? She dredged up her memories of Chase Hamilton's physical description, the sound of his voice. Was he that tall, that broad-shouldered? Was he killing random people in Jules's proximity to send a message? To frighten her away from town? The possibility seemed unlikely, yet chilling.

But, to the best of her knowledge, Chase wasn't aware of who she was, or her position as the manager of the gift shop, and she'd never been in a courtroom with him. She had no social media presence, no photograph associated with her published graduate school research. Did he even realize Abby had a sister?

Hearing a pitiful mewl, her gaze returned to the small black cat, who looked poised and ready to run if she got too close...but also eager to see what food offering Jules had for her. She angled her head as she studied the scruffy feline. "I can't keep feeding you tuna. And you're not really safe out here, even with that house I made."

The cat crept a few steps closer. "Meow."

Joy's high-pitched mewl melted her heart. "I'll bring you some real cat food when I come in the morning. For now, I think there's some Vienna sausage about to expire in the storage room. How does that sound?"

"Merp."

"Okay. I'll be right back." Once she scrounged up an older can of canned sausage from the storage room, she returned to the back door, where the black kitten hovered at the threshold, peeking inside. She dumped the meat on a paper plate, broke it into bites and carried it to the stoop. "Here, you go, Joy. Eat up."

Although the cat scurried away when Jules approached, stopping long enough to hiss over her shoulder, by the time Jules was in her car and pulling out of the parking lot, Joy was gobbling the sausage.

Her heart twisted. She hated to see the poor, cranky kitten scrabbling for food and vulnerable to predators. Could she catch Joy? Bring her inside? What was she supposed to do with a kitten, especially one that was largely wild and armed with four razor-sharp death mittens? She told herself she was cuckoo to pursue this path, but when she reached her motel room, she would place a call to the local animal rescue group to inquire about borrowing a humane trap.

She wrapped her arms around herself to ward off the chill in the air. Casting her gaze around the dark North Dakota plains, she shivered at the vast emptiness of the surrounding grassland. Only last night, two men had met out here at the isolated sculpture, and one man had ended up dead. A man she'd seen alive, talked to just moments before he was killed.

In the distance, a coyote yipped and whined, and a disturbing thought she'd been trying to hold at bay finally presented itself at the fore of her mind. The man in the red hoodie had clearly been concerned about cameras capturing his likeness. And while he had hidden his face from Jules, what was stopping the killer from coming to permanently silence her?

She shuddered and considered calling Cal—no, don't allow yourself to be distracted with his casual manner. She chewed her bottom lip and weighed asking the sheriff about her own safety during this investigation. But all she had to do was remember how dismissive every law enforcement officer she'd trusted with Abby's safety had been to know when it came to her protection, she was on her own.

Chapter 8

Cal whistled to himself as he parked in the driveway of the house he shared with his father, the house where he'd grown up. Sure, he'd have thought by now he'd have his own place, maybe be married with kids. But since his parents' divorce, he'd taken upon himself the responsibility of keeping an eye on his father. Dr. Jonathon Colton was a brilliant physician, but he could be absentminded. A loner. So focused on his work and patients that he sometimes forgot to eat and neglected sleep.

At times, Cal felt like he was the parent, reminding his dad of appointments and apprising him of family news, doing the grocery shopping, cooking and monitoring Jonathon's health. The duty had become second nature since his father had been rather absent throughout Callum's life, and Cal had assumed a number of paternal roles for his siblings. Especially following his parents' divorce.

After his mother left the marriage and the family home, Jonathon had become all the more work-focused and closed off. As the oldest child, Cal hadn't hesitated to step in to fill the void.

Pilot trotted out into the grass and sniffed around, and Cal waited for his dog to finish his business before keying open the mudroom door and standing aside as Pilot squeezed inside first. He was about to flip on the kitchen light when he noticed Pilot's body going still, his ears pricking with alertness to a sound. Pilot gave a low growl that made the hair on Cal's nape bristle.

Someone was in the house—someone that was *not* his father, since Pilot knew Jonathon and his smell as well as he knew Cal's scent. And there hadn't been another car in the driveway, his father's or anyone else's.

Cal unsnapped the strap over his service weapon at his hip and edged deeper into the house, wondering why the security alarm on the house hadn't sounded or sent a notification to his phone.

He heard bumps and rattling sounds coming from upstairs, and he moved quietly through the dark house to the foot of the stairs. Pilot stayed right beside him, his nose sniffing the air, then lowering to follow the scent up the steps, his canine body taut. A light glowed from one of the bedrooms upstairs, though he couldn't tell which one from this angle.

The thumping of footsteps and distinctive squeak of the upstairs hall floorboards told him the intruder was on the move. He hunched low behind the banister and was about to take the stairs when Pilot's body language shifted. Eased.

His dog's ears relaxed, and his tail wagged. He gave a friendly *woof* of greeting.

"Well, hi, Pilot. How are you, ol' boy?" said a voice Cal knew immediately, and he let his tense shoulders sag in relief.

His younger brother Dylan appeared at the top of the stairs and bent to ruffle Pilot's fur. When Dylan noticed Cal standing on the bottom step, his smile faltered, and he raised both hands. "Whoa! Don't shoot, Cal. It's me."

Cal let a low grumble roll from his throat and took his

time putting his service gun away. "I should shoot you on principle. What are you doing lurking in my house without turning on any lights, much less letting me know you were in town? I thought I had a B and E."

Dylan, his dark, shaggy hair currently accompanied by unkempt facial hair, lowered his hands and flashed an apologetic grin. "Sorry, Callum. You're right. I shoulda texted or something. I'm just in the habit of *not* letting anyone know where I am, and so…" He buzzed his lips and shrugged instead of finishing his excuse.

"Did you disable my security system?" Cal asked, arching an eyebrow. His brother, a special agent with the FBI, was perfectly capable of such, and it would explain why the house alarm hadn't alerted him.

"No," Dylan snorted. "I got the code from Dad when I called to let him know I needed to get a few things from my closet. Dad clearly didn't share the news I was home."

Cal snorted. "Come on. You've met Jonathon Colton. Do I really have to answer that?"

"Again. Sorry for startling you. Although," Dylan said, coming down the steps with an easy gait, "if you don't want intruders, you should consider changing your security code now and then. You've had the same one for a few years now, haven't you?"

"I've tried changing it before, and Dad invariably forgets that it is changed and sets it off in the middle of the night. He finally asked me just to leave it alone and keep the old code permanently."

Dylan frowned. "You think that's a sign of early onset dementia? I mean, he's only, what? Sixty-two years old?"

Cal shook his head. "He's mentally as sharp as ever. He's just the same overworked, can't-be-bothered-with-mundane-details-of-life, gives-one-hundred-and-ten-percent-to-his-patients dad we know and love. Learning changed passwords and security codes are mundane details he doesn't want to give the extra bandwidth."

Dylan nodded his understanding, and after a beat in which they simply stared knowingly at each other, Cal grinned and pulled his younger brother into a bear hug. "Damn, it's good to see you! Are you between cases? You going to be in town long?"

Dylan pounded his back. "It's good to see you, too."

As they stepped back from the embrace, Cal chuckled. "So you can't answer my questions, I take it?"

Not knowing where Dylan was assigned or what cases he was working was part and parcel of their brother's job with the FBI. Cal and his siblings had gotten used to the sporadic and surprise visits Dylan paid the family, only when one assignment was finished and his next was still pending. They'd celebrated a number of "Dylan Christmases" in January or even May, and Thanksgiving dinner almost always had an empty seat at the Colton table.

Dylan lifted a shoulder. "Price of the job, man."

Cal sighed. "Yeah, I get it. Although if you are still in town Saturday, the family's all coming here for our annual bash for the Fourth. Fireworks, food, volleyball. The works. Hope you can hang around long enough for that. I know everyone would love to lay eyes on you."

His brother pursed his lips and nodded slowly. "I think I can make that work."

"Great! So are you staying with me and Dad for a few days then?"

"No. I have…other arrangements. I'm doing a little work in the area and—" Dylan waved a hand vaguely.

"No need to explain. We're used to your mysterious

ways. Just do the family a favor and let us know if you ever have a kid or get married or something?"

His brother snorted, then muttered, "Right. As if I could meet someone, much less have a real relationship, with this job."

A pang of regret pierced Cal's soul. As much as Dylan seemed to find his job fulfilling, the notion that his brother might not find someone to spend his life with because of it saddened Cal. He was, frankly, surprised that none of his siblings had settled down yet, although maybe he shouldn't be. Red Grove, North Dakota, was hardly a dating hot spot. Everyone knew everyone else and their business, and anyone he or his siblings might consider dating, they likely already had.

Which brought his thoughts back around to Jules. She had eschewed the idea their dinner out was a date, and technically, it hadn't been. But sitting across from her at the table had felt comfortable. Even her reticence to answer his questions hadn't spoiled the easy mood he'd enjoyed. Instead, the way she'd danced around his probing questions intrigued and challenged him, as if she was playing hard to get and he was taking the bait, hook, line and sinker.

A loud whistle roused him from his musings, and he found Dylan eyeing him. "Huh?"

"Man, where'd you go just then?" Dylan asked. "'Cause you sure weren't listening to me."

"Oh, sorry. Say it again?"

Dylan waved him off, instead fixing a speculative stare on him. "You okay? You had a faraway look in your eyes and were wearing a funny grin." He arched a dark eyebrow. "Are you drunk?"

Cal's eye roll said, *I'm not even going to answer that.*

Hitching his thumb over his shoulder, Dylan started back

up the stairs. "Well, I'm gonna just get a few more summer clothes packed up, and I'll get out of your hair."

"So… Saturday? Come anytime. We'll get started early and go all day."

"Saturday. Wouldn't miss it."

Except Dylan had missed so much in recent years, and Cal hated it. His family meant the world to him. Cal left Dylan to his task and returned to the kitchen.

Jules's impassioned explanation of her move to Red Grove replayed in his mind as he fed Pilot his dinner and set up the coffee pot for the next morning. *My sister needed me. I have to protect her, because no one else will!* So Jules had moved to Red Grove because her sister had, but she'd been vague about why her sister chose to live here.

In a manner of speaking.

What the heck did that mean? Jules clearly had trust issues, and he, as law enforcement, was at the top of her list as untrustworthy. He'd have to work on changing that opinion, because Jules Bailey was someone he wanted to know. Intimately.

Chapter 9

The next day, Cal accompanied Wyatt, who had his own questions for Jules, to the gift shop on the Enchanted Highway. He spotted Jules's car behind the gift shop, as expected, and parked next to her.

"That her car?" Wyatt asked, pointing to the old sedan.

Cal chuckled to himself, remembering Jules's dig last night about him stating the obvious and almost used the Duh 101 line on his brother.

Instead, he just nodded and climbed out of his Jeep into the bright sun. Today would be another warmer-than-usual day by the looks of it.

Wyatt followed him to the back door of the shop and waited while Cal knocked. Cal swept his gaze around the lot, looking for signs anything had changed since yesterday. Tire tracks in the dirt. A bit of trash. Flattened grass at the edge of the lot that could mean someone had tromped through the weeds.

A quiet buzzing brought his attention to a paper plate just down from the back door. Flies and a lone bee swarmed around what appeared to be the remnants of some kind of brown mush. Next to the dirty plate was a chipped bowl with water. She was still feeding the stray then. He smiled, recognizing this kindness to a stray as an indication of Jules's tender heart.

Jules answered the door a few seconds later, looking lovely despite the dark smudges under her eyes that suggested she hadn't slept well. She gave Cal a suspicious scowl, but when she turned to Wyatt, her expression brightened to a welcoming smile. "Hello there. Let me guess. You're Sheriff Colton's brother, the police detective. You have the same eyes."

Wyatt tapped a finger to his nose. "Good guess." He offered his hand. "Detective Wyatt Colton. And you'd be Jules Bailey?"

Her smile brightened as she tapped her own nose, then gripped Wyatt's hand. "How can I help you, Detective?"

Cal frowned as he watched the cordial exchange. What was happening here? Where was the snarky woman he'd met yesterday?

"I know you've already talked with the sheriff, but I'd like to ask my own questions, if you have a few minutes?"

"Certainly. Come in, please." She stood back and waved Wyatt inside. When Cal followed his brother, she gave him a wry look. "You always tag along with your little brother?"

There she was. Miss Sarcasm was back.

He met her jibe with a cocky you-can't-rile-me grin. "When official business calls for it."

She rolled her eyes, then led Wyatt to the break room. "Can I get you something to drink, Detective? Coffee? A soft drink?"

"No thanks," Wyatt said, settling at the rickety Formica table where Cal had sat yesterday to interview her.

"I'd love a cup of coffee. Black," Cal said, testing her.

She gave him a flat look, then hitched her head to the

counter where the coffee maker sat, the pot a quarter full. “Knock yourself out.”

He arched an eyebrow. Why was Wyatt getting the red carpet and glowing reception that he most certainly had not? And why did he care?

She took the chair across from Wyatt, her expression open and pleasant. “Fire away, Detective. What questions do you have?”

Wyatt put a small digital recording device on the table, then stated his name, the date, time and location and asked Jules to state her full name. “Does the name John Harper mean anything to you?”

“Not before yesterday. Cal told me that’s who they identified the man found dead by the sculpture to be.”

Wyatt cast a glance toward him, lifting one eyebrow. “*Cal* told you that, did he?” His brother’s expression and emphasis on his name told Cal it was her familiar use of his first name that intrigued him more than his divulging case information to Jules.

“Yes,” she said.

“Had you seen John Harper before his body was discovered yesterday?” Wyatt asked.

She nodded. “As I told Sheriff Colton yesterday, I recognized the dead man, because he’d come into the gift shop at closing time the night before.”

“Alone?”

“At first. Then another man came in and spoke to him for about thirty seconds before he left again. Then Harper left a minute or so after that without buying anything or speaking to me. That was the only time I ever saw him until the next morning, when he was found dead.” She cocked her head to one side. “I already told your brother all of this. Didn’t he share his notes with you?”

"He did, but I wanted to verify some facts and dig a little deeper," Wyatt said.

She flashed an agreeable, maybe even flirtatious, smile. "And I'd wager you're also checking to see if my story changes, eh, Detective?"

"Just striving for accuracy and some more detail. Right now, you're our best lead, since you saw the man that was last seen with Harper."

Jules nodded. "Understood. Except I don't know how valuable my description of the man could be. I couldn't see him clearly because the hood of his sweatshirt shielded his face, and he kept his back to me."

"You'd be surprised how even seemingly insignificant bits of information can be the piece of the puzzle that brings a case together. Don't underestimate the usefulness of your statement."

She smiled again, and Cal's breath lodged in his lungs. The warmth in her face eased the fatigue that seemed to cling to her. Her eyes sparkled, and her cheeks glowed. She was stunning. "In that case, please proceed."

Leaning his hip against the counter where the coffee pot gurgled, Cal folded his arms over his chest and frowned as he watched Jules answer Wyatt's questions cheerfully, thoroughly and willingly. While he was glad his brother was getting a deeper understanding of minutia regarding the case, he couldn't help wondering what the actual heck was going on here? He'd never had reason to be jealous of Wyatt before, but…

Cal shook his head briskly. *Nope. He wasn't jealous. That was ridiculous.*

Over the next thirty minutes, Jules gave a detailed description of the second man, reiterated that she'd seen nothing suspicious before the men arrived or when she left the shop that night, and provided a timeline of when she'd moved to Red Grove and taken the position at the gift shop. No, she hadn't heard enough of the second man's voice to recognize it again. Yes, she was sure the hoodie had said UNLV. No, she couldn't really say how tall he was. Just… average height.

"Last question," Wyatt said. "In the three months that you've worked here at the gift shop, have you seen anything to indicate that there were regular drug deals happening on the grounds or near the *Geese* sculpture?"

She seemed rattled by this question, as if the suggestion that such illicit transactions and unsavory characters operating under her nose and unbeknownst to her frightened her.

"Not to my knowledge," she said, a frown denting her brow. "During the hours I'm at the shop, I generally only see tourists. Families, guided groups, school field trips, that sort of thing. No one I'd ever considered suspicious."

Wyatt rubbed his chin and considered her answer, then bobbed a nod. "All right then. I think that covers it. If you remember anything else you believe could be helpful—"

"I'll be sure to call you, Detective." Rallying her composure, she flashed a bright grin that made Cal's pulse tick and stumble. She was beautiful all the time, but when she smiled…damn!

When she glanced his way, her eyebrows were raised as if to ask *did you see that? See how helpful I was for him?* Cal's muscles tensed in irritation.

The little vixen was toying with him…

Cal quickly schooled his annoyance and gave her a wink that wiped the smug look from her face.

"Thank you for your time, Jules. I know how busy you are," he said.

Her expression darkened, and she scoffed. "You do remember the shop's still closed. I'm bored spitless."

Cal turned to his brother. "Wyatt? What do you think? Does Forensics need anything else here?"

"I think it'll be safe for you to reopen tomorrow. I'll double-check with the team, but you should be back in business soon," Wyatt said.

As if she had a light switch turning her expression off and on, Jules glanced back at his brother with delight. "Oh, that would be wonderful. Thank you, Detective."

Geez, Louise. He had to get out of here before she saw how her mercurial mood got under his skin.

Five minutes and a few more flirtatious words for Wyatt later, Cal and his brother were back in his Jeep headed into Red Grove.

"So it's Cal, is it?" Wyatt asked, his tone teasing.

"I told her she could call me that. I didn't see the harm, since I'm not leading the investigation," Cal replied innocently. Then, because he couldn't help planting his flag to warn his brother away, he added, "I thought it would make her more comfortable when we had dinner together last night."

Wyatt laughed. "Now I get it. You must have done something to tick her off on your date, based on the cold shoulder she gave you back there."

"Hmm. You'd think, but…" He blew out a speculative breath. "She's been chippy with me from the beginning. Frosty from the moment I introduced myself at the crime scene yesterday morning."

"Well, I guess it's just your winning personality and devastating charms then," Wyatt said, a bit too amused for Cal's liking. "You should invite her to the family barbecue this weekend. She said she's new in town, so she might like to meet some more people."

He chewed on the idea. He *did* want to spend some more time with Jules, and the family's Fourth of July gathering was a good excuse.

Wyatt snorted and playfully punched him on the arm. "If you're thinking I'll try to steal her from you at the barbecue, I promise not to be too interesting and endearing around her. You know, to give you a fighting chance."

Cal's answering laugh was interrupted by the trill of his cell phone. He pulled over to the shoulder in order to take the call. The caller ID said it was the mayor of Red Grove calling, and he breezily greeted the man who was like another brother to him. "Teddy, my man, how's it going? Are we going to see you at the family get-together on Saturday?"

Ted Barrett, who'd been raised in the Colton household after his grandmother passed away, seemed caught off guard by the question. "Um, yeah. I'll be there. I, uh..." Teddy cleared his throat, and in a steadier voice said, "That's not why I'm calling, though."

"Oh? Do tell?"

"I need to see you in my office. ASAP."

Now Cal stumbled, startled by the mayor's stern edict. "Well...sure. Something wrong?" He glanced at Wyatt, who only shrugged.

"We'll discuss it when you get here. Can you come today? After lunch? I can work you in between afternoon appointments."

Cal considered teasing Teddy about being so important that his schedule was packed but decided Ted's tone proved the mayor was in no mood for playful banter. "I'll be there at two o'clock, if that works."

"Two o'clock then."

Chapter 10

Jules chuckled to herself as she watched Cal and his brother drive away. She could see how much her cooperation and kindness toward the detective bugged the sheriff. The inspiration had come to her the instant she opened the door and found Cal grinning his magnetic grin and standing beside a man whose family resemblance was unmistakable. But why had she felt the impulse to needle the sheriff? He'd been nothing but kind and professional with her. She even rather admired his ability to hold his own when she verbally sparred with him.

Maybe that was the problem. She liked the taut exchanges too much. She enjoyed goading a wry laugh from him and seeing the mischievous spark light his blue eyes. While she couldn't let him *know* she was charmed by him—that would only pointlessly encourage him—teasing him was entertaining in a time of her life otherwise filled with disappointment, worry and boredom. She saw no break in that pattern as long as she was in Red Grove, searching for justice and relief for her sister and working this thankless job.

She sighed as she returned to the chemistry journal she'd been browsing when the men had arrived. As long as the store was closed, she could do something to stay current on research and innovations in her field. She didn't even dare to clean up the fingerprint dust on the sales floor until she got approval to reopen.

That permission came a couple of hours later, from Cal, who dropped by in person bearing a sack of hamburgers and cold french fries from a fast food joint in town.

"I have a landline here at the shop, you know. You could have called to tell me," she said as he brushed past her with the greasy bag that smelled heavenly. "And I'm not a charity case that you have to feed."

"Not trying to imply you are, but my mother was big on teaching us not to show up empty-handed. Seeing as it was the lunch hour, and I had to eat as well, I thought I'd share." He unpacked the food onto the tiny break room table, and she pulled a fry from the pack. "Besides, I know the forensic team left a mess in the other room, and I wanted to help clean up. Can't stay long, though. I have a meeting with the mayor at two."

She felt like a heel for rebuffing his gesture, so she mumbled, "Well, thanks. I am kinda starving." After one bite, she tossed the cold french fry back into the pack. "Cold fries are the pits. What a waste."

"True. But this place is a fair hike out in the boonies." Cal took a large bite of his burger. "So I was thinking..."

"I thought I smelled smoke."

He grinned and tapped his head. "Mmm. Faulty wiring up there, you know."

She smiled without meaning to. "Anyway, your brilliant thoughts were?"

Before he could answer, there was a loud pounding on the back door.

Cal held his sandwich suspended halfway to his mouth. "You expecting someone?"

She pushed away from the table. "I wasn't expecting *you*, yet here we are."

When she opened the door, the haggard face that greeted her shot ice to her core.

Chase Hamilton.

She had to dig deep not to show any reaction to the man in his delivery uniform and unkempt hair. Instead, she silently opened the door wider to allow him room to push his loaded dolly inside. He said nothing to her, either, as he strode past, reeking of cigarettes and God knew what else.

When she turned around, Cal was standing in the door to the break room, but his attention was focused on her, not Chase.

Her gut churning, she returned to the break room, trying to hide her agitation, from both Cal and Chase. Letting the jangle of nerves and swirl of acid and loathing in her gut show to either man could be disastrous. Suddenly the aroma of hamburgers and cold fries turned her stomach.

Chase went about his work, unloading cases of snack foods and flats of canned soft drinks in the storage room. When he was done there, he entered the break room without looking at her or Cal. Though Cal was dressed casually, his golf shirt did bear the insignia of the sheriff's department if Chase paid attention to that detail. And how would Chase react to the unexpected presence of law enforcement on his delivery route?

While trying to remain inconspicuous, she monitored Chase from the corner of her eye, all the while feeling the weight of Cal's gaze on her. She heard Cal eating, though she could only pick at her burger.

When Chase walked toward her, she tensed and jerked her attention up to him, on full alert. He held out a clipboard, and she exhaled.

Of course. She had to sign for the delivery. Once she'd scribbled her initials on the sheet, Chase wheeled the dolly around and marched out, letting the door slam behind him. No "thank you" or "have a nice day." Not that she wanted one from him. She didn't want *anything* from Chase Hamilton, except maybe for him to crawl in a hole and die. The bastard.

Keeping her eyes down, she flattened both hands on the cool Formica tabletop and drew a slow calming breath.

Cal set his burger on the open wrapper on the table. His chair squeaked as he leaned back in it. If eyes could drill holes, she'd be Swiss cheese.

"What?" she growled, finally shooting him a glare.

"I didn't say anything."

She stuffed her uneaten burger and fries back in the greasy sack and pushed it away.

"I thought you were starving," he said, picking up his burger and finishing it in two bites.

"Lost my appetite."

He wiped his hands on a napkin then balled the paper wrapper from his sandwich. "Want to tell me what that was all about?" When she opened her mouth to deny she had anything to tell, he held up a finger. "I'm an expert in reading body language and determining when I'm being lied to, so don't even try."

"How about 'none of your business'?" she said, feeling prickly again.

"Maybe so, but considering I could feel the waves of tension rolling off of you while that guy was here, it certainly begs the question."

She stayed silent, although she figured he could probably hear the heavy thudding of her heart.

"I'd like to help if I can." He tipped his head and

scratched his chin. "You know, I have resources at my disposal..."

Resources... Her pulse tripped. Was there a way Cal could help her take down Chase Hamilton? Did she dare trust him with something no one else in law enforcement or the court system had helped her with in the past? Wouldn't she be wasting her breath asking for his help? And wouldn't working with him risk letting down her walls? She'd have to spend time with him, give him private details about her past, her family, her mission.

But hadn't she also promised Abby she'd do anything she could to bring her sister justice and make sure she was safe?

"Forgive me if I'm skeptical of your offer. I've asked law enforcement for help in the past, and they've failed me, spectacularly."

To his credit, Cal didn't dismiss her reply with one of his flippant and breezy responses or diminish her pain with a wink and a grin. "I'm sorry to hear that. How did law enforcement fail you?"

"By failing my sister."

"Is this related to the reason you moved here to Red Grove? You said last night that you came here for your sister. To protect her, I believe was how you put it."

"Yes. To protect her. Because law enforcement and the court system refused to do their job." The old discouragement and anger bubbled up in her, and she balled her hands to keep them from trembling.

Cal leaned toward her, his expression full of compassion. "Is there anything I can do to help?"

She sat back in her chair, debating.

He flipped up a palm. "Tell me about your sister. What's going on?"

To her dismay, tears stung her eyes, and she had to swipe

the moisture quickly to keep them from falling. Clearing her throat, she shoved down the ache and buried it under the layers of resentment and frustration that fueled her fight. For years, she'd used her bitterness as a shield against despair and hopelessness.

She'd never intended to share Abby's story with another cop or lawyer. She'd pleaded with law enforcement and court officials for years, to no avail. And while she knew on a practical level that Cal Colton, sheriff or not, was unlikely to make a difference in Abby's case, she couldn't ignore even the tiniest hope that Cal could help.

She took a beat, reining in the galloping of her heart and her agitated breathing. When she felt she had regained her composure, she said, "My sister is in the mental health facility just outside Red Grove. She had a mental health crisis—what used to be called a nervous breakdown."

Sympathy washed over his face. "I see. Go on."

"Abby was a happy, healthy child, despite our unreliable parents." She waved a hand. "Another story for another time."

He gave her a silent nod.

"Abby is beautiful and sweet and kind and…fragile. She attracted the attention of a man who worked for her college a couple of years ago. He began stalking her. Relentlessly. Frighteningly. Creepily. We knew who he was and called the police every time he escalated or approached her. We tried to get a restraining order against the guy, but the court claimed we didn't have sufficient proof that the guy posed a threat. We used all our money on the first incompetent lawyer we hired and couldn't afford to relitigate. So she moved. She transferred to a new college. Twice. The guy followed her. We called the cops again and again, and they did little or nothing to stop him from showing up everywhere she went and scaring her to death."

"Did he ever physically harm her? That should be enough to—"

"You sound like all the rest!" she snapped, cutting him off. "So we don't get protection from the guy until he rapes or beats her? What about her mental health? What's *that* worth? How would you feel if someone followed you from city to city and taunted you with creepy things left at your home or endless phone calls no matter how many times you changed your number?"

He sighed. "I get it."

"Do you? Because for my sister, it was a living hell. It broke Abby." She balled her hands on the tabletop and battled the bile that rose in her throat. "And no one in law enforcement did anything to stop him."

Cal reached across the table and covered her fist with his wide, warm palm. She should have jerked her hand away, but his long fingers captured hers, and the comfort in his gesture wrapped around her like a blanket. She stared at his hand on hers, a tangle of emotions knotted in her throat.

"I'm sorry so many people in positions of authority and public service have let you down. Your story doesn't reflect well on my profession." He squeezed her fingers adding, "I hope you'll give me the benefit of the doubt and let me see what, if anything, I can do to help your sister."

She lifted her focus from their joined hands to his tender gaze. The spark of hope he lit in her scared her. She didn't want to have faith in anyone again, especially not a small-town sheriff. She refused to risk her emotions, her trust, her soul again. She'd been disappointed, betrayed, failed too many times by too many men like Cal Colton.

So why did something in his piercing blue eyes move

the needle deep in her core? She should be running from him. Raising the drawbridge and lowering the portcullis against him.

She pried her fingers from his and tucked her hands under her arms. "What could you possibly do? The damage has been done. Abby is scared to her core to live beyond the walls of the mental health hospital. She can't sleep. She has panic attacks. She's deeply pessimistic about the rest of her life." Jules let her shoulders droop. "I don't know how to help her anymore."

"It sounds like you've already done the best thing for her, getting her professional help." He twisted his mouth as if weighing his next words. "Dare I ask? Do you know where her stalker is now? What he's up to?"

She barked a scornful laugh. "I'm afraid so. He's here. In Red Grove. He just delivered the gift shop's supply of soda and snacks for the coming week."

"The delivery man?" Stunned, Cal frowned. "Why didn't you say anything?"

"To him or to you?" Jules asked.

"Either. Both."

She scoffed. "I'm telling you now. As for him…" The muscles in her lean jaw flexed as she gritted her teeth. "His name is Chase Hamilton, and I've been very careful not to let him know who I am. If he knows I'm watching him and that I'm Abby's sister, I can't monitor him."

A prickle of alarm crawled up his spine. "Monitor him?"

"Is there an echo in here?" Jules quipped dryly, one eyebrow lifting.

Cal sighed and scratched his chin as he pondered her revelations. Wasn't it bad enough to have a growing drug problem in the county without adding a potentially violent stalker to the local mix? What had happened to the safe and peaceful Red Grove of his youth?

"Well, that changes everything." He leaned back in his chair, ignoring her sarcasm. "If he's here, he's in my jurisdiction, and *I* can keep a watch on him."

"You're going to keep a watch on him?" She pulled a face that said she was unimpressed.

He cocked his head and looked around as if curious. "You're right. I think there is an echo in here."

She snorted and rolled her eyes. "It's just…that's what every other police department in every other city where Abby's lived has said. They'd watch him. All to no avail. *Without proof of unlawful activity*," she said in a deep, mocking voice, "they couldn't do more than that." She scowled and huffed loudly. "I call bull on that! There has to be something the police can do to stop him from harassing her!"

He rubbed his chin, feeling the beginnings of stubble scrape his palm. "Not always. We are bound by the law." She opened her mouth to argue, and he held up a finger to stop her. "But… I will do everything in my power to put an end to his stalking, one way or another."

"Everything within your power…" She turned her head to glare toward the window. "Another trite phrase I've heard too often."

A beam of sunlight streamed through the window, catching highlights in her long chestnut hair. Cal studied her slightly too-lean countenance and the tiny stress lines at the corners of her eyes and mouth. Despite the signs of tension, she was beautiful. The more he learned about her, the more fascinated he became. She presented a hard, cold persona to the world, yet her interaction with Pilot, her concern for a stray cat, her willingness to put her life and education on hold for her sister all spoke of a tender heart and loving soul. In his experience, this sort of prickly behavior indicated a deep pain, a wound that a person hadn't healed from. And if she was dissatisfied with the actions, or inaction, of law enforcement in protecting her sister, he could see why he was caught in that crossfire. Guilty by association.

A deep desire to prove her wrong ignited inside him. He'd show her that he *did* understand her concern, that he wanted to help her. "Today's been a long and stressful day for both of us, so I won't press you on the matter anymore now, but tonight, around seven o'clock maybe, I'd like to dig into your sister's case with you. I'll need the full background on her stalker. I definitely want to monitor his activity."

She turned her gaze back to him and gave him an intense green-eyed stare, clearly weighing his sincerity, his trustworthiness, his honesty. "Fine. Seven. At my motel room."

Something stirred in his chest, a sort of anxiety or hope that she'd found enough merit in him to give him a chance. He wanted to measure up in Jules Bailey's esteem. In more ways than one.

Chapter 11

No one was at the desk of Mayor Ted Barrett's administrative assistant when Cal arrived at five minutes before two. Seeing that Teddy's door was cracked open, Cal strolled past the gatekeeper's desk and knocked on the mayor's door. "Teddy?" He waited to be summoned, and when he heard nothing, he peeked around the open door. "Hey, Mayor, it's Cal. You here?"

Silence.

Cal pushed the door open wider and found the office empty. He checked the time on his phone. He was only a minute or two early, but Teddy had been so emphatic about promptness, Cal was surprised his old friend wasn't in his office. Letting himself in, Cal strolled into the well-appointed room and wandered over to the wall of bookshelves where Teddy had numerous leather-bound volumes, as well as a display of photographs—pictures from his inauguration, candid shots posing with the governor, older memories from vacations. Cal stopped to study one of an older woman that made his heart light.

Ted's grandmother, Annie Barrett, had started working as a mother's helper for the Colton family after Cal's fraternal twin brothers, Aiden and Dylan, had been born. Because Annie had custody of Ted, she brought her grandson with her to the Coltons' home each day, and Ted quickly became like another brother to Cal and his siblings. So much so that when Annie suffered a stroke and was admitted to a nursing home, the Coltons took in Teddy, raising him as their own.

Seeing Ted's picture of the dear lady who'd been like a member of the family brought back many fond memories for Cal. Warm cookies waiting after school. Hugs that smelled like Annie's talcum powder. The sound of her not-quite-in-tune voice singing lullabies to the younger kids.

Cal kissed a fingertip then reached out to touch the kiss to Annie's cheek in the photograph. "Miss you."

"Hello?"

He spun around at the sound of the mayor's voice and shot his friend a grin. "Just telling your grandmother I missed her and taking a walk down memory lane." He held his hand out for Teddy to shake. "How's it going, Teddy?"

The smile of welcome on the mayor's face dimmed with irritation. "I've told you, it's Ted now. I'm not twelve anymore."

Cal held up a hand of apology. "Sorry… Sorry. Old habits die hard." He stepped closer to the mayor's desk and motioned to a chair. "May I?"

"Of course. Please sit down." Ted took his own chair and propped his forearms on the desk.

"I understand Kelly is making strawberry cupcakes from your grandmother's recipe for the barbecue this weekend. Those were always your favorite, weren't they?" Cal asked, leaning back in the leather armchair.

"Hmm? Oh, uh, yeah. Great. But, uh…if we can dispense with the chitchat, this is an official visit. I'd like to get down to business."

Cal straightened, sitting taller. "Okay. That sounds serious. Am I in trouble?" he asked, flashing a lopsided grin.

Teddy…er, *Ted* only gave a weak answering smile. "No. I heard about the body found out at the *Geese in Flight* sculpture earlier. As you can imagine, I was none too happy to hear about a murder in the county, so close to the city limits. What can you tell me about it?"

"Not much at this point."

Ted frowned, clearly dissatisfied with that answer. "Do you have any leads? An ID of the victim? Any surveillance footage to place a suspect at the scene?"

"Well, there are a few leads, but… I'm not heading up the investigation. I'm not in a position to divulge details—"

"I'm the mayor! Don't you think I should be kept in the loop if there's a major crime committed in my town?"

"Technically, this statue on the Enchanted Highway is not within your mayoral jurisdiction." Cal didn't like getting into technicalities or legalities with his old friend. He trusted Ted not to share the information, and he could understand his desire to stay on top of the case, but…

"Who is in charge of the case, if not you?" Ted asked.

"Wyatt. The drug task force."

Ted sat taller, his eyebrows lifting. "Then the case is connected to drugs somehow? A deal gone sour? Smuggling? An overdose?"

Cal didn't say anything, but he gave Ted a telling look that said he was on the right track.

Ted grumbled a curse word under his breath. "I was afraid of that."

Cal weighed his words, then said, "Look, Ted. I know the increase in drug traffic coming in from Manitoba has been a worry for you and your administration, but Wyatt and the task force are doing everything they can."

"Are they? A man was found dead near the main tourist attraction for the area. Murdered!" He paused and tipped his head, inviting Cal to deny this assessment…which Cal could not. Ted gave a disgruntled nod, confirming he'd received Cal's silent affirmation. "You know, you're up for reelection soon as well. This isn't just an issue for my office. We've had a great record before now, lowering general crime and improving parks—"

"I know," Cal said, waving a hand to interrupt the mayor. "You've been a terrific mayor and are well liked. Your landslide reelection is proof of your popularity. And I understand your concern about how the increased flow of drugs reflects on your office and the local law enforcement."

"I'm glad you get the big picture," Ted said. "But what I want to hear is what is being *done* about it?" Ted narrowed a hard glare on Cal. "I want to be kept in the loop with this latest investigation and any other discoveries related to drug traffic in the area. How can I properly do my job and protect the citizens of Red Grove if I'm kept in the dark?"

Cal swallowed the teasing reply that formed on his tongue, knowing Ted wasn't in the mood for the family's usual brand of good-natured joshing. Instead, he cleared his throat and nodded. "I understand. Be assured we—my department and the drug task force—are equally concerned about the surge of drugs. We're doing everything we can to root out the source and stop the flow." He paused, then added, "And we'll keep you informed…to the extent the law allows."

Ted's mouth firmed. "What does that mean? I'm the *mayor*."

Cal was deciding how to explain that being the mayor didn't mean he was allowed access to certain sensitive information that could jeopardize an investigation when the phone on Ted's desk buzzed.

"Sir, the representatives from the state commission have arrived," his administrative assistant announced through the intercom.

Ted stood and buttoned his suit coat. "I have to go. Get me regular updates, Cal. I'm dead serious. This is critical to my administration."

Cal shoved to his feet and headed for the door. "I'll do my best."

"And Callum?"

He turned back to face the mayor from the office door.

Ted cracked a smile. "Tell the ladies organizing this weekend's festivities that I'll bring smoked chicken and lots of it. See you Saturday."

"Good deal," Cal said, giving his friend a casual salute.

Cal arrived at Jules's tiny motel room promptly at 7:00 p.m., as promised. She didn't want to be impressed with something as trivial about him as his being on time, but she'd known too many men who thought their time was more valuable than hers and had kept her waiting for professional appointments, study groups and even dates. Furthermore, she didn't want to be charmed by his warm grin or his teasing words—"I like what you've done with the place"—when she ushered him into the sparse, aged motel room.

"Thanks," she returned. "I call the style Early Dismal."

He laughed, then paused to sniff, his nose wrinkling. "Eww. What is that smell?"

She rolled her eyes. "I try not to think about it. It's the only way I can sleep at night."

He gave her a speculative look. "Would you like to go somewhere else to talk?"

"Yes!" she said, almost before he'd finished his sentence. She grabbed her jacket from the back of the one chair in the room.

He chuckled as he motioned for her to lead the way out. "That's the most agreeable you've been since we met."

"Because that's the first agreeable suggestion you've made," she returned, unable to squash the grin that tugged at her mouth.

He bounced the keys to his Jeep in his hand while she struggled to get the lock on her motel room door to fasten properly. The whole assembly from knob to latch, rattled when she wiggled it, and she feared a strong shake would pop it open without a key. She'd mentioned this failing to the front office, but clearly nothing had been done yet.

She sighed as she followed Cal into the parking lot and inhaled the fresh evening air.

"Where to, then?"

She shrugged. "It's your town. You tell me."

"The Brewery has good local beers if you're in the mood, but I think Cup of Joe would be quieter—fewer people this time of night."

"Cup of Joe, it is."

"Shall we walk? It's only a couple blocks." He hitched his head down the street toward the quaint business district.

"Why not?"

Cal placed a wide, warm hand at the base of her spine, a possessive gesture as he guided her toward the sidewalk. A shiver chased through her despite the lingering heat from the day.

"Have you seen the stray cat again? He still hanging around the shop?" he asked.

"*She* is," she said, emphasizing the correct pronoun. Jules furrowed her brow as she remembered the kitten's pitiful mewls earlier that evening. "I worry about her out there by herself. There are wild animals around the area of the shop and cars on the highway and…"

"I can ask animal control to pick her up—"

"No! Not animal control. They'd shut her in a cage. Maybe put her down." She shook her head. "I can't bear the thought of her…" She exhaled heavily, then admitted, "I'd like to catch her if possible and… I don't know. Maybe take her to my motel room?" She groaned. "Like I need to add a feral pet to the chaos my life is right now. I guess I should try to find someone to adopt her."

"I might be able to get you a humane trap if that's what you decide." He motioned to the front door of a store with a wide picture window.

"I already called the Red Grove Animal Rescue about a trap. I'm picking it up tomorrow at lunch, if I can get Bonnie to watch the shop," she admitted. "Because apparently I have more pity for that cat than I have good sense."

"I tend to think compassion *is* good sense," Cal said, holding the door for her.

Inside, the scents of freshly ground coffee beans and that morning's pastries hung in the air. A much better aroma than the stale cigarette and mystery funk that perfumed her motel room.

Once they'd settled at a corner booth and ordered decaffeinated coffees and sugar cookies, he turned up a hand, inviting her to speak. "Tell me about Abby. When did this guy—Chase Hamilton, you called him?—start bothering her?"

"Bothering…that's such a mild term for *stalking*."

"Stalking, then. And please believe me when I say, I don't take anything about her situation mildly."

His assurance mollified her. Probably more than it

should. Hadn't other police officers and court officials said much the same? So what made Cal different? Shouldn't she be keeping her guard up, instead of letting the compassion in his eyes and the sincerity in his tone lull her?

"Chase worked at the physical plant at the university Abby attended as a freshman. She had an evening class three nights a week, and she noticed he would follow her back to her dorm when the class was over. She tried taking different routes to avoid him, but he still found her and followed. She reported him to the campus security, and they offered to have an officer escort her. She took them up on the offer, and Chase stopped following her at night. But..."

Cal grunted. "But."

Their coffees arrived, and she waited for the barista to walk away before continuing. "He found her at other times of the week. He was just always...there. Popping up at random times and places. She grew scared to go anywhere alone, afraid even to stay in her dorm room alone, because he'd hang out in the lobby or outside her window and just...watch her. And because he never touched her, never verbally threatened her, the campus police wouldn't do anything to stop him. As a campus employee, he had a right to be on campus, in public spaces."

Cal listened patiently as she described how Chase escalated to sending Abby notes, leaving creepy gifts like dolls without arms and dog collars stained with something that looked like blood but proved to be a dye.

"She changed universities, moving to another state, to get away from him, but halfway through the fall semester of her sophomore year, he turned up on that campus as well. And it was a repeat of her freshman year down to the response of the school police and Chase's pattern of behavior."

"How long ago was this? How long has he been…" he caught himself and with a meaningful look, finished his question "…stalking her?"

A bit of the tension that was coiled in her gut loosened with his amended question—his effort to use her terminology and properly identify what her sister had been experiencing felt like a minor victory. Cal was at least trying to give the situation the respect it was due.

"Four years plus. Abby should have graduated this past May, but she left college after transferring a second time and having him find her *again*. Not that her grades would have allowed her to graduate. She was so distressed about his harassment that she couldn't concentrate or get any work done. Which just added to her stress. She'd always been an A student. Failing classes made her feel like she was a failure at life. It became a vicious spiral until she couldn't handle any of it."

Cal muttered an earthy curse. His hands cupped his coffee, though neither of them had even sipped the drinks yet. His countenance was grim, thoughtful. "And is that when you moved her here?"

"Yes. To the Red Grove Mental Health Clinic. I read that it was tops in the field and seemed like a safe place for her. Clean and well-staffed with people who cared."

"And you moved here with her?"

She answered with a nod. "I didn't want her to feel abandoned. And I wanted to keep an eye out for Chase showing up—" she scowled "—which didn't take long. God only knows how he keeps tracking her. She doesn't have social media and changes phones constantly, and we told no one about the move here. I followed him on his delivery route one day, and when he left the gift shop I saw the sign that said the shop was hiring. I needed an income, and now I knew the gift shop was on Chase's route, so…"

His pensive expression sharpened to concern. "Could he have followed you to her?"

Chapter 12

Cal's question was gentle, not accusing. But it reverberated in Jules like a gong. That had always been her biggest fear. That something she did would make matters worse for Abby.

She took a moment to calm her jitters, then shook her head. "He doesn't know me. I was in Canada, trying to finish my own degree. I attended any court hearings related to her cases via Zoom, and did my best to keep a low profile with her legal proceedings, so he couldn't use me as a pawn or a scare tactic with her."

He nodded. "Go on."

"Abby was determined to protect me and her closest friends from Chase, too. When his attentions started escalating her freshman year, she deleted her social media, got rid of photographs of her with loved ones…anything she could think of to keep Chase away from us. The unintended result was it further isolated her. When she worried her cell phone was bugged, we ended up using public phones to talk to each other, the landlines at the university business office and local sandwich shop. Snail mail sent from different postal substations."

"Paranoia or reasonable measures to buffer you and her friends?"

"Again, no proof, but I believe anything that kept her safe was a reasonable measure. She went through burner phones like they were a dime a dozen. She did so much to protect me and her best friends from unwanted attention or threats from Chase." Tears pricked her eyes. "Which is why I can do no less to protect her, to help her heal and to get this creep off the streets."

"And did it work? How sure are you he doesn't know you?" he asked.

"Well, while he knows me *now* as the newest manager of the gift shop, I've never told him my name. I scribble my initials on his sheets. So I have no reason to think he's connected me to Abby."

Cal hummed in thought, but otherwise stayed silent, letting her say all she wanted first.

She stirred her coffee idly. "I know he's likely aware Abby has an older sister, but I, too, have made myself hard to find. No pictures or current updates on social media. Unlisted phone numbers. Other than my name being listed in professional journals when my team published about our research, I can't think of any way he's pieced together who I am." As it often did when she ran through her mental checklist of ways she and Abby had tried to minimize Chase's ability to find either of them, an uncomfortable what-if poked her.

"What?" Cal prompted.

She raised her gaze to him and blinked. "Hmm?"

"You frowned as if you'd thought of something else that bothered you."

Her grip around her coffee tightened, and her gut flip-flopped knowing how easily he'd read her. Of course, he had. It was his job to interrogate people and weed out the liars and dodgers.

"I just can't help wondering what might have been different if I'd not been in Canada. If I'd been around to protect Abby when he started harassing her."

He lifted one eyebrow and leaned forward, then said softly, "I've found what-ifs are a colossal waste of time and energy best spent dealing with things you *do* have some power to change."

She considered this truth and gave him a grudging nod.

Cal finally raised his coffee and drank, then licked a droplet that clung to his lip. The action drew her attention to his mouth, his perfectly shaped lips and the shimmer of moisture left behind. Kissable lips.

What would it be like to kiss Cal Colton? The notion popped into her head before she could block it. A sensation like having the wind knocked from her squeezed her chest, and her pulse rattled through her with an erratic pace.

"I'm in," Cal said, yanking her attention back to his bright blue eyes. Given the recent track of her thoughts, it took her a staggering heartbeat to realize he was talking about helping her stop Chase Hamilton. Not that he wanted to kiss her.

She scowled, irritated with herself for letting her imagination run amok and even madder that he could have sensed where her mind had wandered. Needing to reestablish an emotional distance, she said the first thing that came to mind. "Who says I want you in?"

He barked a startled laugh. "Excuse me? Isn't that the point of this meeting? The reason you were just telling me the history of the case?"

She growled her exasperation and averted her gaze. "Yes."

"Then what's the problem?" He asked the question tenderly, as if he truly cared and not in a way that said, *What's your problem?*

For a moment, she said nothing, but once she felt she had collected her composure, she faced him again. "I have a hard time trusting anyone with this case. I've been let down so many times."

"I get that. I understand your frustration. Given your history, I can see why you crave control."

She tensed and grunted. "Did you just call me a control freak?"

His expression was guileless. "Not in those words, but... am I wrong?"

She wanted to lash out, tell him he was absolutely wrong. How dare he? But deep down she knew he was right. Because since she was young, she'd *had* to take control of things, thanks to her parents' chaotic lives. She'd called it taking responsibility, providing security, holding their home together by sheer will and constant work. But now, especially when circumstances felt frenetic, the spirit of the scared young girl she'd been would clamor for whatever control she could grab.

He reached across the table and covered her fisted hand. The contact was shocking...and pleasant. "Want to know a secret?"

She snatched her hand back from his, wary of the intimacy it implied. "No. I don't like keeping secrets."

His face said he was impressed by her answer, then he gave her that damnable handsome smile. "Actually, it's not such a big secret. It's a truth. We in law enforcement get very discouraged when we know in our souls that someone is guilty, but we don't have the legal evidence to take them off the street. But the rule of law is in place to protect the innocent. It's just a natural byproduct that sometimes the rule of law and due process protect the guilty in a way that seems unfair."

The soothing tone of his baritone voice lulled her, mesmerized her. She wanted to lean closer, inhale his crisp, clean scent, fall into the ocean blue of his eyes. Instead, she marshaled her defenses and sat back, folding her arms over her chest. "Don't go spouting common sense. I know the *why*. I just hate what it's caused for Abby. Besides my love for my sister, my righteous indignation is what fuels my mission to see Hamilton pay for his heinous behavior. Don't try to take that from me."

His grin brightened, and he raised his palm toward her. "You keep your righteous indignation, so long as you remember *I* have to uphold my oath to follow the law."

She gave a small shrug. "Fine. So how will this work…? You helping me? What does that look like?"

"First, I want to do some research on this guy to get up to speed. You can tell me what you know, and I'll dig into national databases to see what pops."

She twisted her mouth in a moue of disappointment. "I meant, what are we going to do to catch him in something wrong *now*, so he can be arrested and taken off the streets? If there'd been something in the past with enough heft to put him away, don't you think I'd have led with that?"

He swirled his coffee mug before taking another sip. "What makes you think he's doing anything arrest-worthy here in Red Grove?"

She scoffed. "Because he's here to begin with. Following Abby. And he's just too shady for me to believe he's not following another girl while he looks for Abby."

"Another girl?"

"I'd bet a year's salary on it." She bit the inside of her cheek, debating, then she said, "I want to turn the tables on him. I was thinking we could observe him. Follow him. See what he does after work."

Cal studied her, his lips pursed as he considered her suggestion, his head nodding slowly. "Okay. Should I have plainclothes deputies staked out along his delivery route?"

She shook her head briskly. "No! That's not the point. *I* want to see what he's doing. I'm not delegating this to anyone else. I thought I'd follow him after he finished his route, see what he does in his off hours."

"All right. It's a date." He grinned and winked. "I'll pick you up in time to follow him after work tomorrow."

A date? Her pulse skittered. Did he have to call it that? Bad enough she found his smile, his bright blue eyes, his muscular physique so distracting without adding a suggestion of a romantic connection. She swallowed hard, trying to squelch the giddy trill tripping through her. A relationship with the sheriff was the last thing she needed to distract her from her obligations to Abby. *The sheriff, for pity's sake!*

She cleared her throat. "Okay. We'll start our stakeout tomorrow. I'd think we should be in place at the distributor's warehouse by four o'clock."

She could have Bonnie cover the afternoon shift at the gift shop.

Cal gave a nod of agreement and finished his coffee in one giant swig. "In the meantime, want to spin by the sheriff's office and see what we can dig up on N-DEx?"

She blinked. "What, now?"

"No time like the present." He pulled out his keys and jangled them. "As the boss, I have full access to the department twenty-four seven."

She exhaled and pushed back her chair. "Okay. You're right—no time like the present."

Chapter 13

Cal typed in his credentials to pull up N-DEx, a national criminal database for law enforcement, while Jules hovered beside him biting a fingernail. "Do you know his middle name? Date of birth? Anything to help narrow down the results, find the right guy?"

"Middle name is Kevin."

She waited while he input that information, then she gave him his August birthdate, and he noted she'd memorized this information, hadn't needed to look anything up on her phone or other files.

"Previous residences?"

She supplied that data as well, and he ran an initial search. Hamilton's previous arrests quickly filled the computer screen, along with the circumstances for dismissed charges, releases on bond, other complaints filed against him. Jules leaned close to read over his shoulder, and he caught a whiff of a sweet floral scent that tantalized him.

He shoved aside the buzz of his arousal, refocusing on the task at hand. But when she reached past him to tap the screen, her breast nudged his shoulder. His libido shifted into overdrive. His skin tingled as if he'd touched a live wire.

"What's this? I didn't know about that."

Clenching his back teeth, he narrowed his gaze on the monitor where she pointed to an arrest in Idaho for drug possession.

He opened a new screen with details of the arrest and read aloud the highlights. "September of last year. Traffic stop for speeding. Officer smelled marijuana." He angled a glance to Jules, "that's probable cause, so he conducted a search of his car. Small amount of marijuana, hydrocodone and drug paraphernalia were discovered. Charges reduced, and Hamilton received only public service."

She flicked her hand toward his computer screen. "See? He gets away with a slap on the wrist. Every. Damn. Time!"

Cal acknowledged her concern with a grunt, while his mind mulled other angles. If Hamilton was still using drugs, could he have any connection to the local dealers? Was there any chance this side mission to help Jules could pay off with unexpected benefits for Wyatt and his task force?

Jules waggled a finger at the monitor. "Keep scrolling. What else is in there on him?"

They continued reading through Chase Hamilton's record, finding one other drug charge when he was in high school and the full history of Hamilton's brushes with law enforcement in relation to his stalking Abby. He could understand Jules's frustration, since time after time, he was questioned and released.

But the man was on Cal's turf now. He would not so easily ignore the pattern of repeated behavior. He'd promised Jules to help get a menace off the street, and that was what he intended to do.

Jules was a jumble of nerves all day at the gift shop, feeling especially testy with tourists who left her displays in a mess or who complained about prices or asked questions about things for which the shop had signs displayed in plain view. When she analyzed what had her so jumpy, she had to face the fact that the plan to tail Chase Hamilton this afternoon wasn't the source of her jitters. She, in fact, had a bad case of Cal-Colton-itis. Thoughts of the rugged sheriff had plagued her last night and kept her restlessly turning in bed. Today, her mind wandered to the moments they'd shared at his office the day before, not because of the work they'd done—fact finding as they built their case against Chase—but because of ridiculous details that she'd been far too aware of. His hands as he typed on his computer. The scents of soap and aftershave that hung in his office, branding it his. The cut of his stubble-dusted jaw.

And, most irritatingly, how his hands might feel on her skin. How the tang of his aroma danced through her and left her nerves tingling. How she longed to stroke her fingers along the scruff on his cheeks and graze his lips with her tongue.

"Excuse me!" The somewhat hostile voice roused her from her daydreams of Cal and snapped her back to the gift shop. A man wearing a scowl waved a handful of postcards at her. "Are you going to check me out or not?"

When the hour finally arrived for Cal to pick her up, she wished Bonnie good luck, reminded her to turn on the security lights and lock up when she closed and hurried out to Cal's Wrangler.

She climbed in the front seat of his Jeep, trying to ignore the whiff of warm, sexy male that greeted her. Bad enough that the mere sight of him now stirred a hum of longing at her core. She tried to push aside all of the distractions Callum Colton presented and focus on the mission ahead.

Tonight they needed to track down Hamilton and see what sort of evil he was up to after hours.

"He should be getting finished with his route in the next couple of hours, according to the dispatcher I spoke to. The company he drives delivery for has its warehouse on Third Street," she said. When she met his odd expression, she paused. "What?"

"First, you look especially beautiful this afternoon," he said, giving her a slow, seductive look.

Her heart jolted, and a wave of sweetness flowed through her like warm honey. She glanced down at her blue jeans and simple pink blouse, and plucking at her sleeve, she asked, "This old thing?"

"I mean *you*, Jules."

Her voice fled, and she felt her cheeks heat.

When was the last time anyone had told her she looked nice? Other than the occasional randy wolf whistle on the street, she couldn't remember. That his tone of voice and expression both sounded sincere made his compliment nestle deep inside her. Finally, she managed a soft, "Thank you."

"Second," he continued as if he hadn't just shaken the foundations of her goal to emotionally keep him at arm's length, "I'm already locked and loaded." He pointed to the screen of his Jeep's GPS that showed the address of Red Grove Food Distributors on the local map.

"Good." She gave him a nod and made a production of fastening her seat belt, buying herself a moment to find her footing again.

You look especially beautiful...

Good grief! Why did such a simple compliment have her insides whirling like a carnival ride? She kept her gaze focused on the passing scenery while she calmed the jitters dancing in her gut.

"I've tried before to follow him home after work, but I was so paranoid about him seeing my car and realizing I was following that I ended up losing him every time."

"Just as well. I don't want you getting in over your head without backup."

She shot him a frown. "In over my head? Are you saying you don't think I can handle myself, or that I'm too stupid to figure out how to—"

"Hey, hey, hey!" He waved a hand to stop her. "No one is calling you stupid. I'd never presume to suggest someone earning an advanced degree in chemistry is stupid. But…"

Her eyebrow sketched up.

"What would you do if he did spot you, and he confronted you? I want you to stay safe." He shot her a pointed glance. "Which leads to my next point. If we *are* able to track him tonight and see anything of note, you stay in the car. Let *me* handle him. I'm the one with the badge."

She compressed her mouth and twisted her lips. She didn't like being sidelined before they even started.

"Got it? I want to hear your verbal agreement, or I'm turning around now."

She heaved a sigh that let him know how her concession disgruntled her. But was she in a position to buck him on the point? "Fine."

Several employees of Red Grove Food Distributors were leaving the facility for the day when Cal parked across the street amid the other cars in the neighboring industrial pipe company parking lot.

Jules took out her cell phone and pulled up a photo of Hamilton. She angled it for Cal to see. "I know you saw him at the gift shop, but as a refresher, this is what he looks like."

Cal took out his own phone and showed her the screen he'd recently pulled up. "Not my first rodeo, darlin'."

Hamilton's grim face stared at her from a previous mug shot. "I did some homework on my own after I dropped you off last night. I wanted to get to know our target a little better for my own reasons. I hate to tell you, but he doesn't currently appear to even have an unpaid parking ticket. I'd hoped we could nab him for some minor infraction. But there was nothing outstanding."

She let a growl rumble from her throat as she glared at him. Then his gaze darted away, and his body tensed. "Looks like we got here in the nick of time. Isn't that him there in the blue shirt?"

She shifted on the front seat and craned her neck to scan the employees' lot across the street. Her pulse jumped when she spotted him, and her stomach roiled. "Yes."

She practically snarled the answer, feeling the heat of fury rise in her blood. Lord, how she wanted to surge from the Jeep and confront the man who'd made Abby's life a living hell. Only Cal's presence beside her and the knowledge that such rash action could ruin any chance of finding justice for Abby kept her anchored in her seat. She watched him climb into a small, rusted-out pickup. "White truck," she said, flapping a hand to hurry Cal. "Go, go, go!"

"Give it a second," he replied, his hand on his ignition key.

"You're going to lose him!"

"Trust me, Jules. I've got this."

She clenched her back teeth as Hamilton pulled out of the food distributor parking and headed down the street out of view. Trust him? *Trust him?* She wanted to trust Cal, but how could she when every other person she'd ever asked for help, from the first time she asked the courts to declare her emancipated from her mother at age sixteen until this moment, had let her down. Trust was in short supply.

But she choked back the snarl she wanted to unleash and sat on her hands as Cal pulled sedately onto the street to follow Hamilton. She spotted the white truck several blocks ahead and kept a vigilant gaze on it. "Can't you go any faster?"

"Not if we want to stay out of his sights and avoid raising red flags. I have done this before, darlin'."

She snapped a churlish look at him. "Did you just call me darling? That's, like, the second time today."

She would not—could not—tell him she rather liked the way it sounded, coming from him. They hardly had an endearments sort of relationship, but somehow, coming after his comment on her appearance earlier, it fell softly on her soul, like a cool rain on parched earth. She'd had little tenderness or empathy or affection in her life for years. Certainly not from her parents. Or from her one failed, serious relationship during her undergraduate years.

He cut a quick, startled look toward her, as if only then realizing what he'd said. "No offense intended. Sorry. It's just…something I do. I—"

She waved off his explanation and pointed down the street. "Left. He's turning left!"

"I see him."

In her chest, her heart was thumping wildly, and she struggled to stay still in her seat. The adrenaline pumping through her made her want to shift restlessly or climb up the dashboard. Cal took the left turn when they reached it and stayed discreetly behind Hamilton until Abby's stalker pulled in behind a row of shrubs in an otherwise empty lot. Jules frowned. "What's he doing?"

Cal cruised past the lot without slowing and kept going.

"Don't know, but what do you say we circle around and watch for a while?"

He drove several blocks before making a right and doubling back on a street that paralleled the one where Hamilton had parked. When they'd circled the block and were approaching the area where they'd seen Hamilton park, Jules noticed what was diagonally across the street from the white truck. A high school with baseball diamonds, buzzing with activity. A summer tournament or team practice, she supposed.

"Damn it! I knew it!" She slapped a hand on her lap and grimaced.

"Want to share?" Cal asked.

"Well, with Abby in the health facility, I guessed that maybe Hamilton had shifted his attentions to other girls. Not that he was giving up on Abby, but just…finding new targets for his sick hobby."

Without her having to point out the obvious, Cal turned to look at the high school where a few teenagers were leaving the fields.

Cal tapped a fist on the steering wheel, his brow furrowed. "And he's here in time to follow some unsuspecting teenager home from summer practice or a tournament game."

"That'd be my guess." She clamped her back teeth so hard, she felt the pressure shoot through her skull. She took off her seat belt and reached for the Jeep door. "We should warn them. If he's fixated on one of them—"

Cal put a staying hand on her shoulder. "Hold on. You go out there now, he'll see you, and you'll not only blow our cover, you might trigger him to do something rash. Not to mention alarming the girls before we have the facts, before we know who he's got in his sights."

She considered his points and flopped back against the seat, dividing her attention between the clusters of students leaving the school and the parked truck barely visible through the scraggly hedge. She tried to guess which of the girls climbing into her parents' car or wandering in pairs and trios to the parking lot had become Hamilton's new fixation. When a tall girl with rich auburn hair scurried into view, her heart jolted. The red highlights of the girl's hair reminded her vividly of Abby's, and she knew…

"That girl." She pointed out the teen to Cal. "She looks like Abby, from her tall lean frame to her reddish hair."

Cal said nothing, though he joined her in watching closely as the redhead climbed into a convertible VW Beetle with her friends. The driver of the Beetle whizzed out of the parking lot and headed past where Chase had parked. Sure enough, within seconds, Hamilton pulled his white truck onto the road again and followed the Beetle.

"Son of a biscuit," she grumbled.

Without her needing to say a word, Cal pulled into traffic behind Hamilton, once again staying a fair distance back. They tracked the Beetle and white truck to a small residential neighborhood where the girl with the bright auburn hair, a softball mitt under her arm, climbed out of the car, waved to her friends and loped toward her front door. Hamilton cruised past the girl's house and pulled his truck into the parking lot of an apartment building just down the street. Cal didn't stop.

Jules grunted her dismay as he sped down the block, and she lost sight of Hamilton. "Please tell me you're turning around! He's clearly stalking that girl! We have to—"

She fumbled to finish the sentence.

What could they do? If they gave themselves away too early, before they had solid evidence of Hamilton breaking the law, he'd just get away again, and she'd have blown her cover. But sitting on her hands while she knew he was, even now, probably hiding in the girl's bushes and peeking in her window—or something equally pervy—rankled.

Cal looked over at her, his expression inviting her to finish her sentence.

"I don't know what, but we should do something!"

"What happened to you trusting me?" he asked.

She snorted. "I've told you before—"

"Right. Right. You were burned by other folks in law enforcement. I am not other law enforcement." He wheeled the Jeep into the driveway of a doughnut shop, closed for the day. As he cut the engine and unbuckled his seat belt, he sent her a playful grin. "Go ahead. I know you're dying to make a crack about cops and doughnuts."

She had been, but she swallowed the remark and instead asked, "So what's your plan then?"

"It's a nice afternoon. Care to go for a walk?"

Chapter 14

As they started down the sidewalk, back toward the apartments where Chase Hamilton had parked, Cal took Jules's hand, lacing their fingers as if they were lovers. She, of course, tried to snatch her hand back and frowned at him, but he only smiled. "Our pretext as we do a little espionage."

She pulled a dubious face before relenting and falling into step beside him.

He cut a side glance to her scowling countenance and chuckled. "We'd be more believable as a happy couple if you didn't look so pissed off."

Her steps faltered, and she gave him an even darker look before conjuring a cheesy grin. "Better?"

"Geez Louise, Jules. Someone needs to teach you how to relax and have a good time."

"I suppose you're volunteering?"

"Would that be such a terrible thing?" He cast a quick glance at her, noting how the sunlight found gold strands in her brown hair and highlighted the sharp lines of her too-thin face. Even with the obvious signs of stress and poor sleep that shadowed her eyes, his heart thudded erratically as he drank in her beauty. As much as he found their barbed repartee amusing, he'd much rather see her smile. Jules

Bailey had clearly suffered more than her share of grief and worry in her life. From his core, Cal wanted to be the one to give her the kind of joy that shone in her expression, the inner peace that eased the crinkles framing her eyes.

"I don't have room in my life for anything besides work and Abby. My time is completely full earning enough to pay my way and taking care of my sister."

He blinked, mentally backtracking to the last question he'd asked her to make sense of her comment. *Oh, right. His offer to show her a good time.*

"The gift shop closes at night. Surely you can take some time to sit back with some friends and enjoy some food and music?" When she turned a withering glance his way, he elaborated. "My family is having a cookout at my dad's place on Saturday. Come as my guest. No need to bring anything. The Colton siblings will have more than enough food and drink there."

She shook her head. "No, thank you."

"And cornhole and volleyball and a bonfire in the evening for roasting marshmallows." He tugged her hand, guiding her around a pothole in the sidewalk. The apartment building was in sight now, and he narrowed his gaze on the front seat of the white truck. Empty. Where had Hamilton gone?

"No, Cal. I'm not crashing your family party."

He lifted her hand so that he could kiss her knuckles, then grinned at her stunned expression. "You're not crashing. You're my guest. My brothers have bought fireworks, and my sister is making a batch of strawberry cupcakes that will make you think you've died and gone to heaven."

She arched an eyebrow.

"Yes," he said, answering her unspoken question, "they really are that good."

She sighed. "Fine. I'll come. But only if I can bring something. Is anyone bringing a watermelon?"

"I hear you are," he quipped as they reached the red-headed teenager's house.

Jules craned her head and scanned the yard, peering back at the white truck and angling a glance at the upstairs windows.

He squeezed her hand. "Cool it, Sherlock. You're being too obvious."

"I—" Color filled her cheeks, and she met his eyes, obviously abashed.

To cover her goof and lend credence to their pretense, he bent to drop a quick kiss on her cheek. When he raised his head, her wide-eyed surprise tugged a chuckle from him.

She arched an eyebrow and appeared ready to scold him when she tensed and her gaze darted to the lawn they were passing. Her steps slowed. "He's in the side yard, behind that family's trash can."

"Keep walking," he said, tugging her forward.

"Can't you arrest him for trespassing or something?" she whispered.

"I could, but I think the smarter move is to wait and get him on something that carries more heft, bigger consequences. I'm sure you don't want to spook him and waste the chance to get him off the streets for good. A petty charge will likely only cost him a fine and tip his hand to us."

Her shoulders slumped, and he released her hand in order to put his arm around her shoulders. "I know you're frustrated, but to do this right will require some patience."

"My patience ran out a couple years ago. My sister has been hounded for too long."

They continued walking, and he noticed she not only

didn't shrug away from his arm, but she also actually leaned into him a bit. She felt good in his embrace. She fit perfectly under his arm, and he reveled in the sensation of her body nestled close to his as they strolled down the sidewalk. She smelled fresh, like lemons and flowers.

"Do you think she knows about him? The girl who lives in that house?" He could hear the concern that trembled in her voice.

"Don't know."

"Did he meet her in town somehow or just camp out across from the school, watching the kids leave until he found someone who looked the most like Abby?"

"Don't know." He gave her shoulder a squeeze, wanting to comfort her. Now, she did shove away and, stopping, she faced him with a scowl.

"What *do* you know? Where's the help you promised? I can follow Hamilton around and stew about him by myself."

Without answering her directly but holding her gaze, Cal slid his cell phone from the clip at his hip. When the sheriff's department dispatch answered, he identified himself and said, "Send a patrol car out to Oakmont Street. Have them cruise the street real slow a couple times. Make it a regular patrol, several times a day until further notice. Yeah, thanks."

"Does that mean you changed your mind about picking him up for trespassing?" she asked.

"It means I want him to be real uncomfortable with hanging around watching her. As far as her knowing about him, I do think it is wise to alert her and her parents. We can get her softball schedule and have a plainclothes deputy at her games to keep an eye on things."

She exhaled. "Good. So now what?" She glanced to the

end of the block and then back in the direction they'd come. "Are we going to find a place to watch him?"

He shook his head. "We are going to get ice cream."

Her jaw dropped. "What?"

"If we linger around here, he'll see us and get suspicious. We can follow him again when he returns to his car…which, as I recall, is parked at apartments across the street from Dairy Queen." He offered her his crooked arm as if to escort her. "Shall we?"

The next afternoon, Jules left Bonnie in charge of the gift shop in order to follow Chase again…without Cal tagging along. This was her mission, and she didn't need the distraction of him and his square-cut jawline. She'd reached the parking lot across from Chase's employer and was intently watching the workers leave the building when someone knocked on her passenger-side window.

She yelped her surprise and clapped a hand over her racing heart. When Cal waved at her and popped the door open, she glared at him. "Way to give me a heart attack, Colton. Don't you know better than to sneak up on a woman?"

"I was hardly sneaking. When you're on a stakeout, it's not good to get so laser-focused on one thing that you ignore your periphery."

Turning her attention back to the employee exit across the street, she grumbled, "Why are you here?"

"Why are *you* here without me? We had a deal."

"I—" A niggle of chastisement pulsed in her chest before she shoved it down. "I only wanted to see if he followed that same girl again today."

"Zoey Rogers."

"What?"

"Her name is Zoey Rogers. She's seventeen. I did a little work overnight. First, I stopped by the girl's house after I dropped you off and talked to her and her parents. I advised them we were actively working to bring Hamilton in, and that we'd monitor her situation. They promised not to confront Hamilton or do anything to blow the investigation."

A mix of feelings pummeled Jules. Relief that the girl had been warned. Irritation that Cal had acted without her. Hope that they were a step closer to stopping Chase Hamilton. Disappointment that she'd missed the opportunity to spend more time with Cal.

She shook her head. *No.* She couldn't get used to being around Cal Colton. She stared at him silently, unsure what to say besides… "Good."

He flashed his incredible smile before his gaze darted to something outside and he directed her attention across the street. "Our man is on the move."

Sure enough, Chase Hamilton was climbing into his white truck. Jules quickly started her engine, and Callum laid a hand on her wrist. "Easy. Don't get too close."

Her nerves jangled as Chase drove away before she pulled out and turned in the same direction their target had gone. He drove toward the high school again, pulled off the road in a different spot to watch the teenagers leaving the school grounds.

Jules spotted the redhead at the same time Cal said, "There's Zoey."

Plastic wrap crinkling, he casually popped a peppermint candy in his mouth. She sent him a scowl as if the crinkle were loud enough to scare off their target.

"Want one?" he said, patting his pocket.

She scoffed and turned her attention across the road again. "No thanks, grandpa."

Her comment earned a chuckle from Cal.

Zoey stopped and searched the parking lot, her expression nervous, as she was clearly looking for the perv who'd been tracking her. A police car cruised through the parking lot then and slowed to talk to Zoey.

Jules cut her gaze back to Chase's truck in time to see him speed out of his hiding place and drive away. She exhaled her relief. "The cop spooked him."

"Good. Let's see where he goes."

But Jules had to wait on traffic to pull onto the road, and Chase was gone. "Damn. Should I drive by the Rogers' house? See if he's there?"

"You can," he said, sounding skeptical.

"What's wrong?"

"I just want to be careful that he doesn't catch on to us following him. He's not stupid." He motioned vaguely toward the school parking lot. "The officer will follow Zoey home. Her mother will be there when she gets to her house. Let's call it a day."

Jules stopped at a traffic light and drummed her fingers on the steering wheel. She was antsy to see where Chase had gone but conceded to Cal's expertise. An odd sort of tug-of-war in her core left her feeling unsettled. Trust Cal or follow her own instincts? What did it say about her that she'd so easily capitulated to him?

Tears of frustration pricked her eyes, and she gripped the steering wheel so hard her knuckles blanched.

He reached over and gave her shoulder a squeeze. "Jules?"

"I just want to get him off the street so bad. Abby has suffered so long. I have to make sure she's safe from him!"

"We will. I promise," Cal said, his tone so warm and certain she almost believed him.

We. She concentrated on that tiny word as the light changed and she headed back to the lot across from Red Grove Food Distributors. She wasn't in this alone anymore. Cal was doing more to help, to listen to her, to problem-solve than anyone in law enforcement or the court system had ever done. Gratitude swelled in her, and she had to blink hard to fight back the gathering tears.

When they reached the parking lot where he'd left his Jeep, Jules caught Cal's arm before he could slide out of her car.

He turned to her with a question denting his brow, and she leaned over to catch his mouth with hers. Just a quick kiss. An expression of her thanks. An impulse driven by emotion she couldn't voice. An experiment…

At the touch of his lips, heat exploded in her veins, and a primitive hunger clawed inside her. She could feel him jolt in surprise, and she met his startled eyes as she drew back.

A blue flame lit his gaze as he stared into her eyes. She didn't say anything. Couldn't say anything, because her breath seemed to stop in her throat and back up in her lungs. Her heart thumped so loudly, she was sure he could hear it as loudly as it drummed in her own ears.

She wanted to hide. Wanted to take back the foolish and impulsive act. But mostly she wanted to kiss him again. So she did.

This time, he plowed his fingers into her hair and captured the back of her head with his palm, anchoring her. He slanted his mouth over hers and returned her kiss with a greedy one of his own.

He tasted like peppermint, like summer sun, like…sweet seduction. Her whole body craved him in a way she'd never experienced before.

But he pulled back, brushed his knuckles along her cheek

and gave her one of his wide grins. "Not bad for a grandpa, huh?"

Her mind was so muddled with lust, she didn't catch his meaning until he'd slid out of her car and closed the door. She'd called him that when he offered her a candy earlier. Now, her heart stumbled with a flash of panic. She blew into her hand, testing her breath. Did it smell of coffee? What had she eaten for lunch? Did she—

Another knock on the car window.

She gasped and felt her face flush, knowing he'd probably seen her testing her breath. She rolled down the window.

"I'll come by to pick you up at noon tomorrow for the shindig with my family. Casual dress. Okay?"

"Uh..." Her head was still spinning from their kiss. How could she think clearly enough to make a cogent decision?

"I'll take that as a yes."

She still couldn't form words but found herself nodding.

His smile brightened. "Great. See you and your watermelon then."

She watched him stride away, her foggy brain registering that she needed to find the farmer's market and buy a watermelon.

As she drove out of the parking lot, her phone rang, and the caller ID read, Red Grove Mental Health Clinic.

Her heart leaped. Abby!

Jules stopped the car in a small lot, snatched the phone from the seat and answered, "Is Abby okay?"

"Ms. Bailey?"

"Yes, that's me. Is my sister okay?"

"Yes, ma'am. She's fine. This is Sylvia at Red Grove Mental Health Clinic. There is a gentleman here who says he's your brother."

She shook her head, confused. "We don't have a brother."

"Well, I knew you hadn't listed one in her admission paperwork," the woman on the phone said, "but he was insisting on seeing her, and I wanted to—"

"No!" she blurted when it clicked.

Chase! Somehow, he'd tracked Abby to the mental health facility. When he'd struck out with Zoey this afternoon, he'd turned to Abby.

Damn it! Jules had thought Abby would be safe in the hospital. How in the world had Hamilton found her there? It was one thing to know she was in Red Grove, and quite another to learn she was a patient at the mental health facility. What had happened with HIPAA?

"Well, that's why I called. I wanted to—"

"Call the police! And for God's sake do not let any man in to see my sister!"

"The police?" Sylvia asked. "But—"

"It's him. It has to be him! The man who's been stalking her is here in town. Do not let anyone but me in to see her!" Her hands were trembling, and she fumbled to put the phone on speaker, so she could drive to the hospital. "I'm on my way! Call the police!"

"Well, actually, when I told him I had to call Abby's family and get your approval, he turned and left. I only wanted to alert you."

Another thought came to her that made her gut swoop. "Does Abby know he was there? Did she see him?"

"Well, no. He didn't—"

"Don't tell her. It would only upset her and…she's been making progress. If she knew Chase was in town—" Bile reached Jules's throat. "Oh, geez. Do not tell her! And do not let anyone but me in to see her. Alert your staff to this guy, and if he shows up again, call the cops. All right?"

"Yes. I understand."

Jules took a deep breath and thanked Sylvia for calling as she fought down her own panic attack. She knew she was too upset at the moment to drive. Which meant she was also too upset to visit Abby. Her sister would sense something amiss, and the last thing she wanted was to be the reason Abby became agitated.

Closing her eyes, she drew long deep breaths, exhaling though pursed lips. Once she had control over her heartbeat again, she headed to her motel to recalculate. Knowing Chase had located Abby upped the stakes. The sooner they caught him and got him off the streets, the better. But was this slow and painful stakeout with Cal going to be enough? Why did the wheels of justice have to move so slowly where Chase Hamilton was concerned?

Tomorrow, she'd make it clear to the sheriff that time was not on their side. She needed action from him or she would take matters into her own hands.

Chapter 15

Jules was restless the next morning, struggling to maintain her patience with wishy-washy tourists and the slow movement of the clock. She told herself she wasn't looking forward to the Colton family picnic, but neither could she stop thinking about the opportunity to spend the afternoon with Cal.

The Fourth of July holiday brought a steady stream of customers into the gift shop, and though Bonnie was happy to get the extra hours of work, Jules was wary of leaving the teenager in charge for the afternoon a third day in a row. She could back out of the Colton family event, but part of her wanted to meet Cal's family. She'd spent so much time working at the gift shop since arriving in Red Grove, she'd barely had time to visit Abby, much less make any local friends.

Abby. The incident yesterday—knowing that Chase had tried to gain access to her sister had kept her awake last night. Now another twang of guilt plucked at her. She'd spent all of her time off recently tracking Chase. Though she phoned and texted her sister regularly and kept in touch with her sister's doctors, she hadn't been to visit Abby in person in over a week. She'd remedy that tomorrow, she vowed.

Seeing Cal's Jeep arrive in the gift shop parking lot, Jules tucked a wisp of hair behind her ear that had come free from her single, low-maintenance ponytail. She collected the sweater she'd brought from the motel in case it got cool in the evening and opened the back door of the shop before Cal could knock. He'd already spotted the watermelon she'd set out by the door and hoisted it into his arms.

"I don't know about this," she said in lieu of a greeting and pressed her lips in a taut line.

Cal's golden retriever expression didn't dim. Instead, he chuckled a bit and tipped his head as he eyed her. "I've already told the family you're coming, and they're eager to meet you. Don't disappoint them."

"Why would they be eager to meet me? I'm no one."

With a hitch of his chin, Cal moved toward his Jeep, and she followed.

"One, you're not no one. Two, Wyatt told everyone we'd been spending time together, and now the family thinks we're an item."

She sputtered and stumbled to a stop. "What?"

He nudged her with his shoulder, propelling her forward again as he juggled the watermelon in order to open the Wrangler's back door. "Don't panic. No one's expecting us to get married."

She snorted. "I'd hope not. Good grief. Now I'm doubly nervous about meeting them all."

He glanced past her, and his smile shifted. "I see your little friend is still hanging around."

She turned and spotted Joy eating kibble from the bowl she'd set out. Jules's spirits lifted. "Oh, good. I didn't see her yesterday, and I was worried about her. I've been so busy, I keep forgetting to pick up the humane trap and get her to the local rescue."

Cal closed the Jeep door behind her, and she watched Joy through the window, her heart melting as she studied the thin, dirty kitten.

"I can help with a humane trap. I'm sure the sheriff's department or city police has one somewhere. Give me a day or so to round it up, and we'll get the little hellion to safety."

"She's not a hellion," Jules countered.

"Her hissing and claws say otherwise."

Jules fastened her seat belt. "She's just scared."

Callum's only answer was a knowing grin.

When they arrived at his father's house, where Cal lived, too, it turned out, Jules gaped at the large yard and numerous people already gathered.

"I need to grab the watermelon out of the back seat. If you'll wait a second, I'll introduce you to the gang," he said as he parked.

Their arrival was clearly noticed. Jules's gut churned, and she took a deep breath to marshal her composure.

Pilot loped out to meet them, and Jules bent to give the Labrador a scratch behind the ears. Following Pilot was a stream of people with bright smiles and warm greetings.

Cal handed the watermelon off to Wyatt and said, "Since you've already met Jules, you can put this on the food table."

Wyatt rolled his eyes. "Oh, can I? Please?"

"Will you, please?" Jules asked with a tip of her head and a sweet smile.

Wyatt winked at her. "For you, yes."

Cal handed off the melon. "And stop flirting with my date!"

Jules jerked a startled gaze toward him. "Your date? I never said—"

"Dad, Kelly, Dylan, this is Jules Bailey," he said, cutting off her objection. He motioned to an older gentleman with graying brown hair and eyes the same dramatic shade of blue as Cal's. In fact, as she glanced from face to face, she realized the sky-blue eyes were a common trait for the Coltons.

As she shook hands with one family member after another, she tried to remember names and the tidbits of introduction Cal gave. The youngest, Matilda, had messy curls, was a social worker and went by Matti. Kelly's hair was longer, and she was an attorney. Dylan was a fireman, one of fraternal twins. No, wait. His twin, Aiden, was the fireman. Their father, Jonathon, was a physician, still practicing at the local hospital. How would she ever keep it all straight?

And then a man with blond hair and green eyes stepped forward and offered his hand and a smile.

"You're not a Colton," Jules blurted. She winced, then amended, "I only mean, you don't match. You don't have the giveaway brown hair and blue eyes all these others I've met have."

The man laughed. "You're right. Ted Barrett, honorary Colton. I grew up with these guys, and they're kind enough to continue to include me in family functions."

"Because you are family!" Kelly insisted, throwing her arm around Ted's shoulders. "He's the mayor of Red Grove, and we are proud to claim him as ours."

"Aw, shucks," Ted said, playfully ducking his head and giving Kelly a peck on the cheek.

"Come on, Jules. I saved a chair for you in the backyard. Would you like a beer or a soft drink?" Dylan said, motioning for her to follow him.

She cast a side glance to Cal as she fell in step with his younger brother. "A diet cola if you have it would be great.

I'm sorry, Dylan, I've already forgotten what you said you did for a living."

"Because I didn't say," he returned, then called to Wyatt. "Grab a diet cola for Jules, Wy."

She frowned. He still hadn't answered the question. Well, whatever. She wouldn't pry.

As she settled in the lawn chair Dylan offered, an older woman with a stylish, short haircut emerged from the house carrying a large bowl that she set on the picnic table already burdened with a variety of food. Cal walked over to hug the woman and said, "Hi, Mom. You look lovely today as always. Let me introduce you to my date."

Jules clenched her teeth. She wished he'd stop calling her his date. His family would get the wrong idea about them. Shoving down her irritation with Cal, Jules gave his mother a smile and stood as Cal made the introduction.

"Call me Emily," his mother said. "We're so glad to have you here today."

"Emily Colton…" Jules repeated, the name stirring something in her brain. "Why do I know that name?"

"Do you read mysteries?" Cal asked. "Mom's written several. She's really good."

Jules brightened. "Oh, my gosh! Yes! I love your books."

Emily thanked her and took a seat beside her, then answered Jules's questions about publishing and where she got her story ideas. "Before I leave tonight—" Emily reached over to the arm of Jules's lawn chair and covered Jules's hand with her own "—find me again, and I'll send you home with a signed copy of my new release. I have my author copies in my car."

Jules was so distracted by the comforting feel of Emily's hand holding hers that she almost missed two key bits.

Emily Colton was gifting her a signed book. Before Emily *left* tonight? Was this not her home?

Jules beamed at Emily. "Oh, thank you! I'd love that. I— But what do you mean when you leave? I thought this was your house."

"Used to be, but Jonathon got the house in the divorce."

Jules felt like she was mentally running behind a moving train, trying to catch up as Emily detailed things about Cal's family dynamic he hadn't shared. His parents were divorced. Yet Emily was here sharing the family holiday party, so…maybe it had been a civil parting?

"Callum lives here now with his father, keeping Jonathon on track. I swear that man would work himself to death given half a chance."

"Cal?"

"No, Jonathon. Callum is a hard worker, no question, but their father would live at the hospital and never sleep or eat if Cal didn't keep after him." Emily sighed and glanced across the lawn to the grill, where Jonathon stood with Aiden and Dylan cooking the meats for the picnic. "His work habits were one of the key factors that split us up. He was an absentee husband and father, and I'd had enough of feeling abandoned and alone."

Jules watched the older woman's face and sensed a grief there as Emily spoke. "I'd hoped my leaving him would be the thing that woke him up and made him change his ways, but Callum says he still burns the candle at both ends." Emily finally tore her gaze from her ex-husband and met Jules's eyes. "And to be honest, I still worry about him. So…fine lotta good it did me to leave, huh?"

Jules stacked a second hand on top of the one Emily still had on hers and squeezed. She wasn't sure what to say, so she whispered, "I'm sorry."

What did she know about family dynamics or marriage? Her parents had been so wrapped up in themselves, so uninterested in actual parenting, so distant and…well, *dysfunctional* was the word her counselor had used. A pretty way to say negligent and alcoholic.

Emily closed her eyes and gave her head a brisk shake. "Good lord, I'm the one who should be sorry. You didn't come today to hear me air old grievances. Forgive me, dear. Please, tell me about *you*. How did you and Callum meet?"

While she was glad to move on from the awkward conversation about Emily's divorce, she was disappointed when Emily withdrew her hand to smooth imagined wrinkles from her skirt.

Jules chuckled wryly. "It's not like that. We're not…" Jules paused, considering how her denials would sound to Cal's mother. "We only have a professional relationship. We met…well, over a dead body."

"Oh, my! That sounds like something I'd write about in my novels! So then…you're in law enforcement?"

"No. I'm currently in retail. I'm managing the gift shop by the *Geese in Flight* sculpture, where the dead man was found earlier this week."

Emily pressed a hand to her chest. "Heavens! I hadn't heard about *that*. I don't live in Red Grove anymore, and Callum hadn't mentioned— But enough of that." She waved a hand, dismissing the topic. "Let's talk about something more pleasant, eh?"

Cal moseyed up at that moment, and Jules caught her breath. He looked so…delicious, standing there, the breeze lightly ruffling his chestnut hair, and his smile beaming as bright as the July sun. How could she have forgotten in ten minutes how handsome the man was?

"Can I steal Jules for a moment, Mom?" Cal offered

his hand to Jules. "We need another volleyball player. You game, Bailey?"

Jules accepted and joined the match in progress. Ted Barrett quickly claimed her for his team, and Cal grunted a protest. "Hey, I recruited her. Why do you get her?"

"I know the winning team when I see it," she quipped, and high-fived the mayor as she took her place at the net.

For the next hour, she laughed and exerted herself more than she had in years. Beyond team camaraderie, Cal's siblings and Ted made her feel like she belonged. When Pilot stole the ball, tail wagging and looking as impish as a puppy, she had to wipe her eyes from mirth. Matilda draped an arm over Jules's shoulder at one point, congratulating Jules on her last spike. "Well done. I want you on my team every time."

Jules started to tell Cal's youngest sister there wouldn't be another time, that today was a one-off, but she swallowed the words. Why ruin her compliment? And...why did the idea of not gathering with the Colton family bring a knot to her throat? Sure, she was having fun, felt welcomed and was grateful for the invitation, but as she'd told the family all day, she and Cal were not a couple. They weren't really even friends...were they? He was just helping her get Hamilton off the street. A strictly professional transaction.

She angled a glance past the net and found Cal staring at her. He smiled his devastating grin and winked. And her pulse tripped.

Darn him! She hated how easily he undermined her control of her composure. This was why he was dangerous for her. She'd already spent her childhood and one disastrous relationship feeling lost and vulnerable. As much for Abby's sake as her own, she had to be strong, stay focused and hold Callum Colton at arm's length.

Chapter 16

When the volleyball game ended, with Jules's team the victors, Callum trotted up beside her and planted a quick kiss on her cheek. "Congrats. You played well. I see you are as competitive as any Colton."

"Competitive?" She blinked. She never thought of herself in that light. "I don't know. I just like to give my all to anything I undertake. If I'm competitive, it's with myself." She'd had to give her all her whole life to make up for the lackadaisical and half-hearted efforts of her parents. So much of her family's survival had depended on her.

Cal cast a glance about as he ushered her up to the food table. His mother was taking the lids and covering off the food as hungry volleyball players gathered around. "Where's Dad?"

His mother shot him a withering look. "Two guesses and the first doesn't count."

Cal groaned. "Seriously? He went to the hospital? The whole family is here!" He waved a hand down the line of Coltons serving plates of food.

"You know your father. He said it was an emergency," Emily said. "Swore he'd be back before the fireworks started."

Jules put an ear of corn on her plate, sidled closer to Cal

and whispered, "If it's an emergency, shouldn't we cut him some slack?"

"If it were an emergency, sure." Cal scooped a huge glob of potato salad onto his plate and jammed the spoon back in the serving bowl with an irritated huff. "But everything is an emergency to my dad. He spends more time at the hospital than he does at home. More than any other doctor or nurse. He's been known to sleep there. His workaholic habits are the reason my family was split up, but he didn't learn."

"Dedication to his profession and patients is admirable," Jules defended.

"Even a good trait can be taken to extremes and become a vice." Cal served himself a piece of chicken. "Can we talk about something else?"

She glanced at the faces of the other Coltons, saw frowns and eye rolls, heard grumbles of "hospital" and "again." Clearly Cal wasn't the only one frustrated with Jonathon's work habits.

As she left the food table with a plate full of delicious-looking treats, Ted Barrett called to Jules and patted the arm of a lawn chair. "Saved a seat for the winning team's MVP."

She joined Ted, Cal taking the seat on her other side as he balanced a loaded plate.

"Aren't you awfully young to already be the mayor of Red Grove?" she asked her teammate.

Ted laughed. "If you give the people what they want, in my case the promise of lower crime and a better, more prosperous town, age is just a number."

"Ted's always been driven," Cal added. "And with his charisma, we knew early on he'd either be a politician or an actor."

"Or a used car salesman," Wyatt quipped.

Ted arched an eyebrow at Wyatt, then turned to Cal. "I'll take that as a compliment." Then, aiming his fork at Wyatt, he added, "And you need to remember who signs your paycheck."

"The city controller, as I recall," Wyatt returned, smirking.

Jules angled her gaze past Ted to Cal's youngest sister, Matti. "Tell me more about your work. You're a social worker?"

Matilda covered her mouth with one hand as she chewed, then after swallowing, she nodded. "I am. I work mostly with at-risk children, placing them and monitoring them while in foster care. It's very rewarding, even when it's heartbreaking. Sometimes I'm the first stable and loving adult these children have known, and getting them to a safe placement means so much."

"I bet so." She had wondered, too many times growing up, if social workers might show up one day at her own house and split up her family. She'd have fought tooth and nail to stay with Abby and protect her, but no one had ever bothered to look too closely at the Bailey household.

Now, she smiled at Cal's youngest sister, whose messy curls somehow made her look younger than Jules guessed her to be. Matti had one of those friendly faces that she could imagine served her well in earning the trust of her young charges.

"Enough about me," Matti said. "I want to hear more about the special project you and Callum have been working on together."

Jules's pulse stumbled. She shot Cal a side glance. "Special…project?"

"Mmm-hmm." Matti curled up one side of her mouth in

an impish grin that looked just like her brother's. "Unless there's another reason you two have been spending evenings together?" The teasing lilt in her voice left no question what she was asking.

"Uh…"

Cal cleared his throat. "Matti, down, girl. Sit. Stay."

Matti dug an ice cube from her drink and threw it at Cal. "Okay. Okay! Excuse me for hoping you finally had a love life!"

Jules ducked her head, feigning intense interest in scratching Pilot behind the ear. But his sister's comment sparked a curiosity in Jules. Why didn't Cal have a wife or girlfriend? He was…what? Between thirty-three and thirty-six years old, she'd guess. Handsome as the day was long. Cheerful. Employed. Intelligent by all indications. Responsible. From a good family. Thoughtful—

She interrupted her laundry list of attributes when she realized she was checking off all the sorts of things she admired and looked for in a man. Not that she'd been looking for a partner in many years…

She was saved from further discussion or contemplation of the topic of her relationship with Cal, when someone turned on music, loud enough to make conversation difficult and dancing inevitable. ABBA's "Dancing Queen" led the playlist, and when Cal stood and held his hand out to her, Jules happily followed him onto the makeshift dance floor.

The family and their closest friends danced and sang and laughed until dark, when Dylan, under fireman Aiden's…er, *supervision* lit up the first fireworks. Colorful rockets filled the night, and a sense of contentment and joy swelled in Jules. She was having *fun*. A rarity for her. And she felt welcomed and wanted in a way even her own family hadn't made her feel. Except Abby. She and Abby had been a team, supporting and loving each other when their parents had not.

Abby. Battling down a surge of guilt, Jules reminded herself she wasn't in Red Grove to have fun or find a surrogate family or a love match with a hot sheriff. Her sole reason for putting her chemistry research on hold and moving to North Dakota was to protect Abby. Cal and his family, welcoming as they were, could not sidetrack her from that goal. She had to make the world safe for Abby again.

And no blue-eyed man with a devastating smile and earthshaking kiss would stop her.

Chapter 17

The gift shop was dark when Cal dropped her off to collect her car. She sighed. "I told Bonnie to leave the sales floor light and exterior lights on for security."

Cal folded his arms on the steering wheel of his Wrangler and leaned forward to peer more intently through the windshield at the dark building and empty lot. "How old did you say the girl is you have working for you?"

"Seventeen, I think. Why?"

"I just don't like the idea of her being alone out here anymore than I like the idea of you being alone until our killer is caught." He glanced at her. "I could assign a deputy to come out and watch the premises around closing time."

Jules opened her mouth to refuse, but how could she deny Bonnie the extra protection? "You'd ask them to be discreet? I don't want to scare Bonnie."

He arched an eyebrow. "Bonnie knows about the murder at the sculpture, doesn't she? She knows to be alert and careful?"

Jules glanced away. "She knows. You can't keep something like finding a dead guy a secret in a small town, but… I downplayed it." She'd thought she was protecting Bonnie's mental health by keeping unsavory truths from her.

Hadn't Abby, when overloaded with too much frightening reality, cracked under the pressure?

Cal grunted. "Jules, Bonnie deserves to know what really happened just yards from her place of employment. More important, she needs to be fully briefed how to stay safe and what to look out for. And I think I'd hire another employee so you can work in teams."

Jules shook her head. "I've asked the store owner about more help before, especially with the store closing for a couple of days at the height of tourist season. He always says it's not in the budget."

A muscle in Cal's jaw ticked. "Then the deputy is a done deal. At least until we catch our killer."

"You really have a man to spare for that from your small staff?" she asked.

His brow creased as if considering the hardship it would cause the department. Then, squaring his shoulders, he said, "I'll find a way, or I'll do it myself."

She studied him and the resolve that sculpted his face and shone in his eyes. Had she ever known this much dedication and responsibility from any man, much less from an officer of the law? Had she met someone as reliable as Cal in the past, Abby's life could have been so different.

Of course, she'd heard promises before, assurances that weren't worth the breath that spoke them. Did she dare put any belief in Cal's promises?

She gave a tight nod and opened the passenger door. "All right. Thank you. For the extra security for the shop and for today." She took a beat and curled up a corner of her mouth. "I had fun. Your family is great."

"I had fun, too." He shifted in his seat and reached for her, but Jules scuttled out of the Jeep before he could do more than brush her cheek with his knuckles.

Had he been trying to kiss her? Her heart scampered at the notion. Facing him again, she sent him a brief smile and wished him a goodnight before closing the door.

She hurried to her car and climbed inside, hoping he couldn't tell her limbs were trembling. Wasting no time, she started her engine and pulled out on the highway. She monitored his headlights behind her until he turned off on the side street at the edge of town that led back to his house. She touched her cheek where his fingers had grazed her skin and felt a pleasant hum stir inside her.

If such a light and casual touch from him had her body buzzing and hypersensitive, how much more would she enjoy having him stroke her bare body, kiss secret places?

She was still pondering those tantalizing questions when she pulled into the motel parking lot and realized her motel room door was ajar.

She'd already complained once to the motel manager that the lock was flimsy, and since she could see the night manager in the front office watching something on his little TV, she detoured to speak to him about the lock.

The manager glanced up from the television screen, his expression saying he was irritated by having his show interrupted.

"When are you going fix the lock on my door?" she asked without any niceties.

He sighed and heaved himself out of his chair to stroll over to the counter. "There's nothing wrong with your door. I already looked at it."

"Really? Then why is the door partially ajar now, when I locked it as I left?"

"Maybe housekeeping didn't close it when they finished?"

"If that's true, you need to have a word with housekeeping about securing residents' doors."

The man gave her a flat look and a shrug. "Noted."

"Meanwhile, I still say the lock is wobbly and insecure. Grab your toolbox and come fix it, please." Her tone said it was not a request. She was fed up with the rickety lock.

The manager cocked his head to the side. "What, now?"

"Yes. Now." She waved a hand to the small TV and added, "While I see that you're *extremely busy*—" her tone and the sour look she gave him contradicted her words "—I'm sure you and the Better Business Bureau would agree that your lodgers' safety and comfort is your first priority."

The man glared at her for a few seconds before shuffling to a closet and removing a small rusty toolbox. "Fine."

Jules outpaced the manager and reached the door a good ten steps faster. She wiggled the knob in demonstration, and with a gentle nudge, the door opened.

"See?" she said.

The word was barely out of her mouth when a tall man in a ski mask lunged from inside her room and wrapped his arm around Jules's throat.

She saw a flash of metal. Screamed.

"Shut up!" the man growled.

"Hey! What the—" the manager shouted.

The man holding her tensed, then shoved her aside. The masked man knocked into the night manager so hard as he fled that the manager stumbled backward and fell on his back. His toolbox clanked to the ground next to him, the loud noise almost as jarring as the initial assault.

Jules shook from head to heels, but she hurried to assist the manager. "Are you all right? Did he cut you?"

The manager craned his head to stare in the direction

the man had run, grumbling an epithet under his breath. Only then did he blink at Jules like an owl. "Cut? He had a knife?"

"I think so. I saw something—" Her knees gave out, and she crumpled heavily on the sidewalk. After taking a moment to catch her breath, she angled a glare at the manager. "I'm fine, by the way. Thanks for asking."

"Huh?" The manager paused as he struggled to his feet and dusted his hands.

Around them, a few of the other room doors opened and concerned faces peered out.

"Pardon the disturbance, friends. Everything's fine," the man said, giving a small wave.

"Fine?" Jules hissed. "A man was waiting in my room with a knife, because your sorry door lock didn't keep him out!"

The man offered his hand to help Jules to her feet, and she brushed it aside as she clambered to her feet again. "Are you going to call the police or am I?"

The night manager's gaze jerked toward her. "The police? No, no, no. We can't do that."

She blinked hard. "Excuse me?"

"Look, I'm already on notice with the boss. If he hears there was an incident on my watch that required the cops being called, I'll be canned for sure."

"And that's my problem because…?"

He scowled. "Look, if you'll let this go, no harm no foul, I'll get a new lock on your door first thing in the morning when the hardware store opens. I promise."

She continued to stare at him in dismay. "I had a man with a knife in my room."

Although she said it to make a point to the manager, she

heard the words she was saying, and a fresh wave of terror rolled through her.

Over the heavy thud of her heartbeat in her ears, she absently heard the manager still pleading his case. "I'll comp your rent this week…no, the whole month. And get new pillows for the bed."

Who had the man been? Had Chase Hamilton figured out who she was, what she was doing and where she was staying and come after her? If he'd learned where Abby was, who knew what else Chase had figured out. Yet… somehow that explanation didn't feel right. Why the ski mask and—

Shut up...

The low pitch of those two words, snarled by the attacker, rolled through her head. They didn't match Hamilton's voice, one she'd long ago memorized, having listened numerous times to the voice mails he left on Abby's phone.

"It's not like there's much the cops can do, anyway. That room's full of fingerprints, and he was wearing a mask, so it's not like you could identify him. Huh?" the manager continued. "Besides, he's long gone now. Come on. I need this job, lady. Can we just let this little incident go this time?"

The man's wheedling tone grated her nerves, but a couple things he said reverberated inside her.

Not much the cops can do…

Would any report she filed be dismissed as easily as had the complaints Abby filed against Chase Hamilton? She didn't like to think Cal or—being within the city limits and in the city police's jurisdiction—Wyatt would be as cavalier about dismissing the incident as those other law enforcement officers had been. But since Wyatt was a detective, working a special case with his task force, it was more likely a rank-and-file patrolman would respond if they called this in. Her gut turned as she remembered how little previous encounters with the police had netted her or Abby.

The night manager was sweating. "No one was hurt, so really—"

"Fine." Jules pinched the bridge of her nose. "No police."

The manager looked so relieved she thought he might cry.

She aimed her finger at the door. "But that better be fixed with a deadbolt by the end of the day tomorrow or the deal's off."

He raised a hand. "I swear it will."

"And I want that free month's rent and new pillows you offered."

A gift shop salary didn't go far and she had to pay Abby's expenses after all.

The man's shoulders slumped, but he nodded. "All right."

As he noisily collected his scattered tools, something else the night manager had said replayed in her head.

He was wearing a mask... It's not like you could identify him...

The second man who'd been in the gift shop five nights ago, the man Cal and his brother suspected had killed John Harper, had worn a red hoodie to hide his face. Had that second man realized she'd seen him and considered her a threat? Had the murderer discovered who she was and come to kill the only witness from the night of his crime?

The notion chilled her to the marrow, and she knew she wouldn't sleep a wink tonight—especially without a strong lock on her door.

Chapter 18

When Cal got back home from dropping off Jules, he spent some time puttering around in the kitchen, cleaning up dishes and savoring the happy memories made that day. When he heard the front door close, he carried a towel with him, drying his hands as he met his father in the foyer.

"You missed a good party," he told his dad, scowling his disappointment.

"Yeah. I hate that. But my patients needed me." His father brushed past him, headed to the kitchen. "I'm starving. Any food left from the party?"

Cal rolled his eyes. "There is. Mom made sure we fixed a plate for you and set it aside."

Jonathon raised a startled glance. "She did?"

"Of course she did. She spent decades of her life taking care of you when you worked all hours at the hospital. Old habits die hard." Callum opened the refrigerator and took out the aluminum-wrap-covered plate. "Here. Everything on this plate is microwavable. The cold stuff is on the bottom shelf." He pointed to another dish with foil wrap on top as he handed off the plate to his father. "She still cares about you, despite the divorce."

His father shot him a withering glance. "Dear boy, I

think you spent too long in the sun today. You're not making sense."

Cal moved aside so his father could get to the microwave. "I'm making perfect sense. What doesn't make sense is you disappearing from a family event for hours. You already missed most of your kids' childhoods. When are you going to prioritize your family over the hospital?"

"I swore an oath to give my patients the best care I could, Callum. I know you, of all people, understand the importance of upholding oaths. You're doing the same thing as sheriff."

"But I know when to delegate so I don't exhaust myself. You have nurses and interns at the hospital who are equipped to deal with most everything that could arise—"

His father snorted and shook his head. "You sound like Emily. Your mother used to nag me, too."

"And when you ignored her pleas, she left you. What does that tell you?" Cal asked, feeling his temper rise.

"I'm not in the mood for lectures, Callum. I've had a long day." With that, his father turned his back to get a beer out of the refrigerator.

Cal sighed. Why did he think his father would change? And why was he still living with his dad, taking care of him and trying to keep Jonathon from working himself into an early grave?

To his dog, who was lying on a dog blanket at the foot of the stairs, he said, "Come on, Pilot. Let's go to bed."

With a scrabble of claws on hardwood, Pilot rose and trotted up the steps toward Cal's bedroom.

Hearing his father's low voice, Cal paused on the stairs to listen.

"Did I wake you?" Jonathon said to someone. "I'm sorry. I'll let you get back to sleep. I just...well, I wanted to thank you for saving me a plate of food today. You've always been good about that, and… I wanted you to know…" His dad cleared his throat. "I appreciate it. Have always appreciated it."

There was a silence, and Cal gripped the stair railing harder. He hadn't known his father still called his mom. Maybe the lingering feelings went both ways.

"Yeah," Jonathon said, "You, too. Good night, Em."

Cal gave his head a shake as he continued up the steps, not knowing what to make of the call he'd overheard. Maybe his father wasn't a lost cause after all.

Jules didn't see Cal again until Monday, when he strolled into the gift shop, looking as cool and tempting as ice cream on a July afternoon. She hadn't talked with him since he'd dropped her off on Saturday. She'd decided not to text him about the man who'd been in her motel room. While she had moments when she regretted not reporting the break-in to the police, the night manager had lived up to his end of the deal. She had a secure door lock now and free rent until the end of the month. Perhaps by then she'd have the evidence against Hamilton that would get him off the streets, and she and Abby could get out of this desolate town.

As far as the incident Friday with Chase at the hospital, she'd checked on Abby on Sunday and reiterated to the staff the importance of calling the police if Chase showed up again. She'd then spent most of the day with her sister, determined to make up for her prolonged absence. Abby seemed well, unaware of Chase's attempt to gain access to her. Jules told her sister about the Colton family celebration, and Abby's eyes had become animated.

"Were there more sparks at that picnic than the fireworks, Juju?" Abby asked, her tone lilting.

Jules had blown a raspberry and waved off the notion, then added, "But Cal *is* hot. I'll give him that."

Now, she watched Cal scan the quiet gift shop as he strode up to the sales counter, and she squashed the sizzle that fired in her veins.

"Is it always this slow on Monday?" he asked.

"People tend to come in waves. Busy early, as tourists start out on the highway, and often a second rush in the evening, if they drove the route in reverse, or they want to end the day with a treat or a souvenir."

"Ever think of closing the shop during the midday doldrums?" he asked, a suspicious lift at one corner of his mouth.

She narrowed her eyes. "Why would I do that?"

He checked behind him again as if reassuring himself they were alone. "So you could join me in the break room for a little…treat?"

The seductive way he said *treat* and the wicked grin that lit his face sent tingles of anticipation through her. Gripping the edge of the counter to steady herself, she lifted her chin. "If that's your idea of a sexual proposition—"

"Only if you want it to be. Otherwise, I meant I have a picnic lunch waiting in my Jeep including leftover desserts from Saturday."

Jules thought about the paltry cold cut sandwich she'd brought for herself, and her stomach rumbled.

Cal laughed. "I'll take that as a yes to lunch and cupcakes."

Seeing no good reason not to join him for lunch, she turned over the *Open* sign and stuck a handwritten note on the door that read, Back at 1:00 p.m.

From his Wrangler, Cal retrieved a cardboard box laden with fruit, cheeses, fried chicken and potato salad. And three kinds of dessert—chocolate cake, peanut butter cookies and Kelly's divine strawberry cupcakes. Jules stuffed herself. On Sunday, between visiting Abby and stressing over the intruder in her room, she couldn't find the appetite to eat. Today, she was ravenous.

"When can you stake out Hamilton's activities again?" she asked between bites of cupcake. "I can't stop thinking about the multitude of ways he could be getting up to no good yesterday while we weren't watching him."

"Who said I wasn't watching him?"

Jules stopped with her dessert halfway to her mouth. "You followed him without me?" She slapped the flat of her free hand on the table and grunted. "Dang it, Cal! I thought we were doing this together. I don't like being excluded!"

He bit a fresh strawberry and let the juice trickle down his chin before slowly wiping the sticky sweetness with his finger and licking it off.

Jules couldn't say if the heat that pulsed through her watching Cal was lust or anger or some confusing combination of the two. He could be the most infuriating prankster and at the same time tease her desires without even trying. Just being… Cal.

Once he'd swallowed, he put the strawberry stem on his plate and held her gaze. "I've made sure the patrols around Zoey Rogers' house, Hamilton's rental and the Red Grove Food Distributors Warehouse were maintained through the weekend. Our friend doesn't appear to have done more than shopped at the Cash Wise Saturday and picked up supper at the Dairy Queen drive-through Sunday night."

Jules leaned back in her chair, only mildly comforted by this news. "So was someone following him all weekend? Even Saturday night?"

Cal dusted off his fingers after selecting a cupcake from

the Tupperware he'd transported them in and tilted his head. "Why Saturday night in particular?"

She stared down at her plate and twisted her mouth as she debated what to tell him.

"Jules? What happened Saturday night?" he asked, his tone brooking no resistance.

She sighed and met his gaze. "When I got back to my motel room after you dropped me here at the shop—" She paused as her lunch rolled in her belly and a shudder chased through her, remembering the man's rough hand, the flash of metal.

"Tell me, Jules," he said, his tone gentler now.

"A man had broken into my room. Not hard to accomplish because the lock was flimsy as hell, but…"

Cal's blue eyes flashed with alarm. "And?"

"He grabbed me. Had a knife, but…the night manager was with me, and I guess he spooked the guy away. He ran when he realized I wasn't alone."

Cal bit out a hard curse, his hands fisting and his face growing rigid. "Why didn't you call me when it happened? Hell, why didn't you call me at all?"

"What could you have done? The guy was gone. You weren't going to isolate his fingerprints in a motel room where there are already traces of dozens of travelers and housekeeping staff."

"Maybe because I care about you, and if you're attacked, I want to know—sheriff or not."

He cared about her? She didn't know what to do with that admission, so she shoved it aside. "There's more."

He folded his arms over his chest and gave her a stern look. "Go on."

"Friday afternoon, after we gave up on Chase—"

He groaned. "What did you do?"

"Uh! Not me. *Chase.* He went to the mental health facility where Abby is and tried to get in to see her! The facility staff called me, because he claimed to be our brother, and I'd said no visitors but me."

He unfolded his arms and leaned forward, his expression creased in concern. "Is she okay?"

Jules nodded. "I saw her yesterday. She doesn't know Chase was there. But…we have to do something about him. Soon! He's a wild card, and I don't like how long this business of watching and waiting is taking!"

Cal sighed. "Okay. I'd planned to visit my mother this evening, but you're right. Dealing with Hamilton is important to you, so it's important to me. We'll see what he's up to after his route today. Deal?"

Something warm spilled into her chest. His concern for her well-being, his prioritizing what mattered to her, his thoughtfulness toward her. When had she ever had this much consideration from anyone? She hadn't. Cal was… an outlier. And he was chipping away at the protective defenses she'd erected around her heart. She gave him her best smile. "Deal."

Three days later, Jules sat next to Cal in the front seat of her car, once again watching Hamilton leave work at the distributor warehouse. They'd followed him every day this week, switching whose vehicle they used, but he'd done little besides drive back to his apartment and stop once at McDonald's.

She was getting impatient, knowing Chase *had* to be doing illegal things worthy of an arrest that would take him off the street. Late at night? Along his delivery route? Because of her own work schedule and Cal's responsibilities with the sheriff's department, they obviously couldn't follow Chase 24/7, so they hadn't yet caught him red-handed doing anything worthy of arrest. Other than the day he followed Zoey Rogers home—which he'd stopped doing, likely because of the increased police presence around the teenager—Chase had been…boring. Humdrum, normal activity during the hours Jules and Cal were watching him.

She knew in her gut he was up to no good. They simply hadn't uncovered it. Yet.

But she would. She would stay on the creepy man's trail until he paid for the emotional distress and life interruption he'd caused Abby.

As usual, when Chase appeared and climbed into his rusted white pickup, they waited an appropriate time, then followed him. Today, instead of going home or to a restaurant or a high school, Hamilton drove to a low-rent part of town, where some windows were shuttered, others broken. Sidewalks sprouted weeds, and pedestrians were few and far between.

"Hang back more," Cal warned. "As unpopulated as this area is, our presence will stand out all the more."

She nodded her understanding, and when Hamilton pulled into an alley and stopped there, she drove past without stopping and sent Cal a quizzical glance. "Do I circle around and find us a place to park and observe or…what?"

Cal scratched his chin. "If you promise to stay close to me and do what I say, I'm thinking our move is to leave the car somewhere around here—" he waved a finger to the side streets "—and walk back. We can find a discreet place to monitor his activity, see if he leaves his truck or meets someone or appears to be stalking someone again."

She considered his suggestion and bobbed her chin. "Okay."

Ten minutes later, they were ensconced in a deserted

building, diagonally across the street from the alley where Chase still sat in his truck. They stayed low, peering through a broken window to monitor their target.

"Hold the phone," Cal said, when a silver SUV arrived and stopped in the alley. Chase climbed out of his truck and approached the driver's window of the second vehicle. "Who have we here?"

Jules tensed, and Cal snapped pictures of the SUV.

"What do we do?" she asked, her nerves jangling, every fiber of her being telling her this was the moment she'd been waiting for. A guy didn't drive to out-of-the-way, seedy alleys to trade baseball cards.

"Patience, Jules. I'm sending pictures of the SUV and license plate to both my office and the city police marked 'priority.' If the owner of the other car has a record, we'll know in a matter of minutes."

"But if Chase is up to no good, shouldn't we act now? Catch him in the act? You can arrest him—"

"Jules." He put a hand on her arm. "I have to have a little thing called probable cause of a crime. So far, he's just talking to a friend."

She narrowed her eyes, studying the interaction. "I don't know, Cal. They don't look so friendly to me. Chase looks angry."

Cal's phone pinged, and he checked the screen. Before he could read the incoming text, his phone rang. Arching an eyebrow when he checked his caller ID, he muttered, "Well, well. We seemed to have poked a hornet's nest."

Chapter 19

Cal raised his phone to his ear. "Wyatt?"

Jules studied Cal's face, trying to guess what his brother was telling him. Cal's end of the conversation gave few clues, consisting largely of "really?" and "I see" and "okay."

"What did he say?" she asked as he disconnected.

"We're to stand down."

"Stand down? Meaning what exactly?" She narrowed a suspicious glare on him. Echoes of past conversations with law enforcement were whispering in her head.

"Meaning Wyatt and the drug task force are quite familiar with that SUV and plate number." He nodded his head across the street to the vehicle Chase still stood beside. "The SUV's owner has been on the task force radar for weeks and is at the center of a sting operation to find the men higher up the chain in the drug trafficking in the region."

Jules's temper swelled. Her gut knotted, and her jaw tightened, knowing where Cal was going. She'd heard similar bull from law enforcement in other states. "So by 'stand down,' what you mean is we're supposed to let Chase go free? He's likely buying illegal drugs over there, and we can't do anything about it?"

Chagrin darkened Cal's face. "Jules—"

She didn't wait to hear him out. Rage boiled over, and

she loosed a frustrated scream. Slapping the flat of her hand against the wall, over and again, she ground out a litany of unladylike curses against both Chase and the police. Soon, to her dismay, she realized hot tears were streaming down her face. Callum noticed, too, and moved up behind her to wrap his arms around her.

"I know," he crooned. "I know."

"You don't know! Don't patronize me!"

"Never. I wouldn't. I honestly do understand."

She struggled to free herself from his grip, but he held tight. "You don't understand! How could you? You're—you're one of *them*! I was stupid to have trusted you. Why did I think you were any different?"

"You can trust me. I want to help—"

"By letting Chase go again? How is that anything but more of the same crap that made Abby feel unsafe, that drove her to an emotional breakdown? Everyone says they understand, but no one does anything! Over and over, Chase just walks away scot-free!" She knew she was shouting, but she didn't care. She was so sick of the double talk and empty promises. Abby deserved better.

She tried again to wrench free of Cal's strong embrace. "Let go of me! I want to leave!"

To his credit, he did release her and said, "Jules, listen to me. There could still be a way we could reel him in."

Her chest was still heaving with fury and sobs, but she quieted, scowling darkly at him. "I've heard that before."

An hour later, she and Cal were sitting across from Wyatt in his office at the Red Grove Police Department. Jules folded her arms over her chest as Wyatt laid down the law.

"We've been looking for a low-level guy with connections to the local dealers who we could persuade to give up information in exchange for reduced or dropped charges. We think this Chase Hamilton guy you've been tailing could be our man."

Jules's jaw was so tight, she thought she might break a molar clenching her teeth. "In other words, you're going to let him get away *again*. This guy is like a cat with nine legal lives. He breaks one law after another and because the police 'don't have sufficient evidence,'" she said in a mocking tone, "or because his lawyer pulls some magic juju to get him off, Chase never serves a day's time behind bars!"

"I understand your frustration," Wyatt said, twisting his mouth with regret, "but in law enforcement, sometimes you have to sacrifice a little fish to catch a bigger, more dangerous one."

"He's dangerous to my sister's mental health! He's literally the wolf at her door. He tried to get to her in the hospital!" She fisted her hands. "And what about the other girl he's been following here? What if he escalates and hurts Zoey?"

"Then we'll arrest him and follow due process." Wyatt exchanged a look with Cal. "I know this isn't what you wanted to hear, but we—the drug task force team—need you to back off of Chase Hamilton. Once we've gotten some actionable information from him, he'll be fair game again. But we have a chance to make a significant break in the flow of drugs coming into our community both from Canada and other states. This is big, Jules. It's a priority not just for our department, but Cal's as well."

She glanced at Cal, saw him raise his chin a notch.

"You ran on a platform of stopping the drug trade in the county, remember?" Wyatt asked.

"Of course I remember. And I will leave Chase Hamilton to you and your team." Cal paused, then added, "Until you're done with him. Then I promised Jules we'd get him off the street, so he couldn't stalk her sister or any other women."

Jules huffed her irritation and stood. "This is bull. I'm so tired of being brushed aside as if my concern for Abby and Zoey's lives doesn't matter."

"Of course they matter," Cal countered, even as she walked out of Wyatt's office. She'd heard enough.

"Take me back to the shop, please," she said over her shoulder as she strode out of the police station. "I need to relieve Bonnie. She's been at work alone too much lately."

Jules was sullen on the drive back to the gift shop, and she said little to Cal despite his efforts to mollify her. But when they reached the back lot of the gift shop, she spotted something that lifted her spirits. The humane trap that she'd borrowed from the sheriff's department had snagged the black kitten.

"It caught her!" she gasped, hurrying out of his Jeep the moment he stopped. Jules rushed over to the cage and squatted to coo at the frightened kitten. Joy hissed and spit and cowered in the farthest corner of the cage from her.

"So now what are you going to do with her?" Cal asked as he strolled over to have a look. "She doesn't seem too happy about being caught."

"Of course she's not. Would you be?" Jules stood and lifted the cage by the handle on top. "I'll take her back to my motel room until I figure out a plan or find a home for her." She started across the lot toward her car, and Cal fell in step behind her.

"I'll drive you." He tried to take the cage from her, and she pulled it away from his grasp.

"No need."

"I don't mind. And once you let the hellion out in your room, I'll take the trap back to the department."

"Stop calling her a hellion. She's just scared. Her name is Joy."

He laughed. "Still the most contradictory name in history."

She glared at him. "Maybe I'm manifesting that she'll grow into her name."

"And *that* is the most optimistic thing I've ever heard *you* say."

This time when he reached for the cage, she let him take it from her and load it in the back of his Jeep. She climbed back in the passenger seat and twisted to talk calmly to Joy as Cal drove them back to her motel.

Once in her room, she set the cage on the floor and opened the trap door. "It's okay, baby. You're safe. I won't hurt you."

She reached in to get the kitten, and Joy swatted at her, tiny claws unsheathed. When she picked up Joy and eased her out, the cat continued hissing, wiggling and spitting, a pitiful sound from such a small feline. She cooed some more and stroked Joy's tiny head with two fingers.

"She'll need a bath. Living outside, she probably has fleas and ticks," Cal said.

Jules twisted her mouth, contemplating the task of bathing a wild cat. She angled a glance at Cal. "Will you help?"

"Two against one? Hardly fair odds."

"But the one has claws," she said.

"I meant we might need more than two. Have you ever bathed a cat?"

She arched an eyebrow. "No."

"Brace yourself."

* * *

Thirty minutes and several scratches later, Joy had been cleaned and rid of pests, and she was bundled in one of the motel towels…and was purring.

"Do you hear that?" Jules asked, beaming at Cal.

He studied her smile, one of the few she'd ever given him, and he savored it. Her face transformed when she smiled from lovely to simply stunning. Heat flashed through his veins, and his breath stuck in his lungs. He nodded. "If I were wrapped up and cuddled against you like that, I'd be purring, too."

When she lifted her gaze to him, he curled his mouth in a lopsided grin that said, *Yes, I meant that just the way it sounded.*

Warmth filled her green eyes, and he slid a hand along her cheek to cup her face. "Can I kiss you?"

She swallowed hard, and her smoky gaze invited him in. But after a crackling moment, she blinked, scowled and said, "No. I'm mad at you."

"Oh?"

"Don't think I've forgotten how you caved to your brother's demand that we not pursue Chase Hamilton."

"Oh."

"Yeah, *oh*." She used a corner of the towel to continue drying Joy's head. When the towel loosened, the kitten wiggled out and scrambled to the far edge of the bed. Before Jules could catch her, the cat jumped to the floor and crawled under the bed.

"Want me to try to get her out?" Cal offered.

Jules considered her answer before she responded, "No. Let her calm down. She'll come out when she's hungry."

She settled back against the stack of pillows and closed

her eyes. "Why am I so exhausted all the time lately?" she said, likely more to herself than to him, but Cal answered.

"Stress. Poor diet. Overwork."

She angled her head to look at him. "I used to pull all-nighters with no problem in college. Does this mean I'm old?"

He barked a laugh. "You're what twenty-six? Twenty-seven?"

Her jaw dropped, and her look of horror told him he'd overestimated, even before she said, "Twenty-five! So I look older than my age? Is that what you're saying?"

He chuckled as he shook his head. "No. Not at all."

She grunted and started scooting toward the foot of the bed in a huff.

"Jules, seriously. Come back." He caught her arm, and when she didn't budge, he wrapped an arm around her waist and dragged her to the head of the bed next to him again. When she was beside him, he didn't release her. Touching his forehead to her temple, he said, "Twenty-five is not old. And for the record, despite how I feel some days, at thirty-five, I'm not old, either."

"You thought I was twenty-seven," she grumbled, folding her arms over her chest.

"Only because of wishful thinking," he said, thinking fast for an excuse for his fumble. "Being ten years older than you, I was worried you'd consider me too old for you. Is my age why you're keeping me at arm's length?"

She opened her mouth and closed it again, her brow furrowed. "Age is just a number."

He brightened and aimed a finger at her. "Yes! Exactly. Which is why you should not care whether I incorrectly guessed your age. You could be forty-five and I'd still think you were beautiful."

The frown on her face shifted abruptly. Clearly his comment stunned her. But just as quickly, she shook her head and tried to wiggle loose from his hold. “This is a pointless discussion, and I have to get back to the gift shop.”

“You are beautiful, you know,” he said, catching her hand.

“Don’t patronize me.”

“Never. Wouldn’t dare. I respect you too much to lie to you or butter you up.”

She cast a skeptical side glance toward him, then swung her feet to the floor. “Bonnie’s probably ready to quit by now.”

He hurried to take her arm before she moved away from the bed. “Jules.”

She shot an impatient look toward him. “Cal.”

Tugging her closer, he caught her cheek in his palm. “You *are* beautiful. And if I have left any doubt in the matter, I am very attracted to you.”

Beneath his hand, he felt the subtle quiver that rippled through her, and her gaze dropped away from his.

“Jules.”

She closed her eyes, clamped her lips tight.

“I want to kiss you.” He moved his thumb against her jaw in a slow, tender caress. When she didn’t move, he tipped up her face, leaned in. Waited. When he didn’t move, she canted slightly toward him, angling her chin up. Still he waited.

Finally, she blinked her eyes open and gave him a puzzled look.

“Jules,” he said quietly, “may I kiss you?”

She looked peeved by his question before closing the distance between them. With both hands, she framed his face and seized his mouth in a greedy kiss. Lips parted, she drew on his mouth and teased him with her tongue.

He leaned back, breaking the kiss before placing a finger to her lips. “There's no rush. I'm yours for as long as it takes.”

Moving in again, he kissed her gently, soft nibbles that teased her and promised more to come. Only when a frustrated growl rumbled in her throat did he deepen the kiss. Lingering, his hands anchoring her close, he sampled the mouth that had enticed him for days.

Abruptly, as if someone had thrown cold water on her, Jules jerked back and shoved to her feet. She raised her hand to her mouth and drew a few ragged breaths before stalking away from the bed, not looking at him.

“I, um… Bonnie. I have to… I promised her part-time hours. She's not— She's worked more than I have the last few days.” Then, dropping to her knees, Jules lifted the bedspread and peered beneath the bed.

“You realize she's yours now?” he said.

“Bonnie?” Jules asked, obviously playing dumb.

He chortled and squeezed her shoulder. “Right, Bonnie.” He aimed a finger under the bed.

“No.” Jules shook her head and pushed back to her feet. “I'm not keeping her. I'm not in the market for a pet, especially right now.” She paused and sent him a meaningful look. “Or a relationship. I have too much going on in my life.”

“I don't think Joy cares. I think she's chosen you.” *And so have I.*

Jules shook her head again, but this time when she protested, she sounded less sure of herself. Her kiss certainly said yes, no matter what she claimed.

While she hung the damp towel up to dry, Cal loaded the

empty cage back in his Jeep. Before they left the motel, she set up the litter box and food and water bowls she'd bought earlier, in anticipation of trapping Joy.

As he drove her back to the gift shop, Cal cleared his throat. "I've been thinking."

"Did it hurt?" she asked, clearly trying to reestablish the snarky repartee that she'd been using as a shield.

He acknowledged her quip with a quick grin. "Throbbed." He let the word hang between them a beat, before adding, "All Wyatt asked today was that we back off and not risk blowing what the drug task force is putting in place. He didn't say we can't still go after Hamilton for stalking. Even if they reduce or drop charges for drug possession or sales or whatever he's into, if we collect evidence related to stalking, we could still make sure those charges stick when the time comes."

"But Sylvia, at Abby's hospital, said when Chase realized she was calling family for approval for him to visit, he fled fast. And the police presence near the Rogers' home spooked Chase. He hasn't followed Zoey in the last few days."

"As far as we know. But…we don't know the extent of what he may have done before he backed off." Cal twisted his mouth from side to side and clicked his tongue as he drove, his mind working out details of their next steps.

When he pulled in at the gift shop, she popped open her door and was climbing out even before the Jeep had come to a full stop.

Cal followed, catching her at the back door. "Jules, wait. I have an idea. What do you say we visit Zoey Rogers and her parents again and talk with them? We may be missing something useful."

Jules's fists balled at her sides. Her hands had to be

hurting after the abuse she'd wreaked on them at the warehouse. He wanted to take those hands in his and kiss her scraped palms.

She cocked her head, hope and curiosity flickering in her green eyes. "What have we missed?"

Damn it, she was doing it again! Already! How did she trust a man, *kiss a man*, who just two hours ago had capitulated to Wyatt and betrayed his promise to her? When would she learn?

Cal hesitated, and her frustration bubbled over.

"You don't have anything, do you?" she growled, aiming a trembling finger at him and hearing her voice crack. "Do *not* string me along, Sheriff Colton. I swear, I am *sick* of being lied to and ignored and strung along!"

Not with the case and not in our relationship, she wanted to yell. But she'd told him they had no relationship, and she sure as hell didn't want him to think they might yet.

He caught her finger in his hand and tugged her close. "On my life, I swear to you, I'm on your side, and we *will* get Hamilton, one way or another. I may not know now what we'll find, but let's talk to Zoey and her family. We'll keep watching Hamilton. We'll pursue any lead that even hints of value."

When he tugged her even closer, she wanted to resist, but she was tired. So tired, and her traitorous body went willingly into his arms. With both hands, he dried her cheeks and stroked the hair away from her face. Then, cradling her cheeks in his palms, he ducked his head to kiss her temple.

"I'm on your side, Jules. And I'm not going anywhere until we get Chase Hamilton off the street."

Chapter 20

"Has something else happened? Is Zoey in danger?" Mrs. Rogers asked, perched on the edge of her chair.

"Well..." Jules began, and Cal placed his hand on her knee, silently reminding her she'd agreed to let him do the talking if she accompanied him to the Rogers' home.

"I believe Zoey is safe as long as you all continue to use best practices and caution. The police patrols will continue for as long as necessary, and they seem to have spooked Mr. Hamilton away. We just want to be sure we didn't overlook something that might help us get Mr. Hamilton off the street. We need something actionable."

"Like what?" Mr. Rogers asked.

Cal turned to face Zoey. "Since we last talked, has he contacted you, either in person or through social media? A note on your windshield or text message?"

Zoey's eyes rounded, and she chewed her bottom lip before shaking her head. "No."

Cal rubbed his chin, thinking. "Have you noticed anything amiss in the house or your cars? Your yard?"

The family exchanged glances, concerned and dubious frowns on all of their faces.

"Windows left cracked you don't remember opening?

Strange trash in the yard? Trampled flowers under windows?" he prompted.

More head shakes.

"Not that I recall," Mr. Rogers said. "I mean, we've always thought this neighborhood, this town was so safe. We lock our doors at night, of course, and we've made sure windows were locked since you told us this man followed Zoey. But…"

When Zoey's father let his words trail off, Cal said, "Generally speaking, Red Grove *is* a very safe town. And I'm not trying to alarm you."

"I heard there was a murder out on the Enchanted Highway a few days ago. Is that true?" Zoey asked.

Cal cut a quick sharp look at Jules to stop her from saying too much, then said calmly, "A man was found along the highway, yes, and the proper authorities are investigating the cause of his death."

"Zoey?" Jules said, before any more could be said about the alleged murder. "Has anything gone missing from your bedroom? Even something small and impersonal. A comb or pillow or article of clothing?"

Cal sent Jules a look meant to warn her she was breaking their agreement when Zoey said, "Well…not recently. But a few weeks ago, I couldn't find my favorite scrunchie."

"Scrunchie?" Cal asked, knitting his brow.

"A cloth-covered band to hold back her hair in a ponytail," Jules clarified, then arching an eyebrow, added under her breath, "Come on, Colton. You have sisters, for Pete's sake. Don't tell me you don't know about scrunchies."

He returned a wry look. "I didn't get any more familiar with my sisters' personal business than I had to. Separate bathrooms and the works."

"Is that significant?" Mrs. Rogers asked. "That she lost her scrunchie last month?"

"Are you sure—" Jules began, but Cal cut her off.

"Thank you, Jules. I'll take it from here." He turned to Zoey. "Can you describe the...*scrunchie*?"

Zoey wrinkled her nose and shrugged. "It's just a regular scrunchie. Green and yellow. Our team colors."

Cal wrote this information in his notebook, then asked more questions about when she last saw the hair tie and where.

"Last I remember having it was after our game against Butler. I think I left it in our car, but... I don't know." Zoey glanced to her parents for reassurance then back to Jules. "Why is that important?"

"My sister lost things from time to time, and I believe Chase took them as sort of trophies."

Seeing the horror that filled Zoey's and Mrs. Rogers' faces, Cal gritted his back teeth. "We don't know that's what happened."

Jules glared at him. "Maybe the police couldn't prove it, but I know that's what happened."

"Trophies?" Mrs. Rogers repeated, her voice trembling. "Like a serial killer?"

Cal saw the moment Jules realized how her comments had upset the family. Color drained from her face, and her mouth opened silently, as if she was searching for words.

"I don't want you to be unnecessarily alarmed. As I've said, we have patrols watching your house and Zoey's practices. We also have no reason to believe Mr. Hamilton is violent."

Zoey's parents exchanged dubious looks.

"Zoey, do you have another scrunchie that I could borrow for a few days?" Cal asked, and the teen gave him a puzzled frown.

"I guess. Why?"

"I want something with your scent for my SAR dog."

Zoey nibbled her bottom lip, then removed the hair band she was wearing and handed it to him.

"Don't worry. I'll bring it back," he said with a smile for the girl. Cal stood then and sent Jules a look that said, *We're done here.* "I believe that's all for today. If you find anything else missing, or see him around your property, or have any questions, please contact me immediately. All right?"

Jules rose and smoothed her slacks. After a beat, during which he saw her take a deep breath, she gave the family a tense smile. "Thank you for your time. Try not to worry. We're going to get him. I promise."

With a hand at the base of Jules's back, Cal ushered her out of the Rogers' home and to his Wrangler in their driveway. "I thought you were going to let me do the talking."

"Were you going to ask her about missing items? I knew taking things from his victims was part of Chase's MO."

He paused with his hand on the passenger-side door handle and faced her. "The point is, trust is a two-way street, Jules. We had a deal, and you didn't keep it. I have to protect the legality of this investigation. You're not law enforcement." He sighed. "And I didn't want to alarm them or provoke them into doing anything ill-advised."

She puffed up her chest and lifted her chin. "Maybe they should be alarmed. Maybe if the cops and courts were more alarmed about Chase, someone would have done something about him by now!"

Cal kept his mouth clamped shut, taking a moment before he spoke, knowing an argument was not helpful. "Jules—"

"I'm sorry," she said, dropping her shoulders and glancing away. "I did make a deal with you, and I broke it. And I shouldn't have yelled at you just now. I know you're trying to help. My frustration isn't with you. I just—"

She blew a puff of air from pursed lips and shook her head.

He opened the Jeep door and held it for her. "Apology accepted. And for what it's worth, the missing hair band is a big deal. It's a lead we can follow up on. Let's go get a search warrant."

Chapter 21

The next afternoon, before the end of the work day, Jules accompanied Cal as he brought Pilot out with them to the parking lot of Red Grove Food Distributors, warrant in hand. He led Pilot to the rusty white truck they'd seen Chase Hamilton driving and held Zoey's hair band for his dog to sniff. He gave the command for Pilot to search for anything that smelled like the hair band, and Pilot got to work.

Jules held her breath as Pilot made his way around the tires, tracking to another vehicle briefly before returning to the white truck. The Labrador circled the truck twice before pawing at the passenger-side door.

"Good boy," Cal said before employing a thin rod to pop the lock and open the truck door.

Pilot jumped into the truck and sniffed around the seats, under the seats and finally pawed at the glove box.

With gloved hands, Cal opened the compartment and pushed Pilot's eager head out of the way to pluck out a green and yellow scrunchie.

"Bingo," he said, dropping the scrunchie in an evidence bag.

"*Now* can we arrest him?" Jules asked.

Cal gave Pilot a reward for his good work and closed

the truck door as the dog climbed out. "We can certainly bring him in for questioning, at least."

Jules sighed her relief. Was she finally going to see progress in Chase's capture and conviction?

"So do we go after him, or wait here, or what?" A renewed energy pumped through her, and she shifted her weight to her toes, restless and ready to move out and hunt down her prey.

"*We* don't do anything." He clipped Pilot's lead back on the dog's collar and started back to his Jeep. "You're not law enforcement, so at this point you are out. I'll deal with Wyatt and the drug task force to negotiate how and when Hamilton is brought in."

"Wait. What? You're not going to stick around now and arrest him when he comes back to his truck?" She stopped in her tracks and gaped at Cal. "We have proof he broke into the Rogers' house and stole Zoey's hair band! Why are you hesitating?"

"We have a band that looks like the one Zoey described, but we haven't proven it is Zoey's. I'm taking it back to the crime lab to test for her DNA, a matching hair or fingerprints. Something ironclad to tell us it is Zoey's and not a look alike he bought. Then we have to prove he broke in to take it and didn't just find it lying on the ground at the ballpark."

Jules curled her fingers in her hair and let loose a frustrated howl that made Pilot startle. "Why are you making this so hard? We *know* it's Zoey's! We *know* he took it."

"No, we *assume* it's Zoey's and that he took it, but we need proof that will hold up in court." When he continued across the street to the lot where he'd parked his Jeep, she stalked after him, seething.

"You are the most infuriating man I have ever met, Callum Colton."

He pressed a hand to his chest and smiled. "Why, thank you."

That he could act so calm and dismiss her jibes so easily only irritated her more. "I'm so glad I amuse you. Can we please just—"

She didn't get a chance to finish what she was saying. Cal's face darkened, and he grabbed her arm. She gasped as he pulled her forward and behind the nearest parked car, dragging her down as he tugged Pilot close and crouched at the back fender.

"What the h—"

"Shhh." He pressed a finger to his lips, then aimed it across the street where a silver SUV slowly cruised by then disappeared from view as it continued down the street, beyond a stand of trees.

Her heart was already thumping wildly from anger, then alarm, when he'd yanked her behind the car. Now, she exhaled heavily and sat down hard on the pavement, her legs gone weak. "That was the drug dealer's car, wasn't it? The one we saw him talking to a few days ago?"

"Yeah. Pretty sure." He didn't rise from their hiding spot but pivoted on his toes to face her. "Sorry I jerked you down like that, but I don't want anyone in the local drug market to have any reason to remember you or associate you with anything suspicious."

She raked her sweat-dampened hair back from her face and nodded. "It's okay. You just...startled me."

"You okay then? I didn't hurt you?"

She gave him a wry look. "It takes more than a tug on the arm to injure me. I've survived a lot worse and lived to tell the tale."

He frowned. "That's a story I'd like to hear someday if you're willing."

Jules snorted a laugh and cocked her head. "You have a thing for tales of woe, Colton? Isn't that kinda macabre?"

"What I have a thing for is you," he said gently, his hand moving to her cheek. "And I want to know more about you—the good, the bad and the history of whatever and whomever hurt you in the past."

A shiver raced through her despite the July heat.

"Come on," he said, releasing Pilot's collar and offering her a hand up. "Coast is clear. Let's get this evidence back to the office before Hamilton or that SUV sees us."

Jules dusted grit from her knees, hating that despite what she considered proof of Hamilton's menace to society, they were walking away without putting the man in handcuffs. "I still want to look Chase in the eye and confront him with what we know about him stalking Zoey. I want him to know that what he did to Abby hasn't been forgotten and—"

She stopped abruptly, noticing a familiar figure leaving the distributor building and approaching his white truck. And something inside her snapped.

Her body taut with loathing and frustration, she started marching back across the street toward Chase Hamilton.

"Jules!" Cal hissed in a stage whisper. "Stop!"

But adrenaline and indignation raged in her blood. She trembled with it, thinking of Abby's breakdown, the fear in Zoey's eyes…

"Hey!" she called, her tone dark and angry.

Chase looked up at her, but only for a second. Instead, his gaze shifted to the silver SUV that, with a screech of tires, wheeled around the corner and raced toward them.

Chapter 22

The SUV's tinted window came down. A muzzle appeared. Shots were fired.

Chase dove into his truck.

Jules gasped her shock and ran for the cover of the nearest car, two down from Chase's pickup. Something smacked into her, knocking her down as if pushed. She banged her head on the car fender as she tumbled down.

With another squeal of tires, the SUV roared away.

Kneeling on the hot pavement, Jules struggled for a breath, her brain trying to assess what had just happened. Her thoughts and the world around her seemed to move in slow motion.

She heard someone calling her name. Chase revved the engine of his truck and sped away. A grating ache bit her elbow and hip. A sharper throb pounded at her temple. And her side hurt, burned with a ferocious stinging.

Then Cal was at her side, all traces of his usual happy-go-lucky teasing and mild manner gone. His face was flushed with…what? Anger? Heat? Or was it…fear?

"Jules!" His eyes raked over her even as his hands gently rolled her over on the hot asphalt. "Oh, God! You're bleeding."

His voice sounded winded in a way she'd never heard before.

She tried to sit back up, stunned, her thoughts muddled. She had to do something…didn't she? What had she been doing before she fell?

"Lie still. I'm calling help," Cal said, even as she saw his shaking hand raise his phone to his ear. "Yeah, I need an ambulance at the Red Grove Food Distributors parking lot. GSW and other injuries."

Jules blinked. GSW? Didn't that mean *gunshot wound*? She frowned, an action that made her head hurt more. Touching her hand to her temple, she winced then looked at the blood on her fingers. She was bleeding?

Cal's hand covered the stinging spot on her side, and she yelped when he applied pressure. She reached down to touch her aching side and found a sticky wetness there as well. More blood on her hand.

She was bleeding. *She* was bleeding. She was *bleeding*! Finally, her stunned mind began to clear, and the situation crystalized with frightening understanding. Now, the belated buzz of adrenaline and fear flooded her gut. Nausea swamped her. Her head throbbed.

She angled her head to look into Cal's face. Her fingers reached for him and gripped a fistful of his shirt. "I've been shot?"

After tucking his phone between his ear and shoulder, he used his free hand to gently stroke the uninjured side of her face. "Hang on, Jules. Help is on the way."

"Stay…with me. Please, don't leave." She put her hand on his, and he laced his fingers with hers, squeezing firmly.

"No chance, sweetheart. I'm not going anywhere."

Tears puddled in her eyes for reasons she couldn't explain.

But when she closed her eyes, breathing slowly and clinging to Cal's hand, an unfamiliar peace settled in her heart.

"CT doesn't show any concussion or internal bleeding," Dr. Ryan Palmer, the physician on duty at the emergency room, said a few hours later. "The GSW in your side wasn't deep, and the bullet only grazed you, leaving a flesh wound. I'll stitch it up in just a moment, but we'll want to irrigate and disinfect the wound first."

After a knock at the exam room door, Dr. Jonathon Colton peeked into the room. "May I come in? Cal asked me to check on you and give him a report."

"He didn't want to come back himself?" Jules asked, missing his hand to hold and his smile to reassure her.

"He does, but since he's not family, permission has to come from you and your doctor," Jonathon said.

"Please, send him back," she said, glancing to Dr. Palmer for confirmation.

"Okay by me, now that your assessment is complete," Dr. Palmer said, nodding to the nurse with an unspoken request to allow Cal access.

Dr. Palmer consulted her test results again. "I'm prescribing an antibiotic to prevent infection at the bullet wound. Also, plenty of rest for at least a day or two and someone to stay with you just in case that knock to the head proves more serious than the CT shows."

She frowned, then caught her breath when the cut on her temple pulled again. Why couldn't she remember to keep her face still? "That could be difficult," she told Dr. Palmer. "I live alone."

The nurse returned with Cal, who rushed to her side. "Hi. How are you? Geez, you gave me a scare!"

"And you promised not to leave me," she said, hearing the petulance in her tone.

"The hospital staff wouldn't—"

"I know," she said, cutting him off and forcing a crooked grin at odds with her stinging tone. "I just…" Rather than voice the truth—that she'd missed him, wanted him—she laced her fingers with his and bit her bottom lip to choke back the rise of emotion.

Cal's father said, "Ryan was just telling Jules that she needs rest and some TLC. What do you think of having her stay with us for a few days, since she doesn't have a roommate?"

Cal's eyes never left Jules's. "I was thinking much the same out in the waiting room. For her safety as much as her recovery. If those drug dealers got a good look at her…" He cut the thought short. "Well, I just want her where we can keep an eye on her, for several reasons. Like she said, I promised to stay with her."

Jules grunted, reverting to grumpy-mode. Staying in control of her emotions was easier if she presented a stern, sarcastic version of herself. "You're talking about me, deciding things about me, as if I'm not here and don't have a say in the matter."

"You object to the plan?" Cal asked, pulling a chair closer to the side of the hospital bed.

Jules opened her mouth, prepared to object to the men deciding a plan for her, but she caught the words before they slipped out. She *did* want to stay with Cal and Jonathon. Not only was their beautiful home *way* nicer than the motel, but the shooting had rattled her. Deeply. The idea of going back to her lonely motel room, where the masked man had attacked her a few days ago, unsettled her. She swallowed hard and twisted her mouth as if considering. "What about Joy? I can't leave my cat behind."

"Your cat? So you've decided to keep her, have you?" Cal said with a knowing grin that set her teeth on edge.

Darn him! Did he have to be so smug and...*right* all the time?

Cal sent his father a consulting glance. "I have no objections to a cat. Do you?"

Jonathon shrugged. "Why not? The more the merrier."

"Are you sure?" Her pulse ticked faster, anticipating the move to the Coltons' home. What had she gotten herself into? Was she really going to live with these two bachelors, a large dog and a wild kitten? She hadn't cohabited with anyone since sharing her dorm room in college. The idea both thrilled her and flustered her.

The grin on Cal's face faded, and the muscle in his jaw twitched as he regarded her. "Positive."

"Fine. I'll stay with you. For now," she muttered, adding an eye roll so he didn't think she was caving to his will easily.

Thirty minutes later, she was leaving the hospital and climbing into Cal's Jeep. After a stop at the motel to pick up Joy, the kitten's supplies and all of Jules's things, she was checked out of her temporary home and headed to another.

When they arrived at Cal's house, Pilot gave the kitten a curious sniff and wagged his tail, looking up at Cal as if to say "hey, thanks for the new friend!"

Joy, on the other hand, hissed and swatted at Pilot's nose, her fur standing on end.

"Huh. So it's not just people she doesn't like." Cal headed upstairs with her suitcase. "Give her space, Pilot. She'll come around."

"You don't think he'll hurt her?" Jules asked, following him up the steps. "She's so little."

"Naw. I bet they're friends by tonight. Pilot's gentle as a lamb."

Jules cast a last worried glance toward the animals, who were still sizing each other up uneasily, before she followed Cal. As it turned out, Cal was wrong…

Joy and Pilot had sorted things out before they came back downstairs. Pilot was lying on his blanket at the foot of the stairs, and the kitten had climbed on top of the Labrador. After turning around a few times, Joy tucked herself into a ball to sleep on Pilot's side. Pilot gave a contented dog sigh and closed his eyes.

"Well, I'll be. Joy's certainly made herself at home," Jules said, a grin forming. "Clearly she feels safe with Pilot."

Cal draped an arm around her shoulders. "I think they have the right idea. Want to snuggle on the couch? It's plenty big enough for two, and there's an afghan to keep your feet warm."

"Don't you have work to do? I'll be fine by myself."

He nudged her toward the living room. "For the rest of today, my official duty is protecting and looking after you. Ryan said for you to rest, so consider me your nurse for the next few days."

She went to the sofa willingly. Her head hurt, and she was suddenly beyond tired. As she settled on the couch, she sent Cal a puzzled look. "Ryan?"

"Dr. Palmer. My dad has been mentoring Ryan for the last several months since he moved to Red Grove and just refers to him as Ryan outside the hospital."

"Oh. Right." Jules's side gave a throb, and she eased

back against the cushions. "Did he tell me his first name? It's kind of a blur… And I'm so…" She yawned. "Tired."

"That could be the pain meds. Or just the post-adrenaline slump." Cal sat on the edge of the sofa next to her and helped her adjust a throw pillow behind her head. "Name your poison. Something to drink? Another pillow? A snack?"

She shook her head, then hissed as a sharp bolt ricocheted through her skull again. "I wish I could remember to keep my head still," she mumbled as she settled in.

Cal stroked the uninjured side of her face with his fingers, carefully combing the hair away from her cheek. He sighed and in a gentle tone, asked, "What in God's name possessed you to run at Hamilton like that?"

She let her eyes drift closed, concentrating on the soothing touch of his fingers in her hair rather than the scary images and sound from hours before. "Abby."

"Your sister."

"Mmm-hmm. When I saw him, walking free, knowing how he'd ruined Abby's life, I just…"

She didn't say more, and after a moment, Cal stretched out beside her and pulled her into his arms. "I'm going to get him off the street for you. For Abby and Zoey. I promise. You just have to be patient. Trust me. *Listen to me.*"

She curled against his solid strength and thought that maybe, just maybe, she had found someone she could count on to have her back, to give her faith to and believe in.

"I've been thinking…" she mumbled then yawned.

"Did it hurt?" When she groaned, he chuckled. "Fair is fair. You used that one on me. Go ahead. What were you thinking?"

"Masked man."

She felt him tense. "What?"

"The one in my motel room."

A growl rumbled in his chest. "You didn't tell me he was masked. That makes his presence in your room seem more premeditated. Not just a casual break-in of a guy looking for money or valuables." Cal was quiet a moment. She could imagine he was stewing. "What about the masked man? Has he come back?"

She shook her head. Hissed in pain. "Dang it."

"Jules?"

"The second guy. In the hoodie. Last week when the guy was murdered."

Cal shifted to lean over her. "Yeah?"

"He hid his face, too."

"Go on."

She pushed him off so she could sit up and blinked hard trying to shove back the drowsy haze. "If last week's murder was drug-connected, as you suspect, and now we think Chase is hooked up with drug dealers who seem to want to kill him—"

"Then the drug dealers have seen your face twice."

She frowned, her gut clenching. "That's not what I was going to say, but…yeah."

"What were you going to say?" he asked, stroking a finger along her chin.

"Just…the guy in the hoodie, the masked man in my room could have been in that SUV today. I thought that detail might help Wyatt solve the murder."

Cal nodded slowly. "It very well could. I'll talk to him. Meanwhile—"

He framed her face with his palms, his blue eyes penetrating. "It tells me you could be in danger. Forget a day or two to rest. You're going to stay here, under my protection, until the murderer is caught."

Chapter 23

As much as she wanted to argue with Cal about his high-handed decree, fatigue tugged at her and a shimmy of fear in her core begged for the security he offered. New lock on her door or not, she didn't want to go back to her motel. Especially if the drug dealers were looking for her. Was the attack at her motel room a one-off? A coincidence?

She didn't know, and at this point, with the sound of the gunfire this afternoon still reverberating in her memory, she didn't care to find out.

So she leaned into Cal's embrace and closed her eyes. "Okay."

"Wow," he whispered, pressing a kiss to her hair. "That's a first."

"What?"

"Agreeing with me. Not arguing. You may have brain damage after all."

Jules allowed an amused hum to slide from her throat as she snuggled closer.

Taking the hint, Cal lay back down on the couch with Jules draped over him. For the next several minutes, he rubbed a hand down her back or threaded fingers through her hair, his touch soothing, mesmerizing. And soon, like

Joy asleep on Pilot's warm fur, Jules drifted off, safe in Cal's embrace.

When she woke later that evening, the room was darker, the sun having already set outside, which told Jules it was after 9:00 p.m. Cal was no longer on the couch with her and the house was quiet.

She kicked the afghan off her feet and sat up slowly. Her head throbbed in protest, and she discovered new aches and stiff muscles throughout her body. She moaned softly as she shoved the hair out of her face and massaged the crick in her neck.

With the click of claws on hardwood and a chuff of greeting, Pilot trotted in from the foyer and put his head in her lap.

"Hi, old boy," she said, scratching his head. "You didn't eat Joy while I was asleep did you?"

Pilot wagged his tail, and she gave him the stink eye. "Does that mean yes or no?"

"Does what mean yes or no?" a male voice asked.

She glanced up to find Cal standing in the open arch that led to the kitchen, a drink of some description in his hand. "I asked your dog what happened to the kitten. He didn't eat her for dinner while I slept, did he?"

A crooked smile lifted Cal's cheek and sent a flutter of longing to her core. He was so damn good-looking, so relaxed here in his home, so tempting. How was she supposed to live with him and not end up in his bed? And would that really be such a bad thing?

If she could walk and chew bubble gum, could make good grades in college while parenting a teenaged sister, couldn't she have a temporary fling while she found a way to get Chase Hamilton behind bars?

Cal crossed the room and sat beside her. "Happy to report, your kitten is in one piece and currently devouring a can of chicken flavored cat food like a frat boy eating pizza. I'm not sure she's chewing."

"Poor thing still isn't sure where her next meal is coming from." Jules leaned into him and released a contented sigh.

"Speaking of which, are you hungry? You were out cold when my dad and I ate a couple hours ago."

She pressed a hand to her stomach, admitting she was peckish. "I don't want to be trouble. I can fix myself some cereal or—"

"Chicken and rice. I saved you a plate. You like green beans? I made those, too."

She angled a startled look at him. "You cook?"

"In a manner of speaking. I have to if I want to eat. Jonathon Colton sure isn't going to. I've been in charge of meals for my dad and me since Matti moved out several years back."

She pictured Cal's youngest sister, her curly hair and bright smile, and Jules grinned.

"That reminds me," Cal said. "Both of my sisters have called me tonight, wanting to know when they could come by and visit you. They heard about the shooting and are determined to smother you with food and personal attention. Apparently they think I stink as a nurse."

"Or they're just kind." Her grin brightened when she anticipated more time with Cal's sisters. "I have nothing but time on my hands for a couple days, according to Dr. Palmer. Tell them to come anytime."

He jerked a quick nod. "Will do. I'll go heat up your plate."

Cal spent the next day at home with Jules. She spent a great deal of time sleeping, which initially concerned him, until he saw how the rest erased the dark circles that had lived under her eyes since they'd met and eased the fine lines of tension around her mouth. He made sure she ate well, and her cheeks gained more color. She had, in less than one day, bloomed, like a parched flower finally given water. Jules was even more radiantly beautiful than he'd first believed, and a part of that transformation came from the fact that since yesterday, he'd seen her use her smile. With Pilot, with his father, and even—hallelujah!—with him. Maybe he'd underestimated how much stress and worry she'd been living with all these months.

Well, no more. While she was under his roof, he'd make certain she was well-fed, felt secure and had plenty of sleep. He wanted to see her smile more, flourish, glow.

Late that afternoon, as Jules roused from her second nap of the day, Cal set aside his laptop, where he'd been clearing out his email, and moved to the end of the couch. He lifted her feet into his lap and began massaging her feet while she yawned and gave him sexy, sleepy smiles.

"Oh, that's nice." Her sigh was both seductive and sweet. "I never knew how tired your feet could get until I had to be on mine all day at the gift shop." She arched her feet, then flexed them as he dug his thumbs into her soles. Her brow creased then. "Which reminds me, I need to call Bonnie and let her know I'll be out for a few days." Her shoulders slumped. "I really should go back to work tomorrow. I hate that I can't."

"Or you could hire more help to give Bonnie some relief without killing yourself in the process. You were working too many hours before, Jules. There from dawn to dark."

She stacked her hands behind her head and moaned softly. "Like I told you before," she said. "The owner is emphatic that there's no money for more help in the budget.

The gift shop is popular in the summer but makes nothing for several months over the long winter season. As it is, I'm going to have to find new employment myself, if I'm still here come October."

Cal stilled. "What do you mean, if you're still here? Abby is here. Why wouldn't you still be here?"

Chapter 24

Jules pinned him with an emerald gaze that pierced his heart. “North Dakota is not our home. The sooner we catch Chase and make the world safe for Abby to live her life freely and without the constant strain of always looking over her shoulder, the sooner she can leave the hospital and I can go back to Winnipeg and finish my research, get my PhD.”

The disappointment that prodded him must have shown on his face, because she pulled her feet from his lap and sat up. “You didn’t really think I was staying around here long-term, did you? I mean, that’s why I didn’t rent an apartment or sign a long-term lease. I’d hoped to catch Chase in some manner within a few months and then get my real life back on track.”

“Your real life,” he repeated, his chest tight. Why hadn’t he realized Jules’s presence in his life was temporary? Of course, she didn’t have the roots here in Red Grove that made him love his small town despite, or maybe because of, its slow pace and remote location.

“Cal? What—”

His phone buzzed at his hip, sparing him from further discussion of a topic he didn’t want to address. He checked the caller ID. *Wyatt.*

Forcing a breezy tone, he answered, "Hey, man. What's up?"

"Forensics report on that hair band you turned in came back." His brother's lack of banter told him he wouldn't like what the report had to say.

"Go on." When he stood from the couch, Jules reclined again on the cushions. Cal moved out of the living room, mouthing to her, *Sorry. I need to take this.*

"The lab confirmed that hairs and other DNA trace evidence found on the band belong to Zoey Rogers," Wyatt said, "so I sent a team to the Rogers' house. Fingerprints found on her window frame and on her dresser drawer match Hamilton's. We've got enough to bring him in on B and E and misdemeanor theft, but we can threaten him with more serious charges based on his history and your testimony of seeing him watching the girl, following her."

Cal walked farther down the hall and closed the laundry room door behind him. If Jules caught wind that there'd been actionable progress with Hamilton's case, she'd want to be involved.

Lowering his voice, he asked, "Does this mean you're ready to bring him in?"

"Yeah. Wanna join?"

Irritation plucked at Cal. "What about the drug task force? I thought you wanted to leave Hamilton in the wild for your drug trafficking investigation."

He tried not to sound bitter. While he understood his brother's reasoning, they'd had enough probable cause to get Hamilton on trespassing and other misdemeanor charges for days. If they'd arrested him when he and Jules first asked, Jules wouldn't have gotten hurt. Maybe.

Or maybe the scumbag would have bonded out and still been on the street that day when the shooting occurred. Cal gritted his teeth with frustration. Was he letting his feelings for Jules color his professional judgment?

"The task force investigation is actually what we have in mind. We finally have weighty enough charges and evidence to be a real negotiating tool with Hamilton. We're hoping he'll give up names in a plea."

Cal pinched the bridge of his nose. "A plea? Meaning he could still end up back on the street in a matter of days?"

"Damn it, bro." He heard the frustration in Wyatt's voice. "You know how this works. Sometimes the small fish gets away in order to hook the big fish. I know this guy has a history with Jules, and I'm sorry if she's mad about how this is playing out, but…looking at the big picture—"

"I know. I know." Cal heaved a sigh. "Yeah, I want in on his arrest. Give me the details."

"You're not going to do anything to mess this up for the task force, are you?" Wyatt asked.

Cal blinked. "Did you really just ask me that?"

"You can't bring Jules."

"Wasn't gonna."

"Sorry. I just know how invested you are in this and how much Jules means to you. I shouldn't have questioned your professionalism."

Cal furrowed his brow. Wyatt knew how much Jules meant to him? What did his brother mean by that? What did Wyatt think was going on between him and Jules?

What did *he* think was going on with Jules?

If I'm still here... North Dakota is not my home...

He shoved the ache and the questions aside for another time. Arresting Hamilton was the priority now. "It's all good. Should I meet you at your office?"

"No. Task force is moving out as we speak. They plan to take him at work when he gets back from his route."

Cal checked the time. He needed to hurry if he wanted to be present for the arrest. "All right. Thanks for the heads-up."

On the way back to the living room, Cal went upstairs to his bedroom to get his service weapon, his badge and his uniform hat. With luck, by tonight, Chase Hamilton would be behind bars.

But if that happened, how long before Jules left town and was out of his life?

Cal returned from his call with his campaign hat in his hands and his service weapon strapped at his hip. Jules shivered. The pistol was a chilling reminder of not only the exchange of gunfire when she'd gotten injured, but also the nature of Cal's work. A ripple of disquiet shimmied through her.

"I'm going out. Will you be okay by yourself for a couple hours?" he asked, his expression grim.

Jules propped herself up on the sofa, leaning on her elbows. "Where are you going? You look…so serious."

*So serious…*which alone was cause for concern. Cal typically had a pleasant, even carefree expression. Something was wrong.

He situated his uniform hat on his head and twisted his mouth as if deep in thought. "Department business. Something I need to handle personally instead of sending a deputy."

"Oh." While disappointed he was leaving, she knew she didn't have a monopoly on his time. The man had a job to do, and he'd already taken a great deal of time off for her. But the uneasiness that clawed at her wouldn't abate. "What is it you have to do? How long do you think you'll be gone?"

Why had she asked that? It made her sound…needy. Or

nagging. Or somehow more deeply invested in their relationship than she wanted to be.

He pulled his keys from his trouser pocket and bounced them in his hand once. "Hard to say. If all goes well, I'll be back by dinnertime. I'll bring in a pizza." He cocked his head. "You got everything you need for a bit? I can freshen up your drink or get you more ice before I go."

She waved a dismissive hand. "I'm fine. And I know where the kitchen is if I need anything."

He bobbed a nod, and as he turned to go, an odd shiver chased through her. He hadn't said what his trip was about. An intentional dodge? "Cal?"

He faced her again.

"Is this business…dangerous?" She curled her hands into fists around the edge of the afghan. He was the sheriff. Of course he would occasionally face perilous situations on the job. That was a fact of life she'd have to get used to if…

No. There was no *if.* He was simply a friend she was concerned about. Period.

Except he didn't answer for a moment, and the hesitation didn't bode well. "Cal?"

"Look. I don't want to lie to you. I want our relationship to be fully honest and forthcoming. I want you to trust everything I say and do."

"But?"

"No *buts*. It's only that I can't always know what might happen on any given day or investigation or call. The nature of law enforcement means I encounter a degree of risk pretty often."

She frowned. "So this outing *is* dangerous. Is that what you're saying?"

His lopsided grin softened the serious edge of his expression, though his eyes remained shadowed and intense. He stepped to the side of the couch and bent to kiss her. "I'm saying I'm a trained professional, and I don't want you to worry unnecessarily about me. I will be back with a pizza in time for dinner."

His reassurance did little to quell the niggling in her gut. She forced a smile as he strode back to the door and called, "Extra pepperoni and cheese."

He signaled a thumbs-up as he exited her view, and she flopped back against the throw pillows. He could tell her not to worry all he wanted, but until he was back from this mysterious errand, she would do exactly that.

Cal chewed the inside of his cheek as he drove away from his house. He hadn't lied to Jules…exactly. He'd just been carefully selective with what he'd told her. Because if he'd said Wyatt had tipped him off to the imminent arrest of Chase Hamilton, Jules would have insisted on coming with him. And he'd have had to refuse her. Because no way did she need to be trying to accompany him while she was freshly injured from their last escapade. Which would anger her. And they'd fight about it. And, well…

So he hadn't told her.

When he arrived at Red Grove Food Distributors, where the arrest would be made, Cal found Wyatt and two more plainclothes officers already there. No marked patrol vehicles to tip off Hamilton before Wyatt or the other officers could take him into custody.

The team members had gathered in the company's main office and were in conversation with the distribution manager.

Cal sidled up to his brother, and when the manager offered his hand, Cal shook it and gave a nod of greeting as he introduced himself.

"What sort of deal are you planning to offer Hamilton?" Cal asked Wyatt under his breath.

Wyatt explained that the task force had intel that the local drug ring was buzzing, and Chase Hamilton was likely the stick that had poked the hornets' nest. Clearly the attempt on Hamilton's life that had caught Jules in the crosshairs wasn't a one-off. The hope was that knowing he was persona non grata with local drug dealers and could be targeted again, Hamilton would trade names for safety. The task force, working with the mayor's office and local DA, was willing to drop charges against Chase Hamilton and allow him to secretly relocate to another state.

Cal goggled at his brother. "Hang on. You're saying that not only does he get away with stalking a teenager, Jules's sister and who knows how many other women, he gets to start over in a new location with no strings attached?"

"Callum—" Wyatt began darkly.

"Don't *Callum* me!" He poked a finger toward his brother. Anger boiled up, making his muscles tense. "You can't let this guy get off scot-free! He's a menace to women. At a minimum, he needs to be reporting to an officer of the court, so his location and activities can be monitored!"

Wyatt propped his arms akimbo, glaring at Cal. "I don't like it any more than you do, but can you really see this Hamilton guy agreeing to name names if he thought he could walk out of the police station and be killed for his efforts?"

Cal gritted his back teeth and suppressed a growl.

"We've kept a tight seal on this deal in an effort to keep the guy alive," Wyatt continued. "Only a handful of people know about this plan for a reason. I had to get special permission from the task force to let you in on the operation today. Don't make me regret the courtesy."

Cal met his brother's blue glare, so like his own. "Doesn't it get to you? Seeing people you know are a drag on society, a danger to others, getting off on technicalities or walking on pleas or dodging arrest for lack of actionable evidence?"

Wyatt was serene, but serious, his voice low. "Of course it bothers me. We've had this conversation before. But as you've reminded me in the past, the system works more often than not. And it's set up to protect the innocent."

Cal rolled his eyes. "Yeah, yeah. Save the lecture."

Wyatt cuffed his brother on the shoulder. "I know you're just venting. But I—"

"Detective Colton," one of the plainclothes officers called. "Hamilton just pulled up to the loading dock."

Wyatt straightened his spine and arched an eyebrow toward Cal. "We good?"

Cal's returned nod and expression confirmed his agreement. "Go get the bastard."

Wyatt and the other officers disappeared from the manager's office, and Cal stepped over to the black and white video screens, where the feed from security cameras played in real time.

He set his teeth as he watched the men approach Chase Hamilton, badges out. He saw the moment Hamilton tried to flee, but was tackled by one of the plainclothes officers. Hamilton fought back and eventually had a pair of handcuffs snapped on behind his back.

Cal should have felt a deeper sense of satisfaction at the stalker's arrest. The operation went smoothly. Charges of resisting arrest and assaulting an officer could be added to Hamilton's list of crimes. But knowing Wyatt and the drug task force planned to offer the scumbag a Get Out of Jail Free card gnawed his gut.

Jules would go ballistic.

After returning to his Jeep, Cal followed his brother and the unmarked cars to the police station, where he intended to observe Hamilton's interrogation.

As expected, they had to wait for a public defender to be summoned to represent Hamilton during the plea deal negotiations. During the intervening downtime, which was taking much longer than expected, Cal called Jules to check on her. "Everything okay at the homestead?"

"Yes. Fine. Kelly stopped by to visit. She's challenged me to a game of Scrabble, which I'm losing big-time. I think she's making up words, but she brought cherry cobbler, so I'm letting her play whatever words she wants."

Cal laughed. "Had I known she was coming to the house, I'd have warned you that my sister is a word game Mensa."

"What about you? How is your work errand going?" she asked, and he heard the trepidation in her tone.

"The hard part is over. Just waiting for the strings to all be tied up." He glanced at the clock in the station lobby. "Clearly I'm going to be later than I thought. Maybe you and Kelly should eat without me. Put it on my account."

Hearing the front door of the police station open, Cal glanced up. He stilled and frowned, recognizing the woman who'd just entered the station. "Hey, I've got to go."

"Be careful," Jules said as he hung up.

He approached the woman and asked, "What are you doing here?"

Chapter 25

"That was your brother," Jules said as she disconnected the call and set aside her phone.

"Don't tell me. He's going to be later than expected, and we should eat without him?" Kelly asked as she drew a new set of letters from the Scrabble bag.

"Yeah. Should we order pizza for delivery?"

"Sounds good." Kelly turned the game board to face Jules and asked, "What is Callum doing that's keeping him away from his houseguest?"

"He wouldn't say, other than department business that he had to personally handle. But he took his gun and his badge and acted dodgy when I asked if it was dangerous business." Jules studied the Scrabble board while Kelly placed the order for a large pizza. Finally, Jules played *PAINT* on the *P* of Kelly's last word.

"Dodgy, huh?" Kelly said, picking up the thread of conversation expertly when she finished calling in their dinner order. "Well, I know what it is to worry about loved ones on the job—" Kelly paused to record Jules's score "—having three brothers in law enforcement and a firefighter. But if it's any consolation, Callum is good at what he does. He doesn't take unnecessary risks."

Jules forced a grin and waggled a few fingers dismissively. "Oh, I'm not worried."

Kelly angled a dubious look at her.

"Well, not too worried," Jules amended. "I just don't like being kept in the dark about what he's doing." Shrugging, she tempered that comment. "Not that I'm keeping track of his business or—" She frowned at the Scrabble board where Kelly had just played *QI* on the *IN* of her *PAINT*. "Qi? Now I know you're making up words."

Kelly laughed. "Look it up. It's perfectly legit. And the *Q* is on the double letter, so I get it doubled both ways… And I'm out of letters, so…game over."

"Ugh." Jules rolled her eyes and stretched out on the sofa. "If you hadn't brought cherry cobbler, I'd swear you came to torture me."

"Speaking of…ready for a serving? There's ice cream to put on top." Kelly put the letter tiles back in the game box and stood.

"Now? The pizza hasn't even gotten here," Jules asked with a furrow in her brow.

"True. But the cobbler is still warm, and I'm starving. Besides, haven't you heard? Life is short…"

Jules laughed. "Eat dessert first!"

Kelly flashed a mischievous grin, much like her brother's. "Exactly."

Jules started to get up. "I can come to the table."

"No." Kelly held up a hand. "I'll bring it to you. Enjoy the pampering while you've got it."

Kelly disappeared into the kitchen, and a moment later, Jules heard Kelly coo, "Oh, my goodness! Aren't you precious? Where did this kitten come from?"

"Be careful!" Jules called. "She's still pretty feist—"

Kelly strolled back into the living room with Joy curled against her chest, a docile ball of fluff. "Is it yours?"

Jules gaped. "How did you do that?"

"Do what?" Kelly stroked Joy's fur with her fingertips, and a loud rumbling purr filled the room.

Jules shook her head and chuckled. "You're the kitten whisperer. Joy's been nothing but feisty since we trapped her."

"Feisty?" Kelly kissed Joy's head and walked over to Jules. "Not this little love, surely." She handed the kitten to Jules, who cradled Joy on her chest. "You hold her while I get our cobbler."

Joy stood and turned around once before settling down again and continuing to purr. Tears pooled in Jules's eyes as she cuddled the kitten.

"You were just scared, weren't you?" she whispered as she patted the fuzzy baby. Her heart swelled, knowing the kitten's calm and loving behavior meant Joy felt safe now, could even be forming bonds with her people.

And why did Joy's turnaround make her think of her own experience with Cal? Was she starting to feel safe in their relationship? Was she forming bonds with him and his family? Friendships, certainly. But was it more?

And what if the answer was yes? What did she do with that information?

"Here you go," Kelly announced brightly as she returned from the kitchen with a bowl of warm cherry cobbler topped with a generous scoop of vanilla ice cream.

Jules took the bowl, then waffled as to how to eat it without disturbing Joy, who was now asleep on her chest. "Um…"

Kelly laughed. "Want me to move the kitten?"

"Not on your life! I'm loving this." Jules propped the

bowl beside her and took small bites, taking care not to jostle Joy or drip ice cream on the couch.

"So are things between you and Cal serious?" Kelly asked.

Jules sputtered and choked on her last bite of ice cream, startling Joy away and sloshing a bit of cherry juice on the sofa cushion.

Kelly set aside her dish and came over to help Jules sit up and dab at the cherry stain. "Sorry. That was rather blunt and out of the blue, wasn't it? You can take the lawyer out of the courtroom, but…" She pulled an apologetic face.

"Is this a cross-examination?" Jules asked as she sat up and wiped her mouth on the napkin Kelly had given her.

"Not at all. Just a sister hoping her oldest brother has finally met someone who'll love him and stick around. He deserves to be happy, and his last couple girlfriends weren't in it for the long haul."

Jules perked at mention of Cal's past. They'd never discussed previous relationships, and knowing Cal had been let down twice before pierced her heart. She hated to think of Cal getting hurt, yet…she didn't plan to stick around. If they were able to get Chase Hamilton off the street and Abby felt safe to resume her life outside the hospital, why would she and Abby stay in Red Grove?

When Jules didn't answer, Kelly frowned. "I'm kinda protective of my brothers, I suppose. Not that they aren't capable of taking care of themselves, but…" She shrugged. "Personal relationships are different, and I've already seen him hurt."

"I have no intention of hurting Cal."

"Then you have feelings for him? You plan on sticking around?" Kelly asked, brightening.

Jules's stomach tightened, and she set aside her bowl of cobbler. "Um…"

"It's just that I can see how much Cal cares for you. I think he's got some real feelings for you. Serious feelings." She paused. "And excuse my being blunt again, but…if you don't feel the same way for him, I hope you'll let him know now. Let him down gently and—"

"I do—" Jules blurted before she'd stopped to analyze what bubbled up from her core. "Uh…care about him. A lot. He's been very good to me, and…" Her heart thrashed in her chest. What was she saying? Had she already fallen for Callum Colton?

Kelly leaned forward, her eyebrows lifting. "And?"

"I'm scared," Jules admitted, her hands starting to shake. "Or I was. I don't trust easily. Too many people have used and betrayed me in the past."

"You can trust Cal. My brother is one of the good ones."

Jules nodded. "I'm learning that. More and more every day."

Joy waddled close to Jules's foot, and she scooped the kitten up to hold in her lap. She smiled as she ran a finger down Joy's small back. Like Joy, she'd begun to feel safe around Cal and the Coltons. Optimistic. She'd begun to believe they *would* catch Hamilton. Abby *would* get her life back. And she might—*maybe*—have found someone to build a relationship with, someone to love. And the prospect of sharing herself with Cal didn't frighten her. It gave her hope. It gave her joy.

Chapter 26

"What are you doing here?" Cal frowned at the woman across the lobby of the police station.

His youngest sister, Matti, turned in response to his impertinent question. She arched an eyebrow and tossed her mop of curls back from her face. "I could ask you the same thing, *Sheriff.* This is Wyatt's domain, not yours."

"True," Cal said, stepping close enough to give his baby sister a hug. She might be twenty-six years old now, but Matti would always be the baby of the family in his eyes. He'd helped look out for her from an early age, especially when it was clear their dad put his hospital duties over his family responsibilities. "But if you've been paying attention in recent years, you'd know Wyatt's department and mine often collaborate on big cases that cross jurisdictional lines. Besides, it's late. Police stations are not fun places to be late at night."

"And if you'd been paying attention to me in recent years, you'd know that I often have business at the police station related to my cases. Even late at night. Often late at night." She frowned. "I'm here to pick up a little boy that was found alone at a motel. The desk clerk saw him rummaging in the trash for food and asked him where his parents were. He only shrugged and said they'd been gone since the day before."

Cal pinched the bridge of his nose and mumbled a curse word. "Poor kid."

"Mmm." Matti tugged his arm, pulling him aside and settling in the formed plastic chairs against the wall in the station lobby. Lowering her voice, she continued, "The desk clerk said when she took the kid back to his room, with some fruit and cookies she scrounged from her own dinner and the vending machine, she found a mess in the room. Drug paraphernalia, dirty food wrappers strewn around, unmade beds and no sign of the kid's parents."

"Drug paraphernalia, you say? What is the kid's name?"

Matti checked her notes. "All he told the motel clerk was Sam. He said he's six." She showed him the thin file in her hand and the database pulled up on her iPad. "I'm scrambling to fine emergency foster care for him. At least for tonight. Tomorrow, if the cops can track down his parents, I get to open a whole new can of worms. But for now, my job is to wait here for the responding officers to bring him here. Once I have a foster home arranged, I'll escort him to the emergency placement and help ease his transition."

Cal placed a hand on his sister's shoulder and squeezed. "Matticake," he said, using his childhood nickname for her, "have I told you how proud I am of what you do? I thought I saw the dregs of society in my job, but you see the victims of the worst of humanity."

"Thank you, Cal. I'm kinda proud of you, too." She leaned into him, bumping his shoulder.

They both glanced to the front door as a female patrol officer entered the lobby through the front doors, leading a small boy with wide dark eyes and shaggy light blond hair. Cal took in the boy's bedraggled appearance. He clearly hadn't had a bath in several days, and his lean frame and small size gave him the appearance of being younger than the six years Matti said the child had claimed to be. The terror and trauma in his expression were heartbreaking. Here was a child who had seen and heard far more in his short life than any person should.

Cal heard Matti's soft gasp of dismay before she schooled her expression, fixing a bright smile on her face and moving to greet the child with a calm and warm demeanor. "Hello, Sam. My name is Matti Colton." She held out a hand as if to shake Sam's. "It's nice to meet you."

Sam only stared at Matti's hand and inched closer to the patrol officer.

Cal hung back, watching his sister work. Clearly the boy was already overwhelmed and frightened without adding another adult face to the mix.

The patrol officer crouched and coaxed gently, "Sam, this nice lady is going to take you to a safe house, where you can eat something good and have a warm bed while we find your mom and dad. Okay?"

Sam ducked his chin and slanted a wary look at Matti.

"I know this is all kinda strange for you, but I promise to take good care of you and make sure you are safe until we get everything sorted out with your mom and dad," Matti said.

The boy stuck his thumb in his mouth, and his nose was running a bit, evidence he'd been crying earlier.

Matti reached in her pocket and pulled out a small lollipop. "I almost forgot! I brought this for you. Do you like green apple suckers?"

The boy perked up and reached for the candy. "Red is my favorite."

Matti brightened. "Really? Red is my favorite, too! Cool!"

Sam looked at the candy, then divided a look between the patrol officer and Matti. "Can I eat it now?"

"If you want. It's all yours." Matti ruffled Sam's hair lightly. "Will you come sit over here in these chairs with me while I finish making a few phone calls?"

The patrol officer nodded to Sam as he unwrapped the lollipop. "You're in good hands with Ms. Colton, sweetie. I've got to go do some other things now. Okay?"

Sam heaved a sigh and gave Matti another wary look, then said in whisper, "Okay. 'Bye."

Matti took his free hand as he poked the candy in his mouth and led him to the chairs near Cal. His sister stroked the boy's hair in a motherly gesture that touched Cal's heart. "What are some of your other favorite things, Sam?" Matti asked.

Cal smiled at her tactic, redirecting the boy's thoughts to happier things while also learning tidbits that might help the foster family acclimate Sam.

Sam shrugged.

"Do you have a favorite flavor of ice cream?" she asked.

Another shrug.

"A favorite television show? Favorite color? I'm guessing…pink?"

Sam shot a disgruntled look at Matti. "No-o-o! Pink is for girls!"

"Not always." She tapped Sam on the nose with one finger. "That, my dear, is what's called a cliché."

Sam wrinkled his nose, obviously confused by the new word.

"Okay, you tell me. Green? Brown?" Matti continued, and Cal could see the child relaxing.

"Red," the child said quietly.

"Of course!" Matti said as if it should have been obvious and she'd missed it. "So not just red lollipops. Red lots of things, huh?"

Sam bobbed his head in a nod.

"Good choice!"

Cal heard the door to the back hall of the police department squeak, and he glanced up to see Wyatt waving him over. He left Matti and Sam to continue getting acquainted and stepped over to his brother.

"So Hamilton wasn't such a tough nut to crack," Wyatt said in a hushed voice, guiding Cal even farther away from listening ears. Once they were in an isolated nook by the vending machine, Wyatt continued, "Almost as soon as his public defender arrived, he agreed to give up names."

Cal clapped his brother on the arm. "Good work."

"With stipulations."

"Naturally. No one really thought he'd flip without a cushy deal. What did he ask for?"

"He swung for the fences. He wants a clean slate, all charges dropped. His record expunged."

Cal snorted. "I hope you said no! The greedy bastard."

"The DA is considering it."

Cal goggled, knowing how this news would devastate Jules.

"But," Wyatt added, "given the hour and our current impasse, we decided to let him sleep and have a good meal in the morning before we resumed. His PD requested time to study the charges against Hamilton more closely."

Frustrated, Cal smacked a hand against the vending machine. "So that's it for tonight?"

His brother nodded. "We'll be moving him to a jail cell

soon for the night. If you want to observe the negotiations tomorrow, we've set that up with his PD for nine o'clock."

Cal nodded again. "Yeah. I want to be here."

"Callum," Wyatt said, pitching his voice low again. "Don't say anything to Jules just yet. Like when we arrested him, the task force wants to play this deal with Hamilton real close to the vest. Only a few key players know anything about it."

"Understood."

"In fact, when we move him to his holding cell, because of the chatter we've picked up on from the drug ring, we're not going the usual route out the back door and around the alley to the transport van. That route is known to anyone who's ever had a brush with the law and been taken the same path. Even with body armor, keeping Hamilton alive is too important."

"What then?" Cal asked.

"If you'd help us keep a watch, we'll have the van pull right up to the front door and hurry him through the lobby." Wyatt received a text and checked his phone screen. "They're ready to move now. Will you take a post out front?"

"Sure," Cal said, taking out his sidearm and moving back into the main lobby.

Matti's eyes widened when she saw him return with his weapon in his hand. "Cal? What are you doing?"

"Nothing you need to worry about." He gave the lobby and front doors a visual sweep. The nondescript van used for inmate transport pulled to a stop at the front curb. "Listen, a prisoner is being moved. Perhaps you and Sam could relocate to another room until—"

Before he could finish his sentence, the door to the back hall opened with a clang, and no fewer than five police officers, surrounding a handcuffed Chase Hamilton, entered the lobby. Cal tugged on Matti's arm, pulling her out of the main walking path to the front doors.

Hamilton seemed to be jerking against the guiding hands of the officer beside him. He snarled a curse at the officer.

"Settle down!" one of the policemen barked. "Keep him moving—"

A loud blast and the clatter of breaking glass ricocheted through the entry hall. Then another blast and another—

Chaos erupted around him. Shouts and gunshots. Toppling chairs and splintering plaster. Flying debris and whizzing bullets.

Sam let out a high-pitched and terrified scream.

Matti cringed and yelped her own fright.

"Get down!" Cal yanked Matti's arm, pulling her behind a large potted plant and shoving her down.

His sister fought his grip. "No! Sam!"

The officers in the lobby rushed to take up defensive positions and return fire. A cacophony of voices added to the confusion.

"Where's the shooter?"

"Anyone have eyes on him?"

"Officer down!"

"He's hit!"

Sam's loud wail of distress sounded like a siren, heightening the surreal incongruity of the unfolding tableau. A shooting. At the police station. Cal shook his head to clear the buzz of shock, the ringing in his ears.

His grip tightened on Matti's arm when she tried to rise. "Stay down!"

"I have to get Sam!" Panic was thick in his baby sister's voice.

"I'll go," he told her, his tone commanding. "Stay here!"

The shooting stopped almost as quickly as it started. Like ants whose hill had been kicked, police officers swarmed in and out of the lobby, taking tactical positions and moving in a crouch into the parking lot in search of the shooter. Others gathered around two fallen bodies.

Chase Hamilton, whose head wound left no doubt he was dead, and the police officer who'd been closest to him. The officer clutched his chest while his colleagues administered first aid.

Broken glass and crumbled plaster and drywall crunched under Cal's shoes as he scurried to the little boy. He stayed low until he reached the spot where Sam had curled into a ball on the floor, tucked as far under the row of formed plastic chairs as he could. "Hey, Sammy. Come on out. I've got you."

Sam continued wailing and shrank from his touch.

"I know that was scary, but I've got you. You're okay now." Cal tried again to tug the boy gently from under the chairs.

Then Matti was beside him, reaching for the boy. Because when had his stubborn little sister ever done what he told her to? "Matti…" Cal growled in a low, disapproving voice. "I told you to stay d—"

"Sam? Hey, buddy, are you okay?" she cooed, not only cutting him off, but also shoving her way closer to the frightened child. "It's Ms. Matti. Can you come out here for me? I know that was scary. I'm so sorry, darling. Come on. I've got you."

Cal helped Matti slide the boy's tightly balled body out from the chair legs. Then, again with his help, she lifted the boy, still curled in the fetal position, into her arms.

"Shh, sweetie. I got you. It's over. You're okay." Matti

kept up the litany of murmured reassurances, and Cal's heart broke for the terrified child.

"Matti! What the hell is she doing here?" Wyatt's voice reflected the stress and frustration of the moment as he rushed over.

Cal pulled his brother away from Matti and Sam. "She was picking up the boy for relocation to a foster home."

"You couldn't have told me our sister and a minor were here?" he said, his glare and timbre both accusing.

Cal forgave his brother's attack, knowing Wyatt was as emotionally charged as they all were. Wyatt's entire body, like his own, vibrated with tension, fury and shock.

"I was trying to get them to a safer place when—" Cal waved a hand toward the destruction in the lobby.

"Cal!" The horror in Matti's voice sent a chill to his marrow. He spun to face her and saw the color wash from her face. She raised a stricken expression to him. "Sam is bleeding! I think he was shot!"

Chapter 27

Jules snapped her gaze toward the front hall when she heard the door open and close. "Cal, is that you?"

Jonathon rounded the corner into the living room and flashed a sheepish grin. "Sorry. Just me."

Jules wilted back against the couch. "Oh. Hi."

Kelly rose from her chair and met her father with a hug. "Cal left on a department-related errand a good while ago. He's late returning, and we haven't had an update in an hour or so."

"Is there reason to be worried?" Jonathon asked, emptying his pockets onto the end of a decorative table.

"He tried to convince me there wasn't, but… I'm not sure." Jules twisted her fingers in the hem of her shirt and sighed.

"He'll call soon. Cal's the conscientious sort," Jonathon said with a wink as he started for the kitchen.

Jules forced a smile for the doctor's attempt to allay her fears.

"Dad," Kelly called as her father left the room, "you know if you don't put keys on your dresser, you won't be able to find them later."

Jonathon returned, giving his daughter a wry look. "You

sound like Cal. Since when did you two become the parents?"

She shrugged. "You know I'm right. You lose your keys on a regular basis."

With a noncommittal growl, Dr. Colton rolled his eyes, picked up his keys again and jammed them back in his pocket.

"If you're hungry, there's a little pizza on the counter and cobbler by the stove," Kelly said to her father's retreating back.

Jonathon peeked around the corner again, his eyes bright. "Cherry cobbler?"

"Yep."

The jangle of a phone ringing spilled into the living room, and Jules heard Jonathon groan. "Hello? Yeah, what's happened?"

His voice faded as he moved into the kitchen, and Jules checked her own phone for the time. For missed texts. For any sign that Cal had checked in. Nothing.

"Dad's right," Kelly said. "I'm sure Cal will be home or he'll call soon. He's not one to leave you hanging. You know. First born, hyper responsible. All that jazz. That's my big brother."

Jules stroked Joy's back, the kitten having been curled up asleep on the couch next to her for the last ten minutes. "That's good to know. It's the picture I've been drawing of him. Reliable. Honest. Trustworthy."

Great kisser. Hot body. Gentle hands, she added silently.

"He's one of the good guys, Jules. I know I've said it before, but…because I really like you, too, I want you to know he is g—"

"Well," Jonathon said, reappearing at the living room

door. "I'm headed back to the hospital. No rest for the weary."

"Dad!" Kelly braced her hands on her hips, clearly disgruntled. "Let one of the other doctors handle...whatever it is. You need to eat and...when was the last time you slept?"

Jonathon glanced away, rubbing the five o'clock shadow on his cheek. When he returned his gaze to Kelly, his expression was stark. "I want to be there myself. I..." He sighed and cut a frown toward Jules that sent a ripple of alarm through her. "That was Ryan... Dr. Palmer. There was a shooting at the police station."

Jules tensed, her heart slowing.

Kelly gasped. "What!"

"They're bringing in several people with injuries. At least one law enforcement officer has been shot," Jonathon said. "I want to be on hand, if one of your brothers..."

Jules swung her feet to the floor and scooted to the edge of the couch. "I want to go, too."

"We don't know that it's Cal..." Kelly said, though her eyes said she was as panicked as Jules felt. "I think we should wait here until..."

At that moment, headlights panned across the front window, and Kelly rushed to look out. "It's Cal! Oh, thank God!"

Jules clambered to her feet, ignoring the dizzy spin of her head as she hurried to meet Cal at the door. She fell into his arms as he entered the foyer, a haggard look dimming his typically upbeat expression. Without saying anything, she clung to him, and he wordlessly hugged her back, burying his face in the curve of her neck.

"Callum?" Jonathon said finally. "Can you tell us what happened? I had a call from the hospital about a shooting. Multiple injuries. I'm headed there now."

"Have you talked to Wyatt? To Dylan? Are they okay?" Kelly asked, her voice trembling.

Cal stepped back from Jules and nodded to his sister. "Dylan wasn't there. Wyatt will be fine. He has a small cut on his arm. He thinks he hit the corner of a metal desk as he took cover."

Jules swallowed hard. "Took cover. From gunfire. There *was* a shooting, wasn't there?"

His face remained inscrutable, though she sensed something beyond the shooting was troubling him. "Cal?"

Dr. Colton clapped a hand on Cal's shoulder as he moved past him to the door. "I'm glad to see you're unhurt, son. I need to go now and take care of those that are."

Kelly cleared her throat and edged toward the door. "I'll go, too… Since you're here to keep her company, and… well, I don't want to be a third wheel."

Jules rallied to tell Kelly goodbye and thank her for the companionship, the food, her steadying influence as she waited. When they were alone, Jules faced Cal and drew a breath for courage. "Tell me. Whatever it is you're not saying, just…please tell me."

Nodding, he took her hand and led her into the living room. He gave Joy a cursory glance before moving to the other end of the sofa and pulling Jules down beside him. "Wyatt and the drug task force arrested Chase Hamilton earlier today."

She straightened her back, and hope filled her chest. "They did? Finally?"

But Cal didn't look happy about the news, and immediately her chest squeezed again. *Shooting at the police station…*

Acid pooled in her gut as she shifted to face him more fully. "The shooting. Was that him? He got away, didn't he?"

Cal shook his head. "No. He didn't get away. He...was shot."

Jules took a beat to process this new tidbit of information.

"The task force wanted his arrest for leverage to get him to flip on higher-ups in the drug ring. They were working on a plea deal—"

"Damn it!" Jules exploded. "So he gets off *again*?"

"Jules..."

"What is it going to take to get this guy—"

"Jules, he's dead." Cal's hands tightened on her arms, his keen blue eyes drilling into her. "He was killed by the shooter at the station when we tried to move him to a holding cell at the county facility."

A strange buzzing filled her ears as she replayed what he'd said in her head. "Dead? Hamilton is dead?"

He nodded.

The tension inside her uncoiled a bit. "Well, then that's good news, isn't it? I mean, I'd rather he was incarcerated for the rest of his life rather than being killed. I'm not a monster. But...if he's dead, he can't bother Abby anymore, either. Or Zoey. Or any other woman."

His cheek twitched. "Well, yeah. There's that. But...he never actually gave the task force any names. His lawyer convinced everyone to put the negotiations and interrogation on hold because of the late hour."

She wanted to quiz him further about Hamilton and what it meant going forward, but she could see shadows in his eyes. "Cal? There's something else. Isn't there? You're so...subdued. Distracted."

He nodded and swallowed hard, his Adam's apple dipping.

"What...?"

"Matti was at the police station when the shooting happened." He drew an unsteady breath. "She was in the lobby with a little boy she was moving to foster care, and—" His voice cracked, and he squeezed his eyes shut.

"Oh, no! Was she hurt?" She grabbed his sleeve, her chest constricting with dread.

He shook his head. "But the little boy was. Not seriously, but…"

She'd never seen him this upset. "Cal?"

"Sorry, I just… It was so unnerving. Seeing her holding that bleeding child. Knowing *my sister* could have been the one hurt—or worse—in that hail of bullets."

"Thank God she wasn't." She sat beside him and wrapped her arms around him, trying to comfort him.

"I mean Wyatt, Dylan and I know the risks associated with our job. Even Aiden, for different reasons. We've kind of accepted that one of us could get injured in the line of duty, but…damn it. Not my baby sister. Not Matti. She and Kelly are…"

"Don't you dare say something sexist and spoil my image of you, Callum Colton," she said in a mock chiding tone.

He cut a glance at her and blinked as if needing a moment to let her jibe register.

"It sounded like you were winding up to call your sisters fragile or vulnerable or delicate or some sexist trash like that." She stroked the side of his face and gave him a wry grin to soften her words.

His brow wrinkled, and he snorted a humorless laugh. "No. Not my sisters. They're two of the strongest and bravest women I know. I was going to say they're—" he pressed a hand to his chest "—special to me. I've always tried to look out for them, especially when we were younger. Our dad wasn't always there when he should have been, and I tried to…fill in the gaps."

She pulled a grin. "Hyper responsible."

"Hmm?"

"That's what Kelly called you earlier tonight. Classic firstborn."

He acknowledged her reply with a sad smile before slumping back against the sofa cushions, the troubled look returning to his eyes.

After a moment, her own nurturing and tenderhearted instincts nudged her, so she asked, "How badly was the little boy hurt?"

He turned up one hand in an I-don't-know gesture. "I'm waiting on a report from Matti. She went with him to the emergency room." He gave her a quick side glance before staring straight ahead. "Sam, the little boy, was already so scared, having been left alone in a motel room and brought to the police station, surrounded by strangers. The shooting was the last straw for him." The pain in his eyes said he was seeing the scene again, replaying the horror in his mind. "He was…almost catatonic. Traumatized by it all."

She cuddled closer to him, rubbing his arm as if he were the traumatized boy. "Having been caught in a shooting myself, I can understand that. Poor little guy."

"If that weren't enough," he said and grimaced, "Officer Rutledge, a guy with a wife and two kids, caught a bullet in the chest as well. He's alive but in serious condition. Last word I had was they were taking him into surgery."

"Oh, no! That's terrible!"

He closed his eyes and leaned his head back. She felt a small shudder pass through him, and her heart twisted.

"Tonight sucked," he said in a low voice.

"Sounds like it. I'm so sorry." She squeezed his arm,

then slid her hand down to lace her fingers with his. "I wish I could do something to help."

He rolled his head toward her. "You would?"

She grunted and gaped at him in dismay. "What? Why would you ask that? I care about people!"

Arching an eyebrow, he scoffed. "And yet with me you're the sarcasm queen."

"I'm not that bad!" But even as she defended herself, compunction gnawed at her conscience.

When she opened her mouth to justify her sarcasm, the corner of his mouth twitched, and he leaned in to kiss her. "There she is, the woman I love to spar with."

"So you don't really think I'm…a grump?"

His grin spread. "Well, I might not go that far."

"Ugh!" She frowned and play swatted at him, thankful that his mood had lifted enough to tease with her.

"What I would say is—" he grew serious again, and his fingers plowed into her hair to cradle the back of her head "—I'm learning more and more that your crusty shell protects a soft heart, a kind and caring soul that I find very attractive."

Her pulse fluttered as his attention dropped to her mouth, his pupils expanding like a cat's when it spied prey. This time, she leaned in to kiss him rather than wait for him to make the move. She heard the swoosh of blood past her ears as her head grew muzzy and light. The fevered spike in her pulse fed her, encouraged her, shouted down the persistent squawk in her mind that warned her not to get tangled up with a man, not to risk the heartache.

Cal's kiss deepened, and she felt the tension in his body as she held him. Was his ardor rooted in desire for her or just a release of the stress that had haunted him tonight? And did it matter? He'd supported her through scary times in recent days. She could return the favor. Especially if the favor meant she could scratch an itch without investing too much of herself.

The hotter the kisses grew, the louder the justifications shouted in her brain. A hunger roared to life inside her that only Cal could satisfy. Finally, she rose long enough to kneel on the couch, straddling his lap. Capturing his face between her palms, she pushed him back against the pillows and lost herself in his kiss.

His arms circled her, and he drew her closer, a small moan slipping from his throat as he drew on her mouth.

Amid the rush of sensation, the heady swirl of pleasure that heated her blood, Jules became aware of a wholly different feeling that swelled in her core and demanded attention.

Kissing Cal Colton didn't just feel good, it felt…right. Being held by him, sinking into him, being the one to console him at the end of a terrible day…fit. As if she'd been waiting her whole life for a missing piece of her soul, Cal was comfortable, familiar. The electron she needed to fill her valence shell.

Wow. That was...awful. A laugh tripped from her that sounded more like a cough. She was in deep if she was creating tortured chemistry analogies like that. Clearly she was no poet with the gift of romantic words.

"Oh, man," he said, his brow knitting as he pulled away. "I forgot about your head injury. Are you all right?"

She wrinkled her nose. "I'm fine. I wish I could blame my head injury for what I just thought."

"Care to share?"

"No. I'd like to preserve what little respect you have for me."

He tugged her close again. "Oh, but I have quite a bit

of respect for you, beautiful. Respect and desire. Which is my way of saying I want to make love to you, but the decision is yours."

Chapter 28

His wording stopped her for a moment. Love? Was that what this was for him? An admission of love? Was that what he thought it was for her?

Her rational brain told her what they had couldn't possibly be love. They hadn't known each other long enough. He was only being polite. A gentleman didn't ask for sex using crude terms, and Cal was kind and thoughtful at his core.

This explanation was enough to quiet the blare of sirens that had been triggered by his phrasing. Not love, then. Just a gentlemanly request for no-strings sex.

So why did framing things that way chafe her at her core? She'd never been a no-strings kinda girl. She was an avoid-all-forms-of-attachment, don't-risk-any-pain-or-betrayal kind of girl. Didn't sex imply trust? Didn't the act mean allowing herself to be at least a little vulnerable?

"Huh." Cal's brow furrowed as he sat up, easing her off his lap. "I think your hesitation speaks for itself. Anything you have to think that hard about isn't—"

"No!" She shook her head, then quickly amended, "I mean, yes. I mean, I always think this hard. I'm a scientist. It comes with the territory. I have to analyze decisions."

His expression was skeptical, but he didn't say anything.

She clutched his forearm. "I just want to be sure, you know?"

He held her gaze, his eyes silently asking, *And...?* His eyes…

Eyes that had teased her and mesmerized her and *seduced her* from the first time they met. Heat flashed through Jules, a yearning so strong it left her lightheaded. "Yes."

She answered before she could second-guess herself or question her need.

Now fire shone from those bright blue eyes as he took her lips again, shifted her beneath him and eased her back on the couch.

When items of clothing started being shed, he stooped to lift her into his arms. Once he'd carried her upstairs to the privacy of his bedroom, they were naked in seconds, each helping the other peel off the remaining garments.

Small creases on Cal's face hinted that the night's ghosts still haunted him, and she wanted to banish his demons and comfort him the same way he'd cheered and supported her for weeks.

Wait…was it only days? Had it really been less than two weeks? As he yanked off the bedspread and folded back the sheet, she blinked, gobsmacked by the realization she'd only met Cal recently, when he'd come to investigate the dead man near the gift shop.

So much had happened in the last two weeks that she felt like she'd known him for so much longer.

"Come here," he said, tugging her hand, and she stepped into his embrace. His hands stroked down her back and cupped her bottom, pulling her closer to him. Air stuck in her lungs, a surge of desire stealing her breath when the proof of his arousal nudged her intimately.

When he feathered nibbling kisses along her throat and down to her shoulder, she let her head tip back, her neck arched in invitation. The slow, tender way he explored made her feel cherished, wanted for more than sex, but valued as a woman. *His woman.*

A shiver chased through her, and she took a step back from Cal, her heart thrashing in panic the way Joy had flailed when she first caught her.

He lowered his eyebrows and gave her a look of concern. "Have you changed your mind? Did I do something wrong?" He stroked his palm along her cheek. "You are safe with me."

She saw the moment his words, the implied promise, clanged discordantly in his own ears. He was thinking of the shooting, of Matti being exposed to peril. She knew it immediately.

She framed his face with her hands and pinned a hard look on him. "Cal, you are not responsible for the shooting or the danger Matti was exposed to tonight. You said yourself that she was all right, unhurt. Don't beat yourself up over it."

A muscle in his jaw twitched as he ground his back teeth. He drew her with him as he moved to the edge of the bed and sat. "It's not as simple as that. Besides being her big brother, I'm the sheriff of this county. It is on me if there are violent drug gangs and dealers shooting at each other and putting innocent civilians at risk. I ran for office on a promise to rid this town of the drug crime, and tonight my lack of progress came back to bite me hard on the ass!"

Sarcastic humor and teasing banter had always been her go-to when she didn't know what else to say, so now, she said, "What if *I* were to bite you on your ass? Hmm?"

His chin jerked back, and his cerulean eyes widened. "What?"

She waggled her eyebrows playfully.

A hearty laugh burst from him—rich, deep and enough to waken every cell in her body. She wanted Cal Colton. Now.

Wrapping her body around his, she kissed him thoroughly and clutched him close. When she paused to catch her breath, she whispered against his mouth. "I'm in a mood to be a little reckless, Colton. Don't blow this opportunity."

He needed no more invitation. Pulling her with him onto the bed, he took her lips with his and explored her mouth with his tongue. His hands slid over her, enticing shivers of pleasure from deep in her core. The touch of his hands on her naked skin made her body hum as if electricity coursed through her. Jules's eyes flicked up, searching his face with quiet urgency. The tension between them was no longer polite—no longer patient. It cracked like thunder.

Cal slid his body down hers, stoking little fires as he moved his lips across her ribs, down to her navel. His fingers brushed her breasts, and she arched into his hands. He molded, pinched and tasted her in a way that was both tantalizing and tender, raw and reverent. Her breath escaped in needy pants as his touch moved downward. When his hands settled at her hips, lifting her, arranging himself, the heat between them felt almost unbearable. "You sure?" he murmured, his voice rough as gravel.

Jules nodded, then wrapped her arms around his neck to kiss him. A gasp slipped from her throat when he entered her, and she inhaled the moan that escaped from his. Or was it the other way around? She wasn't sure where she stopped and he started. Her senses blurred, and the world tilted as they moved as one.

Sensations rose as if from her marrow. Her hands moved to his back, her fingertips mapping out the way his back arched toward her. He lifted her easily, her legs tightening around him, and the world fell away with each heartbeat. As skin met skin, their breaths tangled—hot, ragged, real. Just Cal and Jules, as she learned what it meant to finally feel wanted. Safe.

Much later, when their passion had cooled and their bodies were sated, he held her as sleep stole over them. Jules studied the fringe of his dark eyelashes on his cheeks as his breathing grew deep and even. The tension that had lined his countenance had disappeared, his handsome face now relaxed with slumber. In the aftermath, in the stillness of his dark bedroom, she waited for the recriminations, the doubts to creep over her. But they never came. If nothing else, she'd been what he wanted, what he needed after the nightmare at the police station. And being what Cal Colton needed felt pretty damn good.

Chapter 29

Cal's cell phone woke him the next morning, and he dragged himself from slumber to find Jules still draped across him, her thick hair tickling his chin. He smiled to himself remembering the pleasures they'd shared and the erotic sounds she'd made as he'd loved her. But when she stirred, obviously also woken by the buzzing of his phone, he begrudgingly slid away from her to reach for it on the bedside stand.

"H'lo?"

"Don't tell me you were still in bed," Wyatt said accusingly. "I might have to hurt you. I've been up all night, thank you."

Jules rolled away from him, freeing his left arm to stretch and sit up on the mattress.

"You have an update for me?" Cal asked.

"Several. First, Matti is fine, and the boy's—Sam's—injury proved less serious than we feared. He was treated for a surface wound and kept overnight, largely because Matti hasn't located a foster family yet."

Cal twisted at the waist and looked over his shoulder to Jules. She'd tucked the sheet up to her chin and seemed to be dozing again. Her tumble of hair spread out on the pillow, and her fringe of eyelashes fanned across her ivory cheeks. Damn, but he could wake to the sight of her beside him for the rest of his life. She was—

"Cal, did you hear me?" Wyatt asked, interrupting his romantic woolgathering.

He cleared his throat. "Yeah. Sam spent the night at the hospital, but he'll mend."

He heard Wyatt grunt. "That's what I thought. You stopped listening after the first update."

"Uh. Sorry, what?"

"I've had my men scouring the city all night for the shooter. The shots seem to have come from some point across the street from the station, but so far, nothing of note has turned up. Not casings, not trash to indicate where he'd waited, no sightings by people in the area. He's disappeared into the wind."

"A professional, then," Cal said darkly. "Knew what he was doing. Good aim, too, seeing as how he got Hamilton from a distance."

Now, Jules turned her head quickly, her eyes flying open.

He held up a finger, indicating he'd talk to her in a minute after he finished with Wyatt. "And Officer Rutledge? Did he survive his surgery?"

"Thankfully, yes. He's stable and awake last I heard, but he's got a long road ahead to recover."

"Look, I'm sorry I bailed on you last night rather than helping with the search," Cal said, "but… I had other business that I had to handle. Personal business."

"I get that." Then after only a brief pause, Wyatt said, "How did Jules take the news about Hamilton?"

Jules sat up now, raking her hair back from her face with her fingers. The sheet slipped enough that he could see the swell of her breasts, and he instantly wanted her again, despite hours of lovemaking the night before.

"Cal? You there?" Wyatt asked.

"Yeah. I, uh—"

"She's still there, isn't she? She's with you now. Probably naked. Am I right?" Wyatt asked, his voice low and conspiratorial.

"I'll talk to you later. Let me know how I can help with the search for the shooter. I'll make any resources you need from the sheriff's office available to you."

"Your nonanswer is an answer," Wyatt said and chuckled. Sobering, he added, "Thanks for the offer of assistance. We issued an APB, of course, but without a description of the shooter, we're kinda at a loss. I asked Forensics to rush the ballistics report."

"Good."

Wyatt sighed. "Ted called earlier."

"Oh? And what did the good mayor want?"

"You have to ask? While he was in my custody, I lost a key witness in the drug trafficking investigation and had an officer nearly die in the same shooting. Ted wants a meeting. My guess is he's gonna tear me a new one."

The bed jostled, and Cal watched Jules slide from under the covers and pad into the en suite bathroom. He heard the shower turn on and tried not to think about her body slick with soap and—

"Want to come with me?" Wyatt said, pulling him from his sensual fantasy.

"To see Ted? Why? Don't tell me Teddy scares you."

Wyatt scoffed. "Hell no. Ted's not the issue. I want you in on the conversation about what happened last night. You were there. You were one of the few people that knew who and what was being negotiated behind closed doors. I think you could offer a helpful perspective."

He only had to consider the request a moment to know he would help his brother however he could. That's what he did. How he'd always operated. He took care of his family. He jolted then, realizing that was exactly what had driven Jules to pursue Chase Hamilton with such fervor. A love for her sister and compelling need to fulfill her duty to protect her closest family member when their parents had failed.

He set aside his conclusion for the moment, knowing he'd want to address it later.

"Cal? You still there?"

"Yeah, sorry. Sure, I'll go with you. What time?" Cal swung his legs out of bed and checked his bedside clock. It was almost 9:00 a.m.

"About eleven? That work for you?"

"Hmm, sure. I want to go by the Rogers' first and give them the news about Hamilton in person. His name hasn't been in the news coverage, has it?"

"Not yet. I know you drove Matti's car to the emergency room when she rode with the boy in the ambulance, so you weren't there when the media circus arrived. Local stations showed up at the police station twenty minutes after the shooting, demanding details. Heard about it on their damn police scanners," Wyatt groused. "Bismarck TV station even sent someone, probably because an officer was involved. Media loves a police shooting."

Cal rolled his eyes, dismissing his brother's familiar grumpiness and complaints about reporters. They finalized plans to meet at city hall and arrive at the mayor's office together, and Cal hustled to the shower in time to help Jules…wash her back.

* * *

Jules accompanied Cal to the Rogers' house, wanting to be present to offer her support to the family when they learned the emotionally charged news of the shooting and Hamilton's death. While she was relieved to have the threat to her sister eliminated, she was also riddled with a sense of guilt, as if she'd been party to his death and Officer Rutledge's injury. How could she rejoice over the end of Abby's worries, when it came at such a high price?

Zoey Rogers could easily have similar conflicted feelings.

Cal did an admirable job breaking the news gently, but the shock and muted relief the family expressed were largely what Jules expected.

"He was offered a plea deal?" Zoey asked. "On what charges? Stalking me? Breaking into our house?"

"Zoey," Cal said, his tone soothing, "you are not to blame for anything that happened. Don't go there even for a minute."

Jules appreciated his attempt to ameliorate any strife for the teenager, but Jules heard a different truth in the girl's questions. She'd lived with the same feelings for too long not to recognize the sense of betrayal behind Zoey's inquiry.

"I know it doesn't seem fair," she said, placing a hand over the teenager's, "but the police needed his help on a case with bigger stakes and further-reaching consequences."

"So what he did, the way he scared me and violated our home, doesn't matter?" Zoey asked, her anger rising.

"Of course it matters. The way he terrorized my sister matters, too." Jules squeezed Zoey's fingers. "They mattered enough to be useful in the big picture. The plea deal had more weight because of the numerous charges the police had accumulated against Hamilton. Not an ideal solution for either of our families, but one that was meant to be of greater benefit to the community in the long run."

"The important thing is he's not a problem anymore, honey. You're safe now," Mrs. Rogers said, her tone clearly meant to buoy her daughter's mood.

She and Cal left soon after that, driving directly to the Red Grove city hall, where Cal and Wyatt were meeting with Ted Barrett.

Jules reflected on the Colton family party earlier in the month, when she and Ted had been teammates for several rousing rounds of volleyball, and she grinned. As Cal parked and climbed out of his Jeep, she said, "Tell Ted I said 'hi' and that I've been working on my spikes. I'm ready for the next volleyball match."

"Will do. I shouldn't be too long. Cup of Joe is just down the block, if you want to get a coffee while you wait. Their iced latte is the best in town."

"Good to know. I'll meet you there," Jules said, eyeing the other shops along the small-town-vibe thoroughfare. When was the last time she'd shopped for new clothes? Shoes? Too long ago, she decided, savoring a buzz of excitement that she hadn't felt the freedom to enjoy while the question of Chase Hamilton hung over her. Her gaze followed Cal as he squared his shoulders as if marching off to do battle, then set off with her own mission to find a new sundress and sandals.

"Before we see Ted, I want to talk to you about something," Cal said as he and Wyatt took the stairs in city hall.

"About Jules?" Wyatt asked.

Cal pulled a face. "No. Will you stop about Jules?"

"Sorry. It's just obvious to everyone around you she makes you happy, and we don't want to see you mess it up."

"How would I mess it—" Cal shook his head and raised a hand to cut off that conversation. "Never mind that. What I mean is… I'm wondering how the shooter even knew Hamilton was at the police station. If we're working on the assumption the shooting was a targeted assassination to take Hamilton out before he named names or as retribution if he'd already named names, how did the news get to the drug traffickers so fast? My God, the man hadn't even left the police station!"

Wyatt frowned. "That's bugged me, too. I can name the people who knew about his arrest and the plea deal on two hands and have fingers left over."

"So there's a leak within the inner circle of the task force?" Cal asked, but it could have been a statement instead of a query. Wyatt's expression confirmed his belief.

Chapter 30

"You want to be the one to break *that news* to the mayor?" Wyatt asked, shoving his hands in his jeans pockets and hunching his shoulders.

Callum arched a dark eyebrow. The idea of a leak gnawed at him, and while he wanted to step forward and take the lead on finding the leak and fixing the problem, he knew doing so would be overstepping. "Dude, I'm not officially on the task force. If I go to Ted and report a problem, I'm a…what did we use to call it? A tattletale. And you know me better than that. Haven't I kept secrets on you and every other Colton kid that Mom and Dad still haven't heard? Ted, too, for that matter." He scrunched his face and rubbed his chin in a comically thoughtful way. "Come to think of it, I could probably write a really juicy exposé on the Colton siblings' secrets and sell…oh, dozens of copies in town."

Wyatt gave him a deadpan look. "Before you can write a tell-all book, you'd have to learn to spell and put words in real sentences. I'm not scared of that happening anytime soon." Wyatt playfully punched his brother, then grew serious again. "But I appreciate your coming with me to talk to Ted. You have an easier manner with him, and since you know more about Hamilton and his history…"

"It's all right. Shall we head in? Ted doesn't like people to be late." Cal could never tell anyone in his family *no*, whether they needed money, advice, a place to stay, or for him to protect a secret. "Should I have brought Pilot for his tail-wagging diplomacy?"

"Nah." Wyatt slapped his back as took the final stairs to the mayor's office. "You know what a stickler Ted is for the 'no animals other than service animals' policy in city hall. You'd do better bringing Jules. I think Ted was kinda smitten with her at the Fourth of July party."

Cal missed the last step and stumbled. "He's what? Hot for Jules?"

In a false voice to mimic Ted, Wyatt said, "Come be on my team, Jules."

"Oh, good shot, Jules. High five!"

"I saved you a seat over here, Jules."

Ted's office door opened before Cal could reply, and Ted divided a sober look between them. "I thought I heard voices. Come on in. Time is money, and thanks to last night's events, I have a busy day."

Wyatt and Cal followed their foster brother into his office and each took one of the sleek leather visitors' chairs with nail-head embellishments along the arms.

Ted narrowed his gaze on Wyatt. "Geez, Wy. You look like crap."

Wyatt flashed a sarcastic grin. "Aw, thanks, Teddy. I got no sleep last night just so I could impress you with the dark circles under my eyes and day-old beard."

Then, turning to Cal, Ted added, "You don't look much better."

Cal flipped up a palm. "I'll try harder not to look tired next time. But I know you didn't call us for a meeting about our grooming."

"Hell, no, I didn't." Ted closed his office door with a thud and rounded his desk. Standing behind the desk, he braced his arms on the top and leaned forward, challenging Wyatt and Callum. "A man in your custody is now dead. An officer was injured. The police department is under my purview. This is not a good look for the city or my office." He glared at Wyatt, then Cal, and back to Wyatt. His face tensed and he growled, "What happened?"

Wyatt started his version of events in an even and professional tone, until Ted cut him off. "I don't need a dry blow-by-blow recounting of every fingerprint taken and question asked. I need to know *what went wrong*?" Ted roared the final words, his nose flaring and his breathing heavy before he dropped into his chair. Squeezing both armrests until his knuckles went white, Ted glared at the brothers. "Well?"

"We spent most of the night negotiating a plea deal with Hamilton and his lawyer." Wyatt propped his arms on his thighs as he leaned forward. "We'd finally reached terms that Hamilton would get relocation, protection and a cleared record if he gave us top names in the trafficking business coming from Canada."

Cal sighed, knowing how angry these terms would have made Jules.

Wyatt cast a glance to Cal as he continued, "The operation locally is growing. It's a cancer in our community we have to stop, and we suspected he had information on people and locations, processes and products."

Ted frowned. "Who is this guy… Chris Hamilton? I've never heard of him. How did he end up on our radar?"

"It's *Chase* Hamilton, and he had recently moved to town, following a young lady he'd been stalking." Cal waited for Ted to look at him. "Jules's sister, Abby."

Cal elaborated on the investigation he and Jules had been working trying to get enough evidence of his crimes to get Chase put away. He explained how Chase had followed Abby to town and had started following Zoey, stealing her hair band and watching her house. "At some point, he got involved with local dealers for personal use, or maybe he intended to sell drugs as a side hustle or to drug Zoey and kidnap her or..."

"But this new-to-town, drug-using stalker was killed before he gave you any names. Is that right?" Ted looked from Cal to Wyatt. "Is that the bottom line?"

"That's one takeaway, yes." Wyatt pressed his mouth in a taut line, clearly stewing over his part in the breakdown of the operation.

"Ted," Cal said, drawing the mayor's attention back to him. "A more concerning point we should be focusing on is the leak in the drug task force."

Ted blinked and furrowed his brow. "Leak?"

"Someone had to have told the traffickers that we had Hamilton in custody and that he was arranging a deal for us to drop his charges," Cal said.

"We made a point of keeping Hamilton's arrest and our negotiations under wraps. Only a small circle of men on the task force knew what was happening," Wyatt explained, and Ted's head swiveled between the brothers as they continued to spell out the situation.

"And at what exact moment he was being moved," Cal said.

"Including the fact we didn't use the rear door we typically use for prisoner transfers," Wyatt added. "They were able to shoot through the front lobby windows from a location across the street or on a rooftop. We haven't pinned down the shooter's location yet, but his accuracy leads us to believe he could have been a professional marksman or at least had accurate weaponry."

The muscles in Ted's jaw flexed. After a beat, he asked, "What about Officer Rutledge? Do you have an update on his condition?"

"Holding his own for now, but still serious."

Ted's mouth was pinched and his jaw rigid, a testament to the usually affable mayor's consternation. He said nothing for several seconds, but then grumbled, "Anything else?"

Wyatt and Cal exchanged a glance.

"Ted," Cal said, his tone low and grave. "A child was injured as well. A cut from flying debris. He went to the hospital as well, in shock, and was kept overnight."

Ted's expression darkened. "Why in the world was a child at the police station at that hour?"

"He was being moved to a foster home," Cal said, then took a beat before adding, "Matti was with him."

Ted's expression shifted, awash with distress. He slumped back in his chair and swallowed hard, then asked hoarsely, "Was Matti hurt?"

Cal shook his head. "But she was deeply shaken, quite upset when she saw the boy's injury."

Ted gave a jerky nod. "Of course. She would be. She's—" He pinched the bridge of his nose and sighed before glancing up again. "What else can you tell me?"

"Not much," Wyatt said. "The investigation is only a few hours old, after all, but I will, of course, keep you apprised of developments."

Pulling a face of pure disgust with the situation, Ted pushed to his feet and adjusted his waistband.

Taking the unspoken cue that their meeting was over, Cal and Wyatt rose as well.

"Ted—" Wyatt began.

"I have another appointment to get to now," Ted said, walking to his office door.

The brothers followed, but before Cal could leave, Ted growled, "First a man is murdered at a prime tourist location, now *this*. Voters remember mistakes and incompetence. It's in *all* of our best interests that you get your departments cleaned up and fast. I need results, not excuses."

With that, Ted opened the office door and stepped back.

Cal marched out, his teeth clenched, and didn't say anything until they reached the front sidewalk. "Well, that was fun."

Wyatt's hands were fisted, and he shook his head. "A man is dead, two more people injured, another murder unsolved and his complaint is that it looks bad for his reelection?"

"He's a politician. Of course he's thinking about that," Cal said, trying to be the voice of reason. "But it's not his only concern. He asked about the injured cop. He was visibly shaken when we told him about Sam and Matti."

Wyatt grunted. "I guess."

Cal drew a deep breath and let it out slowly. "Look, we're all tense. We're all tired. We're all frustrated. Let's cut him some slack and get back to work. The best thing we can do now for everyone concerned is find the shooter, solve John Harper's murder and plug the leak in the drug task force."

Wyatt arched an eyebrow and scoffed. "Oh, is that all? No problem."

Cal flashed his brother a wry grin. "That's all. Easy peasy." *Right. If only.*

Chapter 31

Cal found Jules at Cup of Joe, an iced coffee in one hand and her phone to her ear with the other. She was smiling, and he took a moment just to study the glow on her face and the new sparkle in her eyes. And the fact that when she glanced up and spotted him, the smile didn't morph into a scowl like it had so often when they'd first met.

He took a seat next to her and waited while she finished her phone call. "Okay. Well, Cal's here now, so I'm gonna run, and we'll see you in a little while. Love you, too."

He tipped his head and gave her a playful frown. "Love you, too? You got another man on the side, Bailey?"

She snorted. "*Another* implies there is a first man. Rather presumptuous of you, Colton. I swear, you sleep with a man once, and they get all possessive of you."

He grinned at her quip, but at his core, doubts niggled. Was she serious? Her tone had sounded a bit too dry, not light enough to mollify him. Did she not think they were a couple? That they had enough connection and chemistry to pursue a relationship?

"The call," she said, wagging her phone once before stashing it in her purse, "was Abby."

"Ah. So…did you tell her about Chase?"

She shot him a look of horror. "God, no! That's not the

kind of news you deliver over the phone. I told her I would be out later to see her." She paused to sip her drink. "I'd like you to come, too, if you want."

He nodded. "I'd love to meet her."

She pushed her chair back and slung her purse strap over her shoulder. "All righty then. No time like the present."

He ordered himself a coffee to-go, and they were on the state road headed to the outskirts of town minutes later.

Cal was largely silent as he drove, mulling over her distancing denials at the coffee shop. He tried to tell himself he was overreacting. She couldn't fake the sort of passion and connection they'd had last night. Right?

"Jules, about what you said—" he began at the same moment she blurted, "I cannot wait to tell the shop owner I'm quitting the gift shop."

He blinked. "You're…quitting?"

"Of course I am. It was never supposed to be a career move, just a source of income that was also on Chase's delivery route. Now that he's not a concern, I can get back up to Winnipeg and finish my research, get my PhD and get on with my life."

She smiled and exhaled in a manner that said she was savoring the relief that plan gave her.

"Oh." Cal gripped the steering wheel tighter and furrowed his brow. "I see."

She gave him a dry laugh. "What? That's good news. Why the pout?"

His frown deepened. "I'm not pouting."

She reached over and rubbed the crease on his brow. "Kinda are."

He took pains to school his face and rein in his disappointment. "Well, maybe I'm just rather surprised to hear you talk about leaving town."

"Seriously? I've told you from the start the whole gift shop business was a stopgap while I caught Hamilton. Abby is safe now. She can leave the hospital, and we can both get back to living our lives."

He pressed his mouth in a firm line and drummed his thumbs on the steering wheel. "I kinda thought I was part of your life now. Last night—"

"Was great. But Red Grove isn't my home. I've told you—"

"I know what you've told me. But that was before..." He dragged a hand over his mouth and scratched his chin, not wanting to sound desperate or needy. If Jules didn't love him, didn't want him, he had to find the courage and composure to let her walk away. He could do it. He could steel his heart and cut ties with her. Sure.

Liar. Just the prospect of losing Jules made him feel like his chest was being carved out with a grapefruit spoon.

Jules angled her body toward him, her fingers fidgeting in her lap. "Cal, look... I appreciate everything you've done for me, and the time we've spent together has been—"

"Don't." He realized his tone had been brusque. Cold. So he forced a weak smile and shook his head. "No justification necessary. Clearly, the feelings were all one-sided. I misread things."

"Cal."

"But I'll be all right."

"Cal, I—"

"This is the turn, correct?" He aimed a finger at the upcoming crossroad, and she nodded.

She sighed. "I'm sorry if—"

"We're good," he said more confidently than he felt. He wheeled his Jeep into a parking space and cut the engine. "Let's go tell Abby your good news."

Once inside the hospital and checked in with the front desk, Cal followed Jules down the corridor to Abby's room. He hung back until Jules gave the all clear that Abby was dressed and willing to meet him. When he rounded the doorframe, the sisters were still locked in a tight embrace.

"I've missed you, Juju. Your one visit in the last three weeks hasn't been nearly enough. I know you said you were busy, but sheesh!" Abby said, her cheeks suspiciously damp.

Jules chuckled. "I know. I'm sorry. You'll understand why in a minute but…three weeks? That's a bit of an exaggeration, don't you think?"

"Sixteen days! That's more than two weeks, so…almost three." Abby seemed to remember Cal was there, and her expression sobered, appearing wary as she backed out of her hug with Jules. "Hello."

He gave her his brightest smile and stepped forward to offer a hand to shake. "Hi, Abby."

Jules made the introductions, referring to Cal simply as "her friend." He tried not to be disheartened by the generic term, but after her announcement in the car that she was leaving town, what did he really expect? He pushed aside his disappointment in order to focus on Abby.

Jules pointed out the best chair in the room for him, while she sat on the edge of Abby's bed with her sister, holding Abby's hand.

"So Cal is the sheriff here in Stark County. I think I told you I'd been working on a project with him?"

Abby sent Cal a timid glance, then nodded to Jules.

"Well, our work has paid off. I have some good news, Ab," Jules said, angling her body toward her sister. "Chase won't be bothering you ever again."

Abby gave her a stark look, then blinked. All color

drained from her face, and she visibly trembled. "Wha— Chase?"

Jules tucked a few loose strands of her sister's hair behind Abby's ear. "You're safe, Ab. Chase can't bother you anymore."

Cal was struck by the tenderness Jules showed her sister, and recognized the careful way she was broaching the topic of Hamilton's death. If he needed any more proof that the crusty shell Jules had projected when they first met hid a soft and gooey center, he had only to watch this interaction with her sister.

After processing Jule's comment for a few seconds, Abby's eyes widened, and she angled her head. "He's in jail?"

Jules's gaze darted to him quickly, as if seeking support before breaking the news to her sister. "He was arrested yesterday. Yes. And then…"

Abby visibly tensed, the same way Jules had whenever she braced for bad news or more discouragement. Jules clearly felt her sister's reaction, saw it for herself, because she rubbed Abby's arm and quickly said, "It's all right, Abby. He— Well, when they were transferring him to the jail, some men involved in drug dealing shot him."

Cal noticed she didn't mention the plea deal that Hamilton had cut for his release. Moot point at this stage, he supposed. Or the fact that Hamilton had been killed. She was spooning the information in bite-size bits and monitoring how Abby reacted.

Together, he and Jules watched as Abby digested this latest tidbit. She frowned as if skeptical, then scrunched her nose and tipped her head again. "Shot? Wh-what are you saying?"

"Honey, he's dead." Jules put an arm around her sister's

shoulders, and the other hand clung to Abby's hand as if she feared Abby might fall apart if Jules didn't hold her together. "Chase was killed by the gunman."

Chapter 32

Abby blinked hard, shaking her head and frowning. "Dead? I didn't want him *killed.* I never wanted..." Then she squeezed her eyes shut and exhaled as if releasing a long-held breath from her very core. "He's really gone? He can't bother me anymore?"

"I know this stirs up a whole bunch of mixed feelings," Jules said, pulling Abby's head down to her shoulder and resting her own cheek on Abby's head. "I've been going through the same weird roller coaster since Cal told me."

Abby suddenly bolted upright, her face pale. "Wait a minute." Her attention shot to Cal. "She said you're the sheriff *here*? In Stark County?"

Cal gave a slow nod. "I am."

Abby scowled at Jules. "Was Chase the project you were working on with him?"

Jules opened and closed her mouth as if unsure what to say. Her silence was answer enough for Abby.

"So Chase was here? In Red Grove? And you knew it? For how long? Why didn't you tell me?" Abby's breathing grew fast and shallow, and Jules took both of her hands and gave them a little shake.

"Abby, honey, I'm sorry I didn't tell you. But the important thing is he can't hurt you anymore. Haven't I always promised to take care of you, to protect you?"

"But he was *here*! He could have—"

"No," Jules interrupted, clearly trying to calm her sister with her tone and soothing touches to her cheek. "Not while you were safe here at the clinic. I've kept tabs on him and worked with Cal to see him taken off the streets. I would never have let him hurt you. I promised you that long ago, and I meant it."

Clearly Jules still wasn't going to mention Chase had made it as far as the clinic. Probably for the best.

Abby's breathing remained ragged, her gaze darting from him to Jules to the window, as if searching for something. What's more, Cal read on Jules's face an understanding that, despite the news of Hamilton's death, her sister still had anxiety issues that needed to be addressed before she would leave the hospital. He sensed her disappointment that eliminating Hamilton's threat hadn't been a miracle cure.

For all Jules's gentle care and comfort to Abby, Jules would need her own TLC today when they left the mental health clinic.

They stayed for another hour, and Jules finally calmed Abby enough to change the subject to her adoption of Joy and the kitten's transformation from a flea-bitten terror to a soft, purring snuggle buddy.

"You should see the way that little cat rules my Lab, Pilot," Cal added with a chuckle. "He's like her grampa or something, and he's wrapped around that kitten's finger… or claw. Whatever."

"I can't wait for you to meet her," Jules said. "And Pilot."

Abby furrowed her brow. "Meet her? But…"

"When you come home," Jules said. "Now that Chase isn't a threat, you can start working toward the day you'll come live with me in Winnipeg. Maybe start school again. Get a job. Get your life back."

Tears formed in Abby's eyes. "I can do that?"

Jules nodded and smiled through her own tears. "You can, Abby. You *can*." Her tone was rich with affirmation and encouragement.

Abby laughed and choked on a sob. "I can!"

As they left the mental health hospital, Cal caught Jules by the arm and tugged her to him. "C'mere."

She tensed at first, but when he folded her in his arms and pressed her close, she melted against him.

"I like your sister," he whispered, nuzzling her hair. "I see a core of strength in her, a lot like yours. Despite everything, I believe she's going to be all right. She just needs a little time."

He felt her sag. "Time." Jules turned her head to bury her face in his chest. "I was so stupid. Why did I think that simply catching Chase and locking him up would be some magic elixir to cure all her anxiety? And now…knowing Chase died is disturbing in itself." She groaned. "Her breakdown didn't happen overnight. It was a thousand little things that wore her down, so of course she'll need more time to regain a firm footing."

He squeezed her tighter and kissed the top of her head. "You love your sister. It's natural you were hoping for the best outcome today. You've been trying to heal her in the only way you knew how. The way that seemed most logical."

"But I should have known her anxiety wasn't all about being stalked. I mean our parents hardly gave her a solid foundation in life. Their drinking and frequent disappearing acts were hardly ideal for Abby's sense of security."

And then it clicked. Had he really thought Jules could put a lifetime of broken trust and instability behind her and give him her heart so easily? She might be able to smile now, with her external stressor gone, but what about the years of damage inflicted by others?

He stroked a hand down her back and asked gently, "And what about you? It couldn't have been a walk in the park for you, either."

She stilled for a moment, then pulled out of his embrace and started toward the parking lot. "Doesn't matter."

He fell in step behind her. "What? Of course it matters!" When she kept walking, he snagged her arm again. He had to make Jules see that he wasn't like all the people in her past who'd hurt her, let her down, betrayed her trust. Their future together depended on it.

"Jules, it matters, and *you* matter." He took a breath then added, "To me. You matter *to me*."

She blinked then glanced away, biting her bottom lip.

"Your parents weren't there for you, either, were they?"

"I managed. I figured out pretty quick I was the only real parent, the only stability Abby was going to have, and I was willing to do what it took to take care of her."

"And who gave you stability? Who did you rely on when your parents didn't?"

She said nothing for several seconds, then cleared her throat. "I relied on myself."

He nodded. So much of her distrust and sour view of people sharpening into focus.

"While raising Abby and earning an advanced degree in chemistry?" he asked, more as a statement of awe than a query.

She slanted him a look. "Didn't finish my degree, remember? I moved here. Besides, by the time I reached college, Abby was older and didn't need as much of my time. Then she went to college—"

Her brow knitted as her sentence fell away.

"And ended up with a stalker," he said, finishing for her.

"Yeah." She shrugged away from his grip and marched to his Wrangler.

When he caught up to her, before unlocking the passenger door, he cupped her cheek. "I know you wish that the news of Hamilton's death had been the medicine Abby needed to move on, but you've done your best for her since—"

Her anger flashed hot and quick, startling Cal with its vehemence. "No! I failed her!" She jerked away from his touch, and her voice trembled as she ranted, "She depended on me! I was supposed to keep her safe, and I didn't. She went to college and was preyed upon by a vile man. And even once we knew who he was and what he was doing, I still couldn't protect her. And it broke her!"

Cal shook his head, drilling her with a stern gaze. "No, Jules. Do not take this on yourself."

"But I failed to protect her, and she wound up in there." She jabbed a finger toward the hospital entrance. "And even then she wasn't completely safe. Chase still found her here. Maybe if I'd been with her when she went to college—"

He scoffed. "Really? Do you really think you could have predicted that she'd be targeted by a stalker? And would she, at eighteen, have thanked you for helicopter parenting her and not allowing her to spread her wings and find her independence?"

"But I—"

He took her shoulders in his hands and gave her a gentle shake. "Stop! You have punished yourself long enough. You can't swaddle the people you love in bubble wrap and think the world will never hurt them. Pain and the occasional trouble are going to find all of us eventually. What matters is having the support of the people you love to help you through it, not save you from it."

Jules drew a shuddering breath, her eyes filling with tears. Was he reaching her?

"Chase Hamilton's actions are not your fault. The failure of the legal system to stop Hamilton is not your fault. Your sister's breakdown is not. Your. Fault." More tears shimmered in her eyes when she looked up at him, her breathing fast and shallow. "Not. Your. Fault."

When her chin quivered, he wrapped her in his arms and pulled her close. With a hand at her nape, he nudged her head to his shoulder. Moisture from her tears soaked his shirt, and her body shook as she released what he could well imagine was years of pent-up emotion.

His heart ached knowing she'd buried her own sense of abandonment and hurt toward her parents for so long. She'd shoved down her fear for her sister and locked up her heart in order to move through the challenges life had dealt her. For too long, she'd believed she had to be strong, hold herself in check for both her sister and herself.

Pressing a kiss to the top of her head, he whispered, "You're not alone in this anymore, Jules. I am here for you. I swear it."

Jules didn't say much in the Jeep as Cal drove back to his house. After her embarrassing meltdown in his arms, she didn't know how to proceed. He'd said all the nice things and made all the pretty promises one would expect. But…

But what? Why was it so hard to believe him, to allow him past her defenses? She didn't like the idea of being vulnerable to him. Exposed. Her soul naked and fragile.

Although…hadn't she already let him crack open those doors when she made love to him? Maybe she should regret having slept with him. But she couldn't. Losing herself in his kiss, his touch, his tender ministrations as they'd come together had made her happier than she could ever remember. More than sex, being with Cal had made her feel seen, appreciated, cherished.

Other than Abby, who'd loved her the way a little sister would, she hadn't felt cared for or wanted since…well, if she had to think that hard to remember, it had been too long.

But every time she thought of letting down her guard completely, something cold and poisonous filled her, whispered to her of all the pain of her past.

No, she was much better off trusting what was fact based and logical. Not people. Science. And the logical thing to do, the best way to move on with her life was to finish her PhD research, publish her work and find a position in a lab somewhere that she could make a difference in the world of chemistry….which meant the only logical thing to do was return to Winnipeg, where her professors would welcome her back. Thus…leave Red Grove. Leave the tedious gift shop.

Leave Cal.

Once her thought process had gone full circle with the same result a second time, she shut down the circling maelstrom and tamped down the raw emotion that had cracked embarrassingly open in the hospital parking lot. She just prayed Abby hadn't seen from her window the way she'd disintegrated into tears. Abby didn't need that to grapple with.

Protect Abby, her brain said.

Your parents weren't there for you either, were they? Cal's voice answered in her head.

And in her heart, a more insidious voice hissed, *Protect yourself.*

Chapter 33

When they arrived at Cal's house, an unfamiliar car was in the driveway, and Jules tensed. "Who's that?"

"Huh," Cal said, furrowing his brow in surprise. "My mother. What's she doing here?" Cal exited his Jeep quickly, and Jules hustled to follow him inside.

"Mom?" Cal made a beeline for the living room, where they found his mother on the sofa, flipping through a magazine. "What are you doing here?"

Emily rolled her eyes and rose to meet him halfway across the floor. "Good grief, Callum. Is that any way to greet your mother? The woman who's been worried sick about you since she heard you were at the police station last night when the shooting happened?"

Cal hugged his mother and kissed her cheek. "Who told you?"

"Your father did. And he only knew because he was at the hospital last night when Matti brought a little boy into the ER." She backed out of the hug and swatted at his arm. "Why did I have to hear something like that second hand?" She grabbed him with both hands then and gave him an intense up-and-down scrutiny. "And do you promise you're okay? My God, three of my children—*three*—involved with a shooting and I have to learn about it hours after the fact from my ex-husband!"

"I'm fine, Mom," Cal said evenly, while registering on some level her comment that she'd been in touch with Jonathon or vice versa. He recalled the conversation he'd overheard after the Fourth of July picnic between his parents and added another tick to his mental checklist of curiosities for later.

Meeting his mother's disgruntled stare, he added, "And I didn't call because I was *a little* busy dealing with the fallout." He gave his mother a wry grin. "You know, of the shooting. Because I'm the sheriff."

She flapped a hand. "I know. I know. But dear lord, Callum! Do you know how hard it is on a mother having *all four* of her sons in high-risk careers? How I dread a late-night phone call saying—" She raised a hand without finishing the thought. Instead, she cast a startled glance to the foyer door where Jules still stood, watching. "Oh, hello, Jules dear. I didn't see you. How are you, darling?"

Jules twitched a half grin. "Fine, thanks. It's nice to see you again."

Cal propped a hand on his hip. "Mom…how did you get in? I didn't think you still had a key."

Emily faced him again and snorted. "I used the security code," she said as if that should have been obvious. With a droll grin, she added, "I knew it hadn't been changed. Your father would never let it be."

Cal sighed. "Of course." Stepping back from his mother, he said, "Can I get you anything? Tea or water? Maybe something with more kick?" He lifted his gaze to ask Jules the same question, but she was gone. And a gloomy voice in his head said, *Better get used to it.*

* * *

Jules moved to the dresser drawer in what she could only assume had been Matti's or Kelly's room once, based on the bright yellow paint and feminine decor. While she'd spent last night in Cal's bed, going forward she'd sleep here until Abby could move with her to Canada. Might as well start now with habits she intended to carry forward. Leaving Red Grove, leaving this house, leaving Cal, would be far easier when the time came if she hadn't gotten any more deeply rooted in his life.

And she would leave. As soon as Abby had time to process the new reality of Chase's death and come to terms with the return of her safety, they'd both move out of town. If she was lucky, she could rejoin the University of Manitoba program at the start of fall semester. She could restart her paused research and—

A knock roused her from her planning. She glanced over her shoulder to find Emily, standing at the door, holding two glasses of a pale liquid. She extended one. "Lemonade?"

She didn't really want the drink or the company, but neither did she want to be rude to Cal's mother. She moved a cheek in what should have been a smile as she accepted the cold drink. "Thanks."

Emily took a seat at the end of the bed and patted the floral bedspread next to her. "Want to tell me why you're crying?"

Jules's hand tightened, and she almost dropped the condensation-slickened glass. "Wh—"

She swiped at a cheek, stunned to feel the moisture there. What the heck? She wasn't a *crier.* Well, atomic meltdown in the hospital parking lot aside, but…

She used her free hand to hurriedly blot the tears on

her face. She could only assume she was still emotionally overstimulated and her thoughts about leaving town had—

"Cal says you visited your sister today," Emily said gently.

Concerned that her voice wasn't steady, Jules only nodded. To give herself something distracting to do, she took a sip of her drink…and choked as the burn of something that definitely was not lemonade seared her throat.

Emily quickly took the glass from Jules while she sputtered and coughed and caught her breath.

"Oops," Emily said with a wince. "I think I gave you mine by accident. I had Cal spike it with tequila. Sorry, dear." She stood and took a step from the bed. "I'll get you a new glass."

"Mmm," Jules grunted. Dropping on the bed beside Emily, she reached for the drink. "No. I want this one. I just wasn't expecting…the punch."

Emily sat down again, nodding. "Yeah. It's the unexpected punch that gets you every time, isn't it?"

Jules took another sip, prepared this time for the tang of tart lemon and zing of the tequila. When she lifted her eyes to Emily, Cal's mother wore an odd, knowing look.

An uneasy feeling wiggled in Jules's chest. What was happening?

Emily put a hand on Jules's knee. "I understand things didn't go quite the way you'd hoped at the hospital with your sister."

Her eyes widened. "Cal told you?"

"I dragged it out of him. He was uncharacteristically glum, and I was worried. And when he told me how things went, I became worried again…for you."

When Jules only stared at Emily, slack-jawed, Cal's mother patted her knee again and chuckled. "Don't look so surprised. I'm a mother. Worrying about loved ones is what mothers do best."

Jules dropped her gaze to her lap and mumbled, "I wouldn't know about that."

Moving her arm to circle Jules's shoulders, Emily scooted closer, so that her hip bumped Jules's. "Well, get used to it. Because my son clearly cares about you, and so, by extension, you are now included in the circle of my maternal concern."

A cocktail of strange sensations washed through Jules. Warm and soft, while also foreign and scary. And while it might be nice to confess all the things troubling her to Emily, to take advantage of this apparent motherly comfort, her experience with her own mother said that parental security and affection were just as fleeting and unreliable as that of a cold and overworked legal system.

Emily's arm tightened around Jules's shoulders, drawing her into a half hug. "Don't panic. He didn't spill anything overly personal. Cal's not the kiss-and-tell type. He just said you were upset because Abby didn't respond to your news the way you'd hoped."

She took another gulp of her drink and shook her head. "No. She didn't."

Emily nodded. "You know what's ironic?"

Jules angled her head toward Cal's mother.

"Unexpected twists are gold for my plots. Catching my characters—and my readers—off guard is what I strive for. But when real life catches you unaware or your heart's expectations aren't met…well, that's less fun. It rather stinks."

"Hmm," Jules grunted, the best reply she could manage due to the sudden lump in her throat.

"For someone who plans, who craves order and needs some measure of control in their life, the unexpected can be especially hard to grapple with. Cal's dad, for example." She laughed lightly and gave her head a subtle shake. "Jonathon needs life to follow rules. As a doctor, he relies on the world adhering to the laws of science. He has a hard time knowing what to do when life doesn't unfold the way he predicts. He has a plan, a road map to life he finds practical. His modus operandi makes sense to him, and any deviation from that path gives him hives. Good grief, the man can't even change his home security password. And change brands of coffee or underwear?" Emily laughed and raised her hands, spreading her fingers to gesture his mind would be blown. "Ask me how I know."

Jules exhaled slowly and muttered, "I get that. I'm… kinda that way, too."

Emily gave Jules another consoling squeeze. "I kinda figured as much. You being a chemist and all." Emily paused, then added, "I'm guessing falling in love with my son wasn't part of your plan."

Jules snapped her head toward Emily. "What? I'm not—Why do you think…?"

Emily smiled and shifted to face Jules. "Well, for one thing…" She carefully lifted Jules's drink from her hand and dabbed at wet spots on the bedspread. "You're trying so hard to deny it, you sloshed your drink."

"Sorry. Sorry, I'm…so sorry."

"It's fine. The bedspread will wash." Emily rose to set both drinks aside and returned to the mattress, angling her body to face Jules. "Let me guess. Your sister's reaction to whatever news you gave her isn't the only thing that didn't go the way you expected today. You're trying to figure out what happens next and how to get your train back on the right track. Am I right?"

Jules laced her fingers together to stop her hands from

trembling. Having Cal's mother read her so well was unnerving, as much as the truths she was forcing Jules to examine. "I think I might love him." Her chest throbbed as she let the reality settle. "But loving him only makes it harder to leave Red Grove."

"So don't leave," Emily said as if it was the obvious answer. "Stay here and explore this love relationship."

"Well, I will for a while, until Abby can be discharged and move with me. But I interrupted my schooling when I moved here. I'm not a gift shop manager. I'm a chemist, and I belong in Winnipeg, finishing my PhD."

Emily nodded slowly, as if considering what she'd said carefully. She dabbed at the damp spots on the bedspread and her slacks. "You know, I've always believed that the best scientists are the ones who find a way to think outside the box. In life, and many times in science, there is more than one solution to a problem."

Jules wrinkled her nose and chewed her bottom lip. "You think there's an outside-the-box solution I've missed?"

Emily raised her eyebrows and gave her a gentle smile that reminded Jules of Cal's.

"I'll give you a hint. The University of North Dakota in Red Grove has a very good science department from what I hear." She handed Jules back her drink and patted her on the knee before she stood. "Just something to think about. I'd hate for you and Cal to throw away love without considering all the options. Hmm?"

Jules couldn't speak. The muscles in her throat had contracted so hard she could barely breathe, much less answer the older woman. She nodded, though, and blinked as she felt tears slide through her eyelashes.

She walked to stare out the window at the greens and

browns of the vast tundra beyond the Colton property. *Stay in Red Grove?*

She shifted her attention to the manicured flower bed and landscaped lawn where the family had gathered for the Fourth of July.

I'm guessing falling in love with my son wasn't part of your plan.

Oh, heaven help her. She loved Cal. But love had never been an emotion she could count on. She'd tried to love her parents, but they'd let her down in so many ways. Emotions were too unreliable, too unpredictable…especially love. So how could she love Cal? Loving Cal was…risky. Scary.

A squeak-like mew pulled her from her deliberations, and she looked down to find Joy rubbing against her leg. The kitten looked up at her with innocent green eyes, and she marveled at how the wild kitten had made a turnaround in just a few days. Because she felt safe now. She wasn't frightened anymore. She trusted Jules…

A new sensation stirred in her belly now. Something in her chest cracked and swelled, filling her to bursting.

Cal was more than an achingly handsome man. More than a cheerful antagonist to her sarcasm and a mood booster when she was discouraged. More than a trustworthy lawman. He was…*so much more*. His honor and integrity were bone deep. His care and concern were genuine.

He was a man she could feel safe with, trust with her future. Someone she could *allow herself* to love.

Jules stooped to pat the kitten and whispered, "I get it now. Thank you, Joy." She lifted the cat for a quick kiss on her furry head, then put her down on the bed. "You stay here. I need to go find Cal."

Cal looked up from his phone where he was texting with Matti, checking on her and young Sam. Jules stood at the door to the family room, her face blotched with red as if she'd been crying again, and her expression as shaken and uncertain as he'd ever seen her. His pulse tripped seeing her this way. Jules was not a timid person. She was brash and bold and confident. What had happened?

"Jules? What's wrong?" He put his phone down on the end table, and as he started to stand, she rushed to him and sat in his lap, hugging him tightly. She buried her face in his shoulder and drew a deep breath. "I'm sorry."

Cal would have sworn his heart stopped. "About what?"

"Pushing you away. I never meant to hurt you." She lifted her head then and met his eyes. "I do trust you. Maybe I didn't at first, but everything you've shown me over the past weeks has proven to me that I can trust you."

He stroked a hand along her cheek and tucked damp hair behind her ear. Her admission did little to quell the uneasy feeling in his gut. He nodded, though, and said, "That's good. I'm glad."

"So… I was thinking about why it was so hard to trust you… Before…"

"Well, your frequent disappointments with other law enforce—"

"No. I mean, that was part of it. Yes. But I mean trusting *you*. Trusting my feelings for you."

His muscles tensed, and she put a hand on each of his cheeks. "Love had never been a safe place for me before. Besides Abby, of course. But…my parents didn't… I was scared to be—"

"Love?" he blurted, and she stilled.

After a few beats, she exhaled and said, "I love you, Cal Colton. And it's still kinda scary for me. But I do trust you. I do feel safe with you, so I want…"

He waited, holding his breath for her to finish the thought.

"I want to think outside the box for another solution. I want to stay in Red Grove with you. I want a future with you and also a chance to be a chemist. To finish my research and earn my PhD."

Her green eyes were wide and expectant as she held his gaze. "Maybe I can do that at UND here in Red Grove?"

He couldn't contain the smile that rose from deep inside him. "I hear good things about their science department."

"That's what your mom said."

He jerked his chin back. "My mom?"

Jules lifted a corner of her mouth. "Yeah. I've never had the kind of mother I could have a heart-to-heart with like that. It was…really nice."

"So then, you're staying?"

"If you'll have me."

He laughed. "You have to ask? Jules, I will have you today, tomorrow and forever. I love you."

Her hesitant expression melted away, replaced by a smile that reflected pure joy. "Good. Because I love you, too. So… you're stuck with me."

Epilogue

Later that autumn

"Novel Process for Photocata— Huh?"

Jules glanced up at Cal, whose expression looked pained as he puzzled out the title of the paper she was preparing to submit for publication. "Novel Process for Photocatalytically Induced Nickel-boron Transmetallation," she said. Turning up an inviting hand, she flashed a teasing smile. "You're welcome to read it, if you want. I could use another pair of eyes on it, to proofread."

He arched an eyebrow and grunted. "Thanks, but I'm in the middle of *Green Eggs and Ham* right now. I'm dying to find out if Sam eats the green eggs or not."

Jules barked a laugh, something she did a lot these days. She loved to rib her fiancé, loved to jest with him and generally not take life so seriously. She loved Cal for many reasons, but bringing laughter back to her life was among the top ones.

He moved to stand behind her where she was busy on her laptop, reviewing assignments her undergraduate students had submitted. When his fingers began massaging her tired shoulders, she moaned her pleasure. She couldn't get enough of his hands on her and had been late to class this morning thanks to their morning assignation.

He bent to kiss her neck, whispering, "Any chance I can steal you away for lunch?"

She angled a glance up at him. "Don't you still have murders to solve? Bad guys to catch?"

"True, but Wyatt knows where to find me if he wants my assistance. Until I'm asked, it's his and the drug task force's case. They'll get their man. I have faith in them. So, lunch, Dr. Bailey?"

She grinned and savored the ripple of sensation that chased through her as his lips grazed her skin. "I keep telling you… I'm not a doctor yet. I have to finish my research paper and get it approved by the doctoral panel. That means at least another couple months."

His arms slipped around her from behind and pressed his mouth to her temple. "And by then you'll be able to call yourself Dr. *Colton*."

She couldn't help the smile that spread across her face when she thought about marrying Cal. Being part of his big, loving family. Spending the rest of her life laughing and making love to the man of her dreams.

"I can go to lunch," she said, trying to type despite his romantic advances, "but only if you let me get these comments back to Nancy first. She has a deadline."

With one last kiss, he released her and took the chair across the desk in her tiny office at the University of North Dakota at Red Grove. When she'd approached the head of the chemistry department at UND-RG about finishing her doctorate degree with them, he'd moved mountains to get her onboard. The department head had seen the research she'd done while at the University of Manitoba and been excited to add her to their program.

"Mind if I call Abby and see if she wants to join us?" Jules asked as she hit Send on the email she was finishing. "I think she has today off."

Abby, who had made significant progress once she'd known she was safe from Chase Hamilton, had been discharged from the mental health clinic last month and taken over Jules's job at the gift shop to earn a little cash before she, too, would return to college in the near future. Some days, when Abby talked about the interesting tourists from around the world she met at the gift shop, Jules missed the little shop. For about five minutes.

Then she'd thank her lucky stars for her chemistry research, her teaching post as a graduate student and her upcoming wedding.

Life was finally good.

* * * * *

Author's Note

Thank you to Dr. Jeffery Cornelison for his assistance with all things chemistry-related in this story. Any errors or misinterpretations are strictly my own.